Also by Otto Coontz

The Shapeshifters
The Night Walkers

THROUGH THE NIGHTSEA WALL

OTTO COONTZ

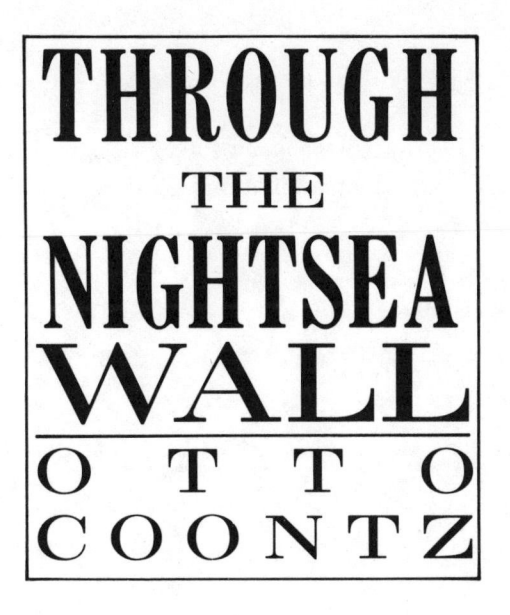

METHUEN

First published in Great Britain 1989
by Methuen Children's Books
A Division of The Octopus Group, Ltd
Michelin House, 81 Fulham Road, London SW3 6RB
Copyright © 1989 Otto Coontz
Printed in Great Britain
by Redwood Burn Limited
Trowbridge, Wiltshire

British Library Cataloguing in Publication Data

Coontz, Otto
Through the nightsea wall.
I. Title
813'.54 [F]

ISBN 0-416-13542-0

Contents

1	Trouble from the Start	*page* 1
2	The Bright Mark	10
3	A Small Dark House	20
4	Night Flight	30
5	Sea Song	36
6	The Mysterious Medusa	41
7	A Jar Full of Stars	45
8	Things of the Present Lost in the Past	58
9	The Stairway Beneath the Falls	66
10	The Seeding	72
11	Tales of Travelers Lost	78
12	The Elusive Quark	92
13	A Trickling of Light	101
14	The Swarm	110
15	A Bat in the Privy	122
16	The Cry of the Chrysalis	131
17	The Chink in the Falls	141
18	Sweet Cravings	146
19	The Secret of Ausable Cavern	152
20	The Hatching	164
21	Where Currents Collide	174
22	The Last Brilliade	180
23	The Starry Armada of Nightsea	194
24	Visions and Voices	207
25	The Wall Between Worlds	214

After all, reality is just a collective hunch.

Lily Tomlin

1
Trouble from the Start

Benjamin Liebling woke with a start to a shrill 'creaking' sound. It reminded him of the noise made by a cricket, only much louder. But whatever it was, it stopped in the time it took him to groggily raise his head and find that he'd fallen asleep on the back seat of his mother's car.

How long he'd been sleeping, he couldn't tell. The hot June sun still poured through the windows, just as it had when they left the motel in Little Rock that morning. His cheek felt damp and prickly and, wiping the sleep from his eyes, he blinked down at the seat. The vinyl where his head had lain was littered with peanuts and cracker crumbs. When he started to push himself up on one wobbly arm crimped under his chest, he heard the crinkling of cellophane and discovered a packet of spilled M&Ms. In fact, the whole seat looked like a rubbish heap with all the wrappings and crumbs from snacks consumed on the long hauls between restaurant meals and motel beds. After the several days and nearly fourteen hundred miles on the road between Cambridge and the Ozarks, he could almost say he'd be glad if he never laid eyes on junk food again. Almost, but not quite, for he wished he had a cold can of Pepsi right then. There was not even a breeze through the open windows, and only on pushing himself to a sitting position did Benjamin realize the reason was because they'd stopped.

'Mom?' he mumbled sleepily as he leaned to the space between the front seats. But both seats were empty, except for his mother's bag on the driver's side, and a hairbrush snagged with curly dark hair, a Madonna tape, and some crinkled up wrappers from sugarless gum and a magazine all crammed together along the crease of the seat where his sister Sarah had sat. Rubbing his fists in his eyes, then yawning and blinking up at the windshield, he found the sun blazing down through towering pines and over a narrow dirt road that wound steeply uphill and through several shimmering puddles of heat mirage. And just ahead, smothered under wisteria vines dripping blossoms like grapes, stood a ramshackle house with a sagging roof and a sloping porch with a trellis. He saw his mother climbing the rickety stairs, then his view was blocked when his sister walked up to the side of the car and leaned there.

'Why did we stop?' Ben called through the window, but Sarah did not seem to hear. She was wearing her Walkman, so Ben crawled in front to the driver's seat and called out again, 'Sarah!' He leaned through the window and tugged at her T-shirt. She jerked around, startled, then frowned. 'What did we stop for?' he repeated when Sarah, scowling, pulled up an earphone. The tinny strains of some rock band poured out of the ear-piece as she replied:

'This is where Dad was supposed to meet us. If Mom hadn't got us lost,' she grumbled. 'We're three hours late and it looks like Dad must have got fed up and left. And if we have to find our own way to Gus's, she'll just get us lost again,' she finished with a look of disgust and readjusted the ear-piece.

'This is it? This is Ausable Center?' Ben mumbled in disbelief, looking around and seeing nothing but the steep hill, the dense forest, the house, and behind him, a tumbledown barn or garage of some sort and what looked like an old fashioned gasoline pump. It wasn't at all the kind of place he'd expected when Gus asked them down for the summer.

He'd imagined a quaint little village surrounded by pastures spotted with picturesque farms, and sheep and cows grazing by sparkling brooks under vast open stretches of sky. But then, he reminded himself, even Gus hadn't known for sure what it would be like. Gus hadn't even been able to locate the place on a map and wouldn't have found it himself if the probate court hadn't sent him directions along with the will. Gus hadn't known he had a great uncle until the court clerk in Arkansas wrote to him in Cambridge to say the great uncle had died, and as the only surviving descendant, Gus would inherit the house and farm. But whatever his father and Gus had discovered, it had been too late to forewarn Ben's mother. They were already on their way by the time his father and Gus had arrived, and as far as anyone knew, there was no phone at the farm. Whatever lay ahead, Ben thought, their meeting spot did not bode well, not if this single rickety house was all there was to Ausable Center.

His hopes grew even slimmer when scanning both ends of the winding dirt road he found he could not even spot a single utility pole. If there was no electricity, it meant there'd be no lights, and worse, no way to run the tiny portable TV they'd brought along. Ben began to wonder just what his father and Gus had roped them into when he caught sight of a gaunt old woman in overalls shambling out of the barn. At least, the long white hair, the gangly shape, stooped shoulders and shuffling gait reminded Ben a little of his grandmother.

'You need fuel?' He'd lost sight of the snowy white head as the speaker stopped at the back of the car, but the voice he heard sounded more like a boy's than a woman's, with an odd sort of warbly edge. Sarah, plugged into her Walkman again, still leaning by the front of the car, hadn't heard, but a thump on the roof sent a vibration through the car which she must have felt for she turned. Then Ben saw her face pull into a knot of surprise as she pulled off her earphones. She looked embarrassed as well, for her curly dark hair had grown wispy and thin and her face looked fat though the rest of her was rail thin, and it made her self-conscious. All these unflattering changes were the result of a medication she took which also made her sick to her stomach sometimes. Chemotherapy, that's what they called it. And though it put her leukemia in remission, it made living with her a trial.

'You need any fuel?' the voice from the back repeated with its peculiar accent, then Sarah, still looking flustered, leaned from the car and shouted up to the house, 'Mom, do you want him to fill the tank?' Then it was a boy after all, Ben thought, and now that Sarah had moved, he spotted his mother with someone up on the porch. When she called back in the affirmative, Ben craned his head out of the window for a better look at the strange-looking boy back by the gasoline pump. He stood a foot taller than Sarah, and his startling white hair was as long as a rock star's, hanging in thick shaggy hanks that hid his face and straggled over his shoulders. Then the boy left the nozzle jammed in the tank, grabbed a pail that hung from the pump and started around the car while Ben and Sarah studied him curiously. But the boy kept his head bowed, his unruly bangs hiding most of his face while he shuffled well around Sarah, as if he was trying to avoid her, then up to the windshield. As he started to wash it, Ben sank in his seat and stared up through the glass at the boy. From his worm's-eye view, Ben now got a much better look at the face beneath the thick bangs.

His skin was nearly as white as his hair, at least from what Ben could see of it, for the youth wore a pair of sunglasses with mirrored lenses that hid his eyes and which were secured to his head by an elasticized band, such as an athlete might wear. Even his shirt was buttoned right up to the collar and his sleeves buttoned down to his cuffs which disappeared under the edge of his grungy work-gloves. He looked as if he were purposely trying to cover himself from head to toe, which made no sense at all, Ben thought, on such a sweltering day. Then, as if he knew Ben was staring, without even finishing washing the windshield he moved to the front of the car and threw up the hood as if to look at the engine, leaving Ben with his own reflection peering down from the rear-view mirror. By contrast, Ben saw his own face was rosy and peeling from last weekend's sunburn, with dark, sleep-tusseled curls licking out from his head and a small green dot on his brow. Picking it off, he saw it was one of the spilled M&Ms from the seat in the back that had got stuck to his heat-flushed face while he was napping. He popped it into his mouth then grabbed his Red Sox cap from the litter in the back, shook off the crumbs, pulled it on and climbed from the car.

The sun was just dragging its belly down to the tops of the towering trees and instead of the stuffy, stale odors from days of fast food, the air outside was redolent with pine and sweet, fresh mossy smells. Ben found the boy now checking the oil while Sarah leaned at one fender, her puffy face gloomily bowed to her chest, pretending indifference to the boy but Ben saw her give him a sidelong glance. Tugging the visor down on his Red Sox cap to cut the glare of the sun, he started toward the house with its sagging roof dripping purple wisteria blossoms.

At the foot of the stairs, he stopped and gaped up at the man on the porch. Though taller, his hair, skin and clothes were exactly like the boy's. Glancing back toward the car, Ben saw that this went well beyond resemblance. The boy looked and dressed like a perfect clone of the man. Then his gaze shot back to the porch as he caught a bit of the conversation above and heard that the man, like the boy, even had the same peculiar warble.

'That was late last night. We haven't seen him hereabouts all day.' Then he paused as Ben started up, but the warble lingered a bit, like the purr of a cat, or so it sounded to Ben as he climbed to the porch and stood by his mother. 'You'd best drive down to Reedsville, like I said, and ask around there.' Staring up at the man, who looked even taller than Gus, who was the tallest man Ben knew, he noticed another odd thing about him. It seemed to him the man's speech was a bit out of synch with his mouth, almost as if he was mimicking speech, sort of like a ventriloquist's dummy. But the words themselves sounded so close and so clear, it was like they were inside Ben's head. But of course, the man's lips only looked out of synch because of his odd, purry accent, Ben thought, like the way the mouth rolls and the words all run together in a southern drawl. Yet, for all the states they'd passed through driving down here, and for all the weird accents he'd heard, none, Ben thought, sounded quite so strange as the one he was hearing in Ausable. Still peering up at the man, he wondered if this was the boy's older brother or father. Only eleven himself, Ben wasn't much good at guessing ages, particularly when it came to grown-ups, who all seemed more or less old. But in spite of his towering height, the face half-hidden by glasses and straggly bangs looked as pale and smooth as the boy's, who was probably not much older than Sarah.

'You need something else before you move on, ask my son,' the man then said, but nothing about his tone seemed to encourage their asking for anything, and watching him suddenly turn and head for the door with the same shambling gait as his son, Ben had an almost physical sensation of being nudged, so intense was the feeling he had that they were not wanted here. It made him remember Gus wondering if the people here would take to him when he moved into his great uncle's house.

'Didn't my husband mention that we were coming?' Ben's mother anxiously asked just as the man shuffled under a sign hanging over the door. 'AUSABLE GENERAL STORE', it read, and beneath this, in flaking paint that seemed to be covering something else that was once printed under it, 'COTTER & SON'. And Mr Cotter, Ben guessed, would have continued inside without even replying if his mother hadn't followed him across the porch to the door. 'Please, we've been driving for days and he promised to meet us in Ausable Center. Are you sure he wasn't by earlier? We got lost so we're later than he was expecting.'

'Ain't no one been by here all day.' The rickety porch gave a creak as Cotter turned back. 'And there's no other road up or down the mountain but this one here. Take my word, he never came back after driving his friend to that doctor in Reedsville, and if you're smart, you'll take my advice and do your looking for him there.'

'Is something the matter with Uncle Gus?' Ben asked worriedly. Though Gus was not his real uncle, he'd been his father's best friend for forever it seemed, and he loved the bear-like man who taught school with his father just like he was family. 'Why did Dad have to take Gus to a doctor?'

'The road down's harder to follow after dark.' Cotter spoke right over Ben's question. 'And the sun's getting low. If you start right now, you might make it down while you still have the light. Believe me, you're best off heading over to Reedsville for the night.'

'My husband said to wait for him here,' Ben's mother replied defensively, for the tone the man had used was more like a warning. 'He might have just had trouble with the van,' she reasoned. 'In any event, I'm sure he'd have called and left a message here if he wasn't coming back.'

'Couldn't call and leave a message here. We got no

phone,' Cotter answered. 'None o' the folks in Ausable got phones. Don't have any need of them here.' Ben looked from Cotter's stolid face, looking all the more stony behind its dark glasses, to his mother, whose face, by contrast, was filling with worry and impatience.

'Mr Cotter,' she said with a trace of coolness herself. Ben could tell she was trying to stay calm but the strain of it was just adding more lines to her already furrowed brow. 'I find it hard to believe, if my husband had to ask you where to find a physician, that you wouldn't have some idea of why his friend even needed to see one.'

'Didn't say,' Cotter shot back. 'And it's not our way to go nosing in others' affairs.'

'Or, I suppose,' she returned in frustration, 'to bother to ask if you might be of help.' Before Cotter could respond to her accusation, both she and Ben gave a start as the same shrill sound that had wakened Ben in the car suddenly filled the air.

'It's a cicada,' Cotter said. Ben didn't know what a cicada was, but it sounded, he thought, like a thousand crickets all making their sound at once. Then, as if Cotter sensed his doubt, he added, 'It's just a bug. Makes that sound by vibrating its belly, sort of like crickets do with their wings.' And sort of like Cotter did with his throat, Ben thought when he heard the faint warble again. And though it still sounded to him like the purr of a cat, it did not sound contented or friendly, but cagey, more like a cat with a mouth full of feathers pretending it hasn't seen the canary.

'All that racket's made by just one bug?' Ben asked in disbelief as he scanned the edge of the woods and the road till his eye finally fell on his sister. She still leaned at the car, her head tilted back to the lowering sun. She did not seem to notice the sound, but then, whenever she had on her Walkman, you couldn't get her attention if you dropped a brick on her head. But Cotter's son now stood stock still, gazing up the road as if listening, until it seemed he sensed Ben watching and ducked his head back under the hood. Ben's gaze swung back to Cotter again just as the sound abruptly stopped.

'I haven't heard one in years,' he heard his mother distractedly murmur. 'And I know they can make quite a noise, but I can't recall ever hearing one quite that loud.'

'They're bigger down here, I expect,' Cotter replied, seeming distracted himself.

'Mr Cotter, you must at least have seen what condition Gus was in. I don't see how you could see him and not even have the vaguest idea how he was. You'd certainly have to notice if he was conscious, or hurt, or lying down or – '

'Didn't see him,' Cotter replied, though the 'purr' sounded cagey again, Ben thought. 'Your husband tore down here in the dead of night and leaned on his horn, and when I got out here to see what the ruckus was, he still had his motor running and all he asked was where he'd find a doctor. That's all, just like I told you. And his friend could have been in the back of the van or sitting beside him for all I could tell. From up here on the porch, in pitch dark, I could scarcely see who was behind the wheel. And as soon as I hollered back where Reedsville was,' Cotter's tone matched his mother's impatience, 'your husband took off down the mountain like a bat straight out of hell.' He paused a moment, as if to collect himself, then added, almost contritely, 'He probably figured we wouldn't have been much help.' But something in Cotter's voice gave Ben the odd feeling he meant that he *couldn't* have helped, as if he really did know what was wrong with Gus but wouldn't say. But one thing Ben was sure of. This man didn't want them in Ausable.

2
The Bright Mark

While Cotter gave his mother directions to find the doctor in Reedsville, Ben's gaze roamed over the porch with its sloping floor and missing rails. The whole building looked closer to falling down than standing up, he thought, with the windows all boarded over and the door missing one of its hinges. Ben doubted that Cotter and Son got much business except for the single old fuel pump next door, and thinking this, his eye wandered back to the boy and his sister down by the car. Watching Sarah, pretending not to notice the boy bent over the engine, made him think of how she'd been up until her diagnosis. Before the symptoms that landed her in the hospital, her hair had been shiny and long, and even he had to admit, in spite of the friction between them, that she had been pretty. She had also had a lot of friends, until she got sick and dropped them all, although she tried to make everyone think that it was the other way around. It was like she had to make things worse to justify feeling so bad for herself, and feeling bad for herself had swiftly become a full-time occupation. And now on top of everything else she'd deliberately flunked a grade in school, at least, that was how Ben saw it, because she hadn't missed that many classes, and his father had bent over backwards trying to help her catch up on the work she had missed. But she hadn't even tried, the way she would not even try with all her old friends, not wanting to talk on the phone when they called or see them on weekends or after school. And sometimes, like now, seeing her watch the boy from the corner of her eye, Ben thought the hardest part of all was having her beautiful hair fall out and her face grow round and puffy and plain, just when all of her friends were starting to date. She probably would have had lots of dates herself if it weren't for the chemo, Ben thought, watching her shyly eye Mr Cotter's peculiar look-alike son. But then, he supposed, looks were only skin deep, and as Sarah had lost hers, who was he to be putting down the Ausable boy for being different. In any case, the boy seemed to pay her no notice, and Sarah was leaving her post, maybe losing interest, hopefully not feeling sick, for he saw her crawl back in the car, then prop her back against the passenger door and crook her legs to rest her feet on the driver's seat, as if trying to lay down. Ben knew it must be hard for her, having something that serious, so bad that she might even die if the chemo ever stopped working. Still, he'd been finding it harder and harder to like her, particularly on this trip, the way she was always so cranky and always expected, and got, what she wanted. Not that he didn't think people ought to try harder to overlook things when you're sick, but still he wished she'd try a little bit harder as well, not to be such a pain.

'I don't know,' he heard his mother thinking aloud as Cotter finished directions, 'I still think it might just be trouble with the van. Or perhaps he lost track of the time.' But that wasn't at all like his father, Ben thought, a stickler for never being late. 'He could have lost track of the time if he misplaced his watch or the battery ran out,' his mother continued, as if she was mulling it over. 'There could be a chance he's up at Gus's great uncle's house right now.'

'Look, I told you, I'd've heard if he came back this way.' Cotter's warbly voice shot back with such impatience that it finally made Ben angry. As his mother lowered her head with a sigh, Ben glared at the man, but the man didn't see. His face was turned away from them as if watching or listening for something. Ben followed his gaze up the road but saw and heard nothing, not even a bird, yet looking back, he found Cotter just as before, his head cocked as if listening. Then one gloved hand rose to his thick snowy hair to give a distracted scratch, and Ben, peering up, was startled to see that Cotter appeared to be missing an ear. He wondered with a wince if it was cut off in some terrible accident, or a fight, or if he was simply born that way. Perhaps that was why both of the Cotters wore headbands to keep their glasses on. If both of them were missing ears, there'd be nothing to hold up the frames of their glasses. Though he knew he shouldn't think such things, Ben half felt it served Mr Cotter right to have lost an ear, particularly after the way the man spoke to his mother. Then Cotter's hand suddenly dropped with his gaze and Ben could nearly feel the eyes behind the mirrored lenses boring into him, like he'd read Ben's mind.

'Ma'am, take my advice and drive over to Reedsville before it's too late.' This time there was no mistaking the warning and urgency in the man's voice. 'You won't want to stay in that house your husband and his friend was at. It's fallen into an awful sorry state since the old man passed away. Go on down to Reedsville. They have a motel with accommodations more like you're used to.'

'We're quite used to roughing it,' Ben's mother cooly replied. 'And in any case, before we spend another two hours back-tracking to Reedsville, I think I should look at the house since I'm here. If my husband's not there, there might at least be a note with some sort of explanation. So, if you'd just point me off in the right direction.' Now Cotter sighed, but he gave them the directions then, if grudgingly. Ben wondered at the man's lack of concern over Gus and their being stranded. It didn't seem to count for much that Gus was the only living relative of the Cotters' recently departed neighbor.

It made Ben increasingly angry, and sad for Gus, who had been so excited, particularly when he learned that a river ran by the house, for Gus and his dad loved to fish. Not that Ben and his parents weren't thrilled just at the prospects of summering up in the mountains. Especially after their last summer, stuck in the city, with Sarah so sick. But Sarah had come through her check-up with flying colors, and arrangements were made by her hematologist with a hospital three hours away if her chemo needed adjusting. But mostly, Ben knew, his parents leapt at Gus's invitation because Sarah was well enough and if they didn't take this badly needed break from all the worry and sadness surrounding his sister to just be a regular family, they might not get another chance.

Though Sarah was doing well enough now, in the sickness department at least, and though his parents were careful not to discuss the matter when he was around, he'd overheard them nonetheless, the night his father left with Gus – the doctor had told them remissions like this rarely lasted very long with the particular type of leukemia Sarah had. And he guessed Sarah knew this as well, for instead of being pleased at the prospects of summering here, she'd grown sourer all the way down. And Sarah alone, it seemed, had guessed what Ausable would turn out to be. While everyone else was picturing something like 'Little House on the Prairie', his sister had imagined a place just like this, overgrown and run-down and populated by rude, eccentric, 'backwoods illiterate types', as she'd put it.

Though Ben had agreed with his father, that Sarah's uninformed judgment was harsh and uncalled-for, looking over the rickety steps to the rutted dirt road snaking up through the woods, he now found he was feeling just like her, as if they'd gone backward in time where the land was still wild and the handful of people who lived there were just as unruly. It wouldn't surprise him at all if Cotter had lost his ear in a drunken brawl. In fact, maybe that was why both of the Cotters moved with an unsteady shuffle, maybe they talked in that warbly way and all but tripped over their feet because their brains were pickled and punchy from too much drinking and too many fights. And though Cotter's son looked no more than fifteen, there'd been kids at Ben's school even younger who bragged about getting into their parents' liquor supply when their folks weren't home. It wouldn't surprise him if Cotter's son was just like those bragging bullies back home. The boy and his father were probably wearing those glasses, he thought, to hide black eyes.

'But I warn you,' he heard Cotter say on completing directions to the great uncle's house, 'the road gets worse going up than it does going down, and you'd better not wander around once you get there 'cause it's easy getting lost and the ticks are bad this time of year, and keep your kids away from the river if you don't want to see 'um drown, 'cause the current up there is treacherous. There's even whirlpools around the falls. And you won't want them climbing around the falls, either, 'cause the rocks are slick from the spray and unstable, and – ' Before he could rattle off whatever else he hoped would scare them away, he cut himself off and looked like he was listening or searching for something again. Once more, Ben followed his gaze but saw nothing but shadows creeping out of the woods and across the steep, winding road that climbed over the mountain.

'Sun'll set in another half hour,' Cotter murmured and there was a chill in his voice. 'You want to be in before it's down, and stay inside till morning.' Then looking as though he was listening again, his head cocked to one side, he said in a harsh, urgent whisper, 'Lady, you better get moving or you'll be driving right into nightfall, and if you miss the turn to Matthew Marsden's place, your kids and you . . .' his odd warbly voice trailed away as Ben finally heard what he'd been listening for. The sound was as faint as the buzz of a fly but Ben knew that it was a motor. It quickly grew louder and soon Ben could see a thin cloud of dust rising out of the trees. Then a glint of metal appeared at a bend in the road and Ben nearly ran down the stairs for it looked like Gus's new van kicking up dust as it bumped its way down the steep grade. But he caught himself when he saw that it wasn't a van but an open-back wood-panel truck with a big spot of rust on the hood that looked, unnervingly, like a puddle of blood. Like the heat mirage Ben had seen earlier, this was only a trick of the light, like the flashes of fire he now saw through the trees, as if the woods were exploding in flames, while it was nothing more than the blazing sun slipping down the side of the mountain.

Peering through the vine-entangled trellis surrounding the porch, he watched the truck come to a lurching halt just to the left of the stairs. Cotter was already shambling down when the door on the driver's side swung out. A woman, who looked about his mother's age, in jeans and a tattered plaid shirt scrambled down from behind the wheel and shook back the longest hair he'd ever seen. Black as night, it caught the light of the sinking sun in fiery sparks as it swept across her shoulders and tumbled past her waist. Though Ben thought his mother was pretty, especially the way she had dressed to meet his dad, with black chino shorts and a peach-colored shirt that looked nice with her tan and her short blonde hair, he thought the woman who'd come in the beat-up truck, despite her shabby clothes, looked about as beautiful as a movie star with her dazzling hair.

'I found Daniel!' the woman shouted as she whisked

around to the back of the truck while Cotter continued to shamble unsteadily down the rickety steps. 'I was bringing a jar of honey to Righteous Hammond when I spotted him, up by the Marsden place, wandering in the woods by the falls! Found him babbling nonsense and clawing his ear like he wanted to rip it right off! Till I got him into the back here, then he got into my honey like he was starved. And when he lost interest in that, he just stared at the sun till I thought he'd go blind. But it calmed him right down, and when I could finally look him over closely,' then her voice grew faint as she breathlessly climbed to the tailgate, but it sounded to Ben like the next thing she said was something like, 'I saw the bright mark.'

'The bite mark?' he heard his mother mumble, then guessed, of course, that he must have heard wrong, for a 'bite' mark made a whole lot better sense than a 'bright' mark. And from the sounds of it, whatever bit him made him crazy to boot.

'Don't know what else it could be, 'cause my healing won't work,' the woman went on as she crouched on the tailgate and Cotter at last reached the back of the truck. 'And it was by the falls, and folks out my way have been saying it's starting up again and driving down I could've sworn I heard . . .' the woman cut herself off when Cotter, leaning over the tailgate now, gestured with a shrug of his snowy white head toward the car by the gasoline pump. This brought the woman's gaze swinging to Cotter's son, heading toward the truck, then up to the porch where Ben and his mother peered down through the vine-tangled trellis. 'I ought to get back,' Ben heard her say softly while lifting something out of the truck. 'Sun's almost down and the others'll prob'ly keep searching till they know he's found.' Then Ben felt his mother's hand on his shoulder just as he saw what the woman passed down. Mr Cotter gently took hold of a boy who looked no older than Ben.

With straw-blond hair, the youth hung limp as a rag doll as Cotter turned toward the stairs. When he started up, Ben saw the boy's trousers and T-shirt were torn and streaked with dirt as if he'd spent the last few days roaming around in the forest. In fact, Ben thought as he felt his mother's hand give his shoulder a squeeze, the boy looked more dead than alive, his face nearly as chalky as Cotter's, his chest barely rising and falling as he jounced in Cotter's arms. As the man approached the top of the stairs the boy's head lolled to one side and Ben saw that one ear was caked with blood and scored with dozens of angry scratches.

'Is it . . . is it starting up again? I heard the chink's come back! You think – ' Her voice broke off as her gaze abruptly jerked toward Cotter. The man had paused on the stairs and despite his dark glasses, Ben had the oddest impression that Cotter not only studied the woman intently, but that he was telling her something, as if he were conveying whatever was on his mind without actually speaking. And indeed, the way she had cut herself off was as sudden as if she'd been verbally silenced. And then, as if hearing Ben's thoughts as well, the woman gave him a nervous glance.

'We'll take care of Daniel.' Cotter's son broke the uneasy silence. 'Now go along, Meg. The sun's near down and you don't want to be on the road after dark.' Ben's mother nudged him away from the stairs as the Cotters stepped up to the porch. The woman was already pulling away in her truck when they went through the door to the store.

'What's a chink?' Ben asked as he watched the old pick-up race back up the mountain road.

'Wait, I still haven't paid you,' his mother's voice rang out just as he heard the door close, and turning, he saw her helplessly staring at one of the boarded windows. 'I guess they'd rather wait until we're back this way again,' she said feebly, then, 'I wonder what sort of a bite would do that to a boy?'

'Maybe there's snakes, like rattlers and things,' Ben suggested.

'Or maybe an insect,' his mother worried aloud. 'He said they had ticks and I know that in some places you can get Lyme Disease and Spotted Fever from ticks.'

'It didn't look like he had any spots,' Ben remarked. 'Just that bloody, scratched-up ear.'

'If it is something like Lyme's or Spotted Fever,' his mother continued, 'or encephalitis . . . sometimes, mosquitoes carry things like that. Although I think it's pretty rare unless they're near infected horses. All the same, whatever it is, it's no wonder that woman's home-healing techniques wouldn't do any good.' She turned back to the stairs. 'And I don't know what good that poor woman thinks that man can do. If that boy's as sick as he looks, he shouldn't be subjected to some primitive herbal remedies. He should be seen by a proper physician who knows just what he's dealing with.' Then after a thoughtful moment, she anxiously added, 'God, I hope Gus isn't that sick.' She prodded Ben down the stairs.

'Could a snake bite make you act like that, too?' Ben asked as she pulled the car door open then stared for a moment at Sarah, sprawled over both seats, her knees up and her nose in a copy of a movie star magazine. Still wearing her Walkman, she didn't even realize they were back and obviously had missed the whole episode with the woman and the sick boy. Ben repeated his question just as his mother pulled up Sarah's earphones, scooting her over so she could sit in the driver's seat.

'I don't know about snakes. I don't even know what kind of snakes they might have here,' she distractedly answered while Ben climbed in the back.

'What snakes? Are there going to be snakes?' Sarah anxiously looked from her mother to Ben.

'All woods have snakes,' Ben replied while she stared at

him squeamishly. 'We just don't know if the snakes around here are poisonous or not.'

'Mommy!' Sarah looked panicked.

'Benjamin, stop it.' His mother gave him a frown before she started the engine. 'Now I don't want you two starting up. I have quite enough to worry about without making things up, and as far as we know there's nothing to be alarmed about in these woods.' Then she met Ben's gaze in the rear-view and gave him another warning look meant to tell him not to frighten his sister, but Ben could still tell that his mother was more than a little concerned herself.

3
A Small Dark House

Ben listened as his mother gave Sarah a watered-down version of what Cotter said, pointedly leaving out details about the boy brought down by the woman named Meg. She did mention, however, the business about the river's dangerous current and how they were not to go near the falls with its whirlpools and loose, slippery rocks. Leaning between the front seats, looking out at the road winding up through the darkening woods, all hopes for this trip grew dimmer while worry for Gus and his father deepened.

'Ouch!' Sarah's cry was followed by a slapping sound. 'Something bit me!'

'Probably just a mosquito,' Ben mumbled off-handedly. 'It won't kill you.' But as soon as the words were out of his mouth, he realized his mistake. He saw his mother's hands grow so tight on the wheel that her knuckles showed white through her tan. When she spoke, his mother's voice came even tighter:

'They come out in droves around sunset. You'd better put up your windows now.' He could tell she was trying, in spite of the strain in her voice, not to sound too concerned.

'It's too hot to roll up the windows,' Sarah replied as she leaned in her seat and began to rummage through the glove compartment. 'Where's that stinky repellent?'

'I'd rather you rolled up the windows,' his mother repeated a little more tensely.

'It's all right. I found it.' Sarah had pulled out a tiny squeeze bottle of Bug-Off and was already starting to slather it over her legs when their mother said stiffly that she wanted the windows closed as well as having them all apply the repellent. 'That's crazy,' Sarah muttered. 'It's broiling in here. We don't have to do both.'

'Mom, we don't even know what was wrong with that kid,' Ben began without thinking again just as Sarah passed back the bottle of repellent.

'What kid?' Sarah turned to their mother, who in turn gave Ben another warning glance in the rear-view, but it was out now, and Sarah persisted until their mother explained about the boy and Cotter's mention of ticks and how it was better just not to take chances.

'But, Mom,' Ben interrupted her as Sarah hurriedly rolled up her window and snatched back the bottle of bug repellent to put it on all over again. 'He didn't even say what kind of bite. It might not even be from a bug.' Then he put his foot in his mouth again, adding, 'He could have meant some kind of animal.'

'You mean they've got something with rabies up here?' Sarah asked, sounding nearly hysterical, and Ben suddenly had the exasperating feeling that they were playing *Telephone*, where the story got steadily worse with every retelling. 'Oh, why did we have to come to this awful place, anyway? First snakes, mosquitoes and ticks, and now we have to worry about – '

'Sarah, stop it!' their mother said sharply. 'Ben's right. We don't know what was wrong with that boy and we'll make ourselves crazy if we start letting everything scare us now.'

'But, Mom, if there's poisonous snakes, or ticks – don't

ticks sometimes carry Spotted Fever? And mosquitoes can carry malaria, and you just said yourself – '

'He didn't have spots,' Ben drolly informed her, 'unless you count a couple of zits. And there isn't any malaria in this part of the world.'

'Please, both of you, stop it!' their mother said firmly. 'I have too much on my mind right now to listen to the two of you bickering. Now, please . . .' Her 'please' sounded close to tears, and it sent Ben sinking back in his seat feeling guilty at what he'd begun, and worried as well, not over bugs and snakes and such, but over what had become of his father and Gus.

While the sky turned a deep, velvety blue and the woods all around them grew darker with shadows, the road ahead grew steadily rougher, just as Cotter predicted. All down the middle, thick clumps of grass sprouted up between the tire-worn ruts, and rocks and branches littered their path as if it was rarely used. Feathery pines brushed the sides of the car and the windows as the road narrowed and twisted, at one moment climbing at such a steep angle the engine would gasp at the effort, at the next nosing so sharply downward it pitched them all forward in their seats. Though the distance they had to travel was probably not all that great, it seemed without end as the day swiftly faded into dusk.

'Watch carefully now.' Their mother broke the silence when the road leveled out and the car passed over a short, wood-plank bridge. Ben could hear the brook underneath, but with the sun now down, what light remained was barely sufficient to see the road, let alone what was around it. The deep forest looked like a solid wall of steadily darkening grays. 'Cotter said there'd be a turn some twenty yards ahead, and then we follow that right down to the river.'

'Who's Cotter?' Sarah asked.

'The man who gave me directions. His son filled the

tank,' their mother replied. 'That's their name. Cotter. They run the general store.'

'That kid was so weird,' Sarah muttered. 'Did you see him? He looked just like an albino.'

'What? You mean like from Australia?' Ben asked.

'That's aborigines, Einstein,' she answered sarcastically, clearly pleased that she knew something that he didn't for a change. 'That's probably why he was all covered up. Albinos get sunburned easy. And their eyes are all pink, just like white mice. I bet that's why he had on those glasses.'

'How do their eyes get all pink?' Ben couldn't help asking her in spite of himself.

'From inbreeding,' Sarah loftily answered. 'Don't you know anything, dummy?' And while Ben was debating whether or not to ask what inbreeding was, which would just give Sarah a chance to make fun of him again, their mother cut in.

'Albinism just means a lack of pigment. It has nothing to do with inbreeding.' And then she braked hard and they all shot forward in their seats.

'Why did you do that?' Sarah grumbled.

'I think that was it.' Their mother backed up till they came to what looked like no more than a hole in the woods.

'I can't see any road in there, Mom.' Ben peered through the window at the dark woods.

'I hear water,' she said, rolling her window down till the others heard it as well, the nearby rush of what sounded like quite a big river. She turned on the headlights then and backed up a little bit further till the beam fell across what looked like an overgrown turnoff. Then they all saw the sign. A small piece of wood crudely painted and nailed to a tree. It read, simply, 'MARSDEN'. 'This is it.' She pulled at the wheel then eased the car forward. Branches slapped at the windshield but with the headlights they now saw the path in fact led to some sort of clearing. 'Let's hope your father's here,' she murmured anxiously. 'Or at least left a note.' The car bucked over heaves in the ground as they crept ahead at a snail's pace. 'I hope there's a kerosene lamp in the house,' she thought aloud, 'otherwise, we'll be falling all over ourselves without any light.'

'You mean there's no electricity?' Sarah asked in disbelief, 'How will we watch TV? How am I going to get my blow-dryer to work?' Why she even bothered to use one at all any more Ben couldn't understand. With or without it her chemo-thinned hair looked the same, all brittle, wavy wisps, as if she'd just come from a pillow fight and a bag of black down had burst over her head. But old habits die hard, he'd once heard his mother say, and vanity, too, he thought, feeling sad at her hopeless efforts at trying her best to look as she used to. 'Why didn't anyone tell us, we could have just left the hair-dryer and TV at home?'

'No one knew,' their mother said quietly, but Ben could still hear the strain in her voice, as though she was trying her hardest not to show how upset she was.

'My hair looks like a drowned rat when it dries by itself!' His sister continued to pout. 'I won't be able to show my face this whole trip.' Ben wanted to tell her the dryer wouldn't make a bit of difference, that she always looked like a drowned rat and that for someone three years older than he, she sounded like a two-year-old brat, what with Gus and their father missing and their mother as worried as she was.

'Who's going to see you, anyway?' he said instead, but she didn't hear, for she'd already pulled on her earphones and turned on her Walkman to console herself. But Ben figured she meant Cotter's son, for who else had she seen since they got here.

'Ben, would you please sit back?' his mother distractedly asked as the headlights bounced over the trees and glinted off what looked like water ahead.

'What's that?' He bounced back up between the front seats just before they pulled free of the trees to a clearing where something flashed back with the beam of their headlights. Then the last of the branches smothering the path scraped over the windshield and they found themselves in a meadow that ran to a river the size of a highway, and just a few yards ahead, shining back in their beams, was Gus's new, black van. Though it didn't look quite so new as when it left Cambridge. It looked dented and spattered with mud. 'Then Dad's here!' Ben said excitedly with his hand all ready to open the door as his mother pulled the car alongside the van. Then they saw the small dark house. And dark was the thing that stood out the most when Ben jumped from the car and raced toward it, scarcely noting the waterfall thundering down from a craggy cliff looming above it.

There was no sign of Ben's father either inside or out of the small dark house, and trudging back from the car with a bag full of groceries, he brooded over Cotter's insistence that his father hadn't come back. With the van here, he couldn't still be in Reedsville. Either the man had been lying, or he'd been away from the general store when his father drove back over the mountain to Matthew Marsden's farm.

Some farm, Ben thought with sarcasm, feeling sadder for Gus by the second as he walked through the small, overgrown field toward a house as neglected as Cotter's had been. Standing between the small field gone to seed and the river, the Marsden house looked more like a garage with a closet-sized wing at one end that barely had space for a single bed. And not only was there no electric light, but the water came from a pump, the stove ran on wood and the only facilities were an outdoor shower which had to be fed by buckets and an uninviting outhouse which made the rest-stop privies they'd used driving down look like palaces. Still, in Ben's mind at least, the surroundings somehow made up for the squalid house, for the forest that bordered the field looked immense and mysterious, begging to be explored, and the rush of the rapids and high above the trees, the cliff with its ghostly white falls were nearly hypnotic between the spectacular view and the lulling, watery sounds.

'Is everything out of the back?' Ben barely heard his mother call from the house as he stared, transfixed, at the rumbling falls that hung like a curtain across the broad cliff. It must stretch nearly twenty yards wide, he thought to himself, peering up from the field, his eyes still sorting it out through the shadows drawing the dusk ever closer to night. Then his gaze leapt off to one side of the falls to something that spiralled up like smoke. An endless black uncoiling of bats taking flight, he suddenly realized, and judging from where the spiral began, he guessed that the falls hid a cave. While watching them scatter like ash as they started their nocturnal hunt for food, his mother called again across the field and he answered that the car was empty and pushed ahead through the waist-high grass, passing Sarah who sullenly straggled along with her backpack, overstuffed with the zipper compartments and tie-top all open and trailing her things.

'What's taking your sister so long?' his mother asked when he neared the door where her silhouette was framed by the gauzy, golden light of a kerosene lamp.

'We've already made five trips apiece for her one,' Ben wryly pointed out. 'You'd think she had a two-hundred-fifty pound bag of cement to lug in.'

'She may be tired from the trip,' his mother replied with a worrying edge that he knew meant she wondered if it was really just all the driving or something else.

'It's heavy!' his sister, who'd heard them, shouted testily

back. 'And I'm trying to be careful of snakes and ticks!' Though for all the repellent she'd slathered on, Ben doubted that anything living would dare to come within a mile of her. His mother took the last bag of groceries from his arms and he sat on the stoop and looked across the field. A mist seemed to be rising off the river and creeping up over the bank, where it started a tentative crawl through the edge of the field where his sister still straggled along. His gaze wandered past her, beyond the car and the van to the pines that loomed like mountains themselves, their pointy tops stretching so high they seemed almost to scratch the dark sky. Then he glimpsed something, pale as the mist sweeping up from the river, but shaped like a diamond and drifting over the trees like a kite, though it looked about the size of a man. Pushing back up to his feet, stepping down from the stoop, he watched it glide, then dip and swoop through the trees right beyond the car.

'Sarah!' he anxiously shouted as she continued to pick her way through the high grass. Whatever it was, it had been far too big for a bird and was now in the woods just behind her.

'I'm coming!' she shouted irksomely back just as something flapped at Ben's head, bringing his startled gaze jerking up to the leathery wings of a fat, brown bat. Ducking through the door, glancing quickly back, he saw it flapping away. It made him think of the sick boy again, and rabies, but then he remembered that bats ate insects and that it was probably after some bug.

'If I have a single tick on me, I'll scream!' he heard his sister cry out, and stepping back out to the stoop, he watched her, her eyes on her feet, wading up through the grass. Then she suddenly froze in her tracks ten yards from the door, her hands flying out in surprise, and then came a bloodcurdling scream as she bolted ahead, arms and legs akimbo, looking for all the world like a wind-up toy with a spring that was wound too tight.

'Snake!' she shrieked at the top of her lungs with her eyes darting frantically over the grass while her zig-zaggy course brought her veering away from the house more often than toward it. 'It's chasing me!' she screamed as her mother came rushing out the door.

'Sarah!' she shouted in panic. 'You're going toward the river! This way, baby! Toward me!' And finally, her face taut with horror, her eyes wide and fixed on her mother, she frantically beat a path back through the overgrown grass to the house. As she shot toward the stoop, Ben glimpsed something long and black jerking after her heels. It slithered right over the threshold when Sarah darted inside the house.

'Mommy, it's still coming after me!' she squealed, just as Ben and his mother rushed through the door and found her scrambling over a chair and on to a table. Then the two of them exchanged glances of disbelief while Sarah stomped at the thing jerking right up from the floor and around her feet. 'Make it stop!' she screamed.

'Sarah.' Ben's mother's voice started to shake as his sister continued to dance on the table. 'It's not a snake.' And the shaking Ben heard was his mother trying not to burst out in laughter. 'Now stop it,' she still strained to control her voice as she walked to the table, 'before you break something.' But Sarah kept up her hysterical tap-dance until her mother grasped the thing then caught her daughter by one wrist to force her to take a good look. Sarah blinked in disbelief at the long black cord with fang-like prongs. 'It was trailing behind you, out of your pack.' Her mother held up the plug.

'You chased yourself with your hair-dryer.' Ben shook his head for he found it more stupid then funny. 'If you didn't stuff your pack so full you could tie the top shut and things wouldn't fall out.'

'Shut up!' Sarah snapped, still shaking but rapidly turning bright red with embarrassment.

'It's all right, baby,' her mother said soothingly, trying to help her down. 'We all make mistakes, and we're all overtired and concerned about Daddy so don't feel too – '

'I can get myself down. And I'm not your baby.' Sarah sullenly cut her off. 'And I'm not concerned about Daddy. He makes me so mad, getting us to drive all the way down here. Just look at this place!' And then she started in on Gus's house. But warmed by the amber glow of the kerosene lamp and with its big wood-burning stove, Ben found it a good deal more inviting from the inside than the out.

4
Night Flight

While Sarah, plugged into her Walkman, rocked in the single most comfortable chair and sulked, Ben helped his mother to sort through the bags for something to make for dinner.

'Dad could be with one of the neighbors,' Ben offered hopefully, for if the van were there, his father couldn't have gone very far. But they hadn't passed a single house the last two miles out of Ausable, and Ben found it hard to imagine the others being any more neighborly than the Cotters.

'And wouldn't it be like your father to walk in the minute I have supper ready?' his mother added with an equally hopeful if somewhat weary smile. Ben nodded, although he did not really think it likely at all.

'How about spaghetti?' She held up a jar of tomato sauce, then she set it down and turned to the wood-burning stove that dominated the room. 'We're going to need a few logs to get this going,' she said as she looked in the oven. 'Did you happen to notice if there was a woodpile outside?'

Again, Ben nodded then pulled on his cap to go outside to fetch some. Of course, he thought, Sarah wouldn't be asked to do anything the entire trip. Even when her white cell count was practically normal, she was still pampered.

'And be sure to bring in enough to keep the stove going

through to the morning. There seems to be a bit of a chill coming on now that it's night.'

If there was a chill, Ben didn't feel it, and glancing back from the door he saw his mother arranging a blanket over Sarah and knew that she'd not felt one either. It was just her usual relentless worrying over his sister, as if even with a good blood count she was more prone to catching things, which she wasn't. 'Sweetheart, are you feeling all right?' he heard her ask, stooped over the girl, pulling up an earphone from his sister's head just to make herself heard.

Sarah practically lived in that headset and it irked him, the way she tuned everyone out, as if no one in the world had problems but her. Not that she didn't have problems. And being sick was just the beginning. Flunking a grade and being kept back while all her friends went on to high school next year was a pretty big deal, he had to agree. But it wasn't his or his parent's fault, and it still didn't give her the right to take it out on everyone else, always moping around. And particularly now. With their father missing and something wrong with Gus and no way of knowing what, things were difficult enough for their mother.

'Will you leave me alone?' his sister predictably whined, pushing the blanket away. 'I'm hot! I don't want it! I'd say if I wanted it! Can't you just leave me alone?'

Ben watched his mother still hovering, one hand in the air over Sarah's head, as if about to rest itself on her forehead to feel her temperature. But she caught herself, letting the impulse pass if still looking worried.

'It is still kind of hot,' Ben fibbed, for if not chilly, things still had cooled down, but he wanted to say something to ease his mother's endless concerns.

'Oh, Ben.' His mother turned, looking surprised and embarrassed at getting caught fussing. Another thing he knew his parents worried about was how *he* felt, with all the attention lavished on Sarah and so little left over for him. 'I thought you'd already gone.' She watched him hanging by the door. 'I really should help you.' He could see her now worrying over whether she'd given him too much to do.

'Mom, it's OK. I saw a wheelbarrow out there. I can manage it easy alone.'

Then his mother crossed the room with a wan, small smile and laid a hand on his cap.

'Three big logs should do it for now. And we're going to need kindling, to get it started.'

'I know that,' Ben told her. 'This isn't the first time we ever went camping, you know.' And it would be more like camping, he thought, what with the stove and the outhouse and pump and having to sleep in their sleeping-bags, which all would have made their visit here fun, if only Gus and his father were there and if Sarah would knock off her gloom routine.

'You sound like your father.' His mother's smile brightened a bit and she gave his cap's visor a tug. 'Can't stand to be told the obvious so I won't even mention the fact that we don't have any paper to start the kindling.'

'What do you call grocery bags?' Ben straightened his cap and opened the door.

'Just like your father,' his mother's voice echoed behind him as he stepped out in to the night. Seeing the van, he couldn't help thinking again that Cotter knew more than he'd told, that he must have known of his father's return, perhaps even lied about Gus going to Reedsville. And thinking again of the Cotters, of how strange they looked and their odd warbly accents, Ben suddenly thought he recalled that the woman they saw spoke quite differently. At least, he could not remember her having that funny sort of purr, unless he had just been too distracted by the sick boy to listen that closely.

Pushing the wheelbarrow around the house to the woodpile, he scanned the velvety darkness of the sky above the trees. A scythe moon hung on a thin dark cloud overhead like a silvery claw and glimmering specks of stars wrapped around the horizon. Dropping his gaze to the woodpile, where mist off the river crept over the first layer of logs, he thought for a moment he saw a star there, too. But of course, it would have to be a firefly, the way it sluggishly swam through the air, drifting up one side of the stack of wood. Letting go of the wheelbarrow, he cupped his hands to catch it, but a flapping sound high above brought his hands down empty and his gaze soaring up.

It was not another bat Ben saw but two pale shapes, like kites, gliding over the roof and out of sight. Racing around the back of the house, he squinted up though the night and just for a moment, he almost thought he could make out the shape of something one of them carried much like a bird of prey might carry a rabbit or mouse in its talons. But whatever it carried was far too big for a rabbit, and if these things were birds, their wingspan and length appeared to be larger than any bird he'd ever seen. In any case, he lost sight of them within seconds when the pair seemed to swoop toward the rumbling falls that towered beyond the trees. Though their shapes had seemed actually closer to a bat's, because of their size he decided they must have been birds after all, like the thing he'd seen earlier, dropping into the trees behind Sarah. Still, they seemed even much bigger than an eagle, which made him uneasy, for no North American bird could be that large.

'Benjamin!' his mother called from the house, and heading back toward the woodpile, he wondered if these birds had a roost at the falls, like the bats. As he hefted a log from the stack and set it down again in the wheelbarrow, he noticed another firefly had joined the first drifting over the pile. The light they emitted seemed closer to blue than white, like the fireflies back home, he thought while hefting another log off the top of the stack. Grasping yet another, he found a third speck of light had joined their ranks and all three were now drifting closer to where he stood. Then he heard a flapping sound again, but this time it was a bat, and ducking his head he watched it glide under the overhang meant to keep rain off the wood. After snatching a pair of the insects in flight, the bat swooped upward again, and again Ben recalled Meg saying she saw 'the bite mark' on the boy, and once more he thought, and more seriously, of his sister's remark about rabies.

Without knowing why exactly – perhaps because the sick boy had been pale as the Cotters – Ben wondered if the reason the Cotters' skin was so white and all covered up against the sun was because they'd been 'bitten', too, by whatever it was that got Daniel. Then suddenly the bites and the strangeness of the Cotters and even the great pale shapes he'd seen soaring off toward the falls all took on a darker dimension. Ben began thinking of horror movies and scary books with settings like this – thickly wooded mountains, far from civilization, where nightmare creatures roamed the night, preying on people who sometimes became just like them. Then something flapped again, and this time it was so close behind and so large that it sent a soft breeze over the back of his neck and made his blood run cold.

'Nice evening.' At the sound of the voice behind, he dropped the log in his arms. 'Sorry, I didn't mean to give you a start.' Then the flapping started again, and sheepishly glancing around at what moments before he'd imagined might have fangs, he stooped to pick up the log and hide his embarrassment. 'What is that, a firefly?' his mother asked, giving the braided rug she held another hard flap. A cloud of dust filled the air around her and she coughed.

'Your father and Gus may be handy with tools, but I

don't think they've cleaned the place once since they've been here. There's a layer of dust an inch thick on everything in there . . . Ben, look behind you.' But by the time he'd turned, whatever she'd meant him to see was gone. Or just out of sight, he realised when she added, 'Now it's on top of your head.' Ben dropped the log a second time, yanking his cap off, expecting another bat, but of course he'd have felt a bat on his head and all it was was the firefly. 'It's only a bug.' His mother grinned, for she'd seen his fleeting alarm. 'It can't bite.'

'I know that,' he said disconcertedly, feeling like Sarah had over the so-called snake, and annoyed with himself for letting his imagination get carried away. The speck he'd shaken from his cap still lazily circled his head as he pulled his cap back on and stooped to pick up the log again.

'Remember to check for ticks when you get that inside,' his mother off-handedly mentioned, but still he could tell she was just as uneasy as he in their new surroundings.

5
Sea Song

'Don't you ever take off that ridiculous cap?' his sister remarked when back in the house, he sat before the stove, tearing up grocery bags to roll into balls. He glanced at her, still rocking and wearing her Walkman and looking as gloomy as ever. 'What's the big deal about the Red Sox anyway?' she testily murmured. 'Didn't they lose the world series last year?'

He might have snapped something back, but she wouldn't have heard, not with the headphones, and he knew she was just trying to pick a fight, and anyway, the reason he wore the cap wasn't because he was crazy for baseball, he wore it for the same reason his father wore one that said Bruins. They were gifts from Gus. He turned back to the stove, and had a good blaze going when he finally realized his mother was taking a long time coming back from shaking out the rug. Closing the door to the stove, he went back out to the rickety steps.

The mist off the river now blanketed everything, spreading across the grass like smoke, rising right over the wheels of the wheelbarrow, looking now like a boat adrift. Then he noticed the old braided rug, folded in quarters, tossed into the cart, as if his mother had just been on her way in with it, then changed her mind. But all he saw when he looked for her was the pale gray mist, like a sheet of ice, and skirting the edge of the field like the wall of a fortress, the pine trees all blurred together, their pointy tops like pinnacled sentry stations along the parapet.

This illusion of some sort of medieval castle sprouting up from these dark, silent hills put in mind old horror movies again, where ghosts prowled dank and dusty halls. Even the rush of the river, lost somewhere beneath the smoldering blanket of gray seemed malevolent now, like the rumblings of monstrous beasts buried under the ground. And still he did not see his mother, and that in itself made the night feel much darker somehow.

The crackle of twigs underfoot sounded much too loud as he crept to the side of the house. Perhaps she'd decided to bring in more wood for the stove, he thought, till he came to the woodpile. There was nothing, except for more fireflies, six in all, and all drifting toward him. Waving them off with one hand he squinted off at the free-standing privy. Nestled right up at the edge of the woods, he saw that the door was closed and wondered if maybe she'd gone to use it, but then the door had been closed when they got there and it was more likely she would have come back to the house for a flashlight, for the hut was in utter darkness.

'Mom?' he called out softly. Listening a moment, he did hear something. But it wasn't what he'd hoped to hear, just a rustling sound from the forest. About to call again, the words caught in his throat when he heard something snap. God only knew what sort of animals lived in these woods. He swallowed hard. 'Mom?' His call this time was even softer than before. In mountains this wild, there might even be grizzlies . . . or worse, he thought, as he swallowed again to clear the dryness from his throat to call once more for his mother. But another call, some distance behind him, broke the stillness first.

'Ray!' It was his mother, calling his father's name down

by the road. The thought of his father finally turning up brought him barrelling back through the field. 'Ray!-ay-ay-' Her call reverberated from every direction, echoing up to the falls and down the river and through the woods. Then he saw her, and the excitement of seeing his father too was nipped in the bud. Instead, he felt as if his heart were a stone dropping into the deep, icy river. Hearing her call again, then the forest mimicking her cry, he plowed through the grass, watching her, arms hugged to her chest, turning in circles and peering off every which way like a very small child that had suddenly found itself lost.

'Mom!' He jogged past the van and wrapped his arms about her waist. 'He'll be back.' He looked imploringly up at her. 'I'm sure of it.'

'It's after nine.' Her voice was raspy and trembling. 'And he should have been waiting to meet us in Ausable since four. Now where would he be?' With the light of the claw-like moon crawling the sky above the falls, Ben saw the shine on her cheeks and knew she'd been crying.

'Mom, the van's here. All their stuff's in the house. He *has* to come back,' he reasoned, then pulling her arm over his shoulder he tried to lead her back to the house.

'I can't even tell if something's wrong with the van,' she went off on her own train of thought. 'I can't find the keys to start it, if it will start at all. It looks like it's been through a lot, all spattered with mud, the right fender dented, and one of the headlights is broken. Maybe,' she went on in a trembly tone, 'maybe they had an accident. Maybe that's why Gus needed a doctor. And maybe Dad borrowed a car from one of the neighbors.' At least this gave some sense to a situation that seemed to make none. Till his mother remembered something. 'No, Cotter said he distinctly recalled the van when your father drove through there last night.'

'Maybe he didn't have trouble with the van till he got back here. Maybe he went to borrow a car from someone who lives nearby.'

'Then he would have met us down in Ausable. Ben, we were three hours late. He could have walked to Ausable in that time.'

'Not,' Ben strained to reason it through, 'not if he went through the woods to find someone. It looks like it would be easy getting lost in there, even in daylight.'

'Why on earth would he go through the woods?' his mother asked disconsolately.

'Maybe there was a path. Like the turnoff to here. It looks more like a path than a road. Maybe there's another one. One that leads to someone's house.' Then, as if in answer, a new sound rippled down through the night. Before it broke into fading echoes, Ben placed the source somewhere up by the falls.

'What was that?' His mother's arm pulled him close to her side when they heard it again, and both of them listened, scarcely breathing, trying to decipher the faint, distant sound. It seemed at first like singing, or music, or both, though it wasn't quite human. Instead, Ben thought, it was more like an eerie mixture of deep oboe sounds, like the wind, and a chirping, a bit like that cicada thing Cotter mentioned, but now it was not so shrill. And there did seem to be a melody to it, weaving between the different tones, and the only thing even remotely like it that Ben could think of would be electronic. But this was alive, he somehow sensed, and then it came to him what it did sound like.

'Last winter my teacher played a record in class,' he said softly, still listening. 'Mom, it was "Songs of the Humpback Whale", and it sounded almost just like this.' And it did, the more he strained to hear. First the deep oboe sounds, then the chirruping peals, like hundreds of thousands of crickets all at once. His mother said nothing, and Benjamin realized, of course, that the thought of a whale was absurd, up here, in the Ozark mountains, hundreds of miles away from the nearest sea. But nothing else he'd ever heard so closely resembled this pairing of sounds, beginning with the melodious thrumming then swelling into that high-pitched trill. In fact, it even evoked in the eye of his mind an impression of something massive, yet gentle and swimming gracefully through the ocean's depths.

This impression was so strong, he wondered at his own imagination, for he'd never actually seen a real whale or how one moved. It was almost as if the singing, or music, projected a picture along with the sound, like something telepathic that touched and awakened in him some brand new sense. But this seemed just as far-fetched as his other imaginings, and in the end, he decided he must have conjured his own image up to this eerie hypnotic music.

'Maybe it was just someone playing a record,' he said after it stopped, feeling strangely sad once it was over.

'I don't see how they could without electricity,' his mother replied. 'Unless they were using one of those hand-crank victrolas.'

'Those what?'

'That's before your time.' Her voice seemed changed somehow, lighter, less anxious. 'As a matter of fact they haven't been used since well before your grandparents' time. Maybe it was a tape cassette, like your sister's, run on batteries. Or maybe, if someone is actually living up there, they have their own generator.'

'Hey! Where did everyone go?' Sarah's shout shattered into a dozen ear-splitting echoes. His mother's arm slid from his shoulder as she shouted back, 'It's all right! We're coming!'

'Mom? Benjamin?' Sarah continued to holler as if she hadn't heard, and sure enough, when they reached the door, they found her still wearing her earphones.

6
The Mysterious Medusa

The kerosene lamp was left burning on the table after they'd all retired; Ben and his sister in sleeping-bags, their mother taking the room with the bed. The bed, of course, had been offered to Sarah, who then surprised them both by refusing, saying she'd prefer her down sleeping-bag on an air mattress on the floor. Ben doubted that she was being selfless, for the bed looked lumpy and sagged in the middle, but his mother, he knew, thought Sarah was actually making a sacrifice for her. In any event, Sarah hadn't grouched through the meal as she usually did, and to whatever they owed her lack of complaints through the rest of the evening, Ben was just grateful.

Over dinner, they had decided to look for a path through the woods in the morning, and if they found one, they'd follow, and hopefully it would lead to some news of their father. If nothing resulted from this, they'd bundle everything back in the car and drive to Reedsville in search of the doctor Cotter mentioned. But even having two different plans didn't make Ben feel any easier, for it wasn't at all like his father to vanish without so much as a note, unless, that is, something truly terrible had happened. Lying awake with that troubling thought, he watched the flickering light from the lamp scatter shadows like scurrying mice over the walls and across the cobwebby ceiling. Though crudely constructed, the house, in Ben's opinion, still had charm.

The walls had almost entirely been papered with pages from magazines, mostly *National Geographics*, and every picture, strangely, was of the sea. Or rather, every picture was of some life form or other found in the sea, but not whales and sharks and seals and other better known salt water denizens. The room was a virtual mural of exotic ocean organisms like Portuguese man-of-wars, anemones, hydras and all sorts of corals. At a glance, most resembled flowers with semi-translucent, petal-like tentacles, and with all the delicate green vegetation swirling up in the water around them, they looked, all together, like snapshots from some murky, mysterious garden. It seemed odd that a man from the heart of the Ozarks would cover his walls with such creatures, and looking around at these marvelous images faded by time to a ripe golden brown, Ben wondered if Matthew Marsden had been a sailor before moving up to the mountains.

In any case, it was clear he had more than a passing interest in creatures like these, and that he did not put much stock in material things, for apart from the stove and the rocker, the rest of the furnishings were scrappy and spare, just a knotted pine table with four straight-backed chairs that looked like crates on stilts, a few shelves and a cupboard cluttered with pots and plates and cups made of tin, and the worn braided rug and a handful of books that looked nearly a hundred years old. And the books: Ben had scarcely been able to make hide nor hair of what they were about, with titles like *The Pathology of Coelenterata Electricus* and *The Mysterious Medusa*, which at first he guessed would be about some woman whose head was covered with snakes and whose glance could turn a person into stone, for his mother once said, after having her hair permed and hating the way it came out, that she looked like Medusa, which his father then explained was a monster from Greek mythology. But both turned out to be about jellyfish, like most of the books in the room, except for a few about things like quantum physics and one that looked newer than the rest. Called *The Elusive Quark*, Ben just managed to understand from the cover that it had something to do with what scientists now believed was the smallest unit of matter, a thing thought to be tinier than the electrons, neutrons and protons of an atom. But all of these books seemed as out of place as the pictures on the walls, for why would Gus's great uncle, a simple farmer, care about 'quarks'?

Turning in his sleeping-bag, he stared through the legs of the table and chairs at the door to the tiny bedroom where his mother, he hoped, was now sleeping. She'd barely picked at the meal she'd made, not that Ben had managed to eat much more, as worried over his mother's state as he was over Gus and his father's absence. All through supper, he'd wanted to talk about the curious pictures and books, but he doubted his mother even noticed them, distracted as she was. As for Sarah, if she did not spend the evening complaining, she also did not seem particularly interested in their surroundings or any too eager even to talk. In fact, she spent the whole evening plugged into her Walkman, off in her own little world, and now she noisily snored from her side of the room, still wearing her earphones.

It both amazed and irked Ben, how oblivious she could be, so wrapped up in herself she did not seem the least concerned with their father's absence. He even resented how easily she slept while he could not. Then, as if all his anxious thoughts weren't enough, he was suddenly seized with another. It came with a rustling sound right overhead, above the beamed roof of the cabin. It brought back to mind the great, kite-like creatures he'd seen gliding over the forest. He still thought they'd looked more like bats than birds, despite their unusual size. Then another rustling sound came from the opposite end of the ceiling, and Ben suddenly pictured a pair of these kite-like creatures perched on the roof. Or perhaps it was only the bats, though the rustling seemed louder than bats might make with a wingspan of only a half dozen inches or so. Then a scratching sound on the roof filled his head with pictures far stranger than those on the walls, pictures of human-like creatures with great fleshy wings with talons and long white teeth.

Trying to focus instead on the faint, lulling rush of the river some yards from the house, he burrowed deeper down in his sleeping-bag till it covered the top of his head, and all he could see was a patch of the braided rug where the light from the lamp dimly flickered. Then the watery sounds from the river and the thin, dancing light at last worked their spell, and he slept, not stirring again still just before dawn, when a distant sound like thousands of crickets broke with the suddenness of an infant's cry at birth.

Benjamin tossed and turned, nearly waking. His eyelids fluttered open a crack. But then, the drowsy heat pouring out of the wood-burning stove dragged him back toward sleep where the faraway, shrill creaking sound grew faint as the creak of an old, turning hinge. His eyelids fluttered shut again on an image that flitted across his subconscious. A pair of nightmarish creatures peered in through the door. But for Ben, it was just a bad dream.

7
A Jar Full of Stars

Although the eerie singing from the night before seemed to come from the falls, the following morning, the only path they found near the house wound away from the river. To Ben's disappointment, Sarah, who'd opted to wait at the house should their father return, changed her mind at the very last minute, her dislike of exercise and fear of ticks apparently giving way to her fear and dislike of being left in a strange place alone. So the three of them set out right after breakfast, hiking through woods that no longer seemed ominous, but magical now, with the dazzling sun streaming down through the leaves to a carpet of bright green moss where feathery bracken and mushrooms and ferns were scattered between the straight-backed pines and the gnarled, twisting trunks of other old trees marching over the hills.

The forest was quiet, however. Too quiet. They neither heard nor saw any birds or any other wildlife usually found in deep woods. And they should have. Despite the gentle beauty surrounding them, the silence made Ben uneasy. If there had been bats by night, by day there should have been other creatures about. But then, animals in the wild often sense when people are about and perhaps they were there, just hiding, he reasoned, for he did have the vague, funny feeling that they were being watched. And though none of them were talking, even he could just make out the faint beat of the rock music seeping out from the earphones of his sister's Walkman.

'Mom,' he quietly started, moving ahead as Sarah brought up the rear. 'That boy we saw, Daniel, the one who was sick, remember what that woman said?' His mother, walking beside him, looked distractedly ahead. 'Remember how she said something about how her healing didn't work?' he went on, and this time his mother gave a slight nod, though she still seemed lost in thought. 'What do you think she meant? About her healing?' Ben persisted.

'People living in places like this often have to make do without doctors,' she answered. 'So over the years, they develop their own kinds of medicine. Often by accident. There's probably a wealth of medicinal herbs growing in these woods.' Ben looked at the assortment of plants poking up through the moss around them. Indian pipe-cleaners, jack-in-the-pulpits, lady slippers and skunk cabbage were the only ones he recognized, and he doubted they'd be much good. 'Unless she meant a laying-on-of-hands,' his mother thoughtfully added, holding back a thorny branch so it didn't spring back and catch Sarah.

'A what?' Ben glanced back at his sister, plodding behind with a pout, still plugged into her earphones.

'It's like praying over someone,' his mother replied as Sarah passed by them. Then Ben was suddenly thinking again of the eerie music or singing they'd heard, for it had had an almost angelic, ethereal sound, a bit like a choir. And then, instead of whales he was picturing people chanting in a strange tongue, all wearing hooded robes and joined in a circle, trying to 'heal' the sick. This line of thought soon had him thinking of voodoo and witches and that sort of thing, but he kept it to himself, for he knew it would sound as far-fetched as vampires and whales.

'How far are we going to go on this trail?' Sarah's trudging pace was slowing them down.

'Until we find something or come to the end,' Ben grumbled, for they'd only been gone twenty minutes.

'What?' Sarah stopped and huffed as if they'd been running instead of crawling along. Ben stomped up beside her and yanked off her earphones.

'As long as it takes to find Dad,' he repeated, ignoring his mother's warning glance.

'I wish,' his mother said gently to Sarah, 'you'd waited at the house, like we planned. For all we know your father could be turning up there now.'

'And if you don't want to keep looking,' Ben irksomely added, 'you'll have to go back by yourself.'

'We don't even know where this goes.' Sarah looked at her mother. 'We could be walking for hours.'

'We aren't going to give up just because you want to,' Ben grumbled back. 'You can go back alone. It's only a little way and you'd have to be blind to get lost on this path.'

'Mom!' she all but pleaded now, and their mother looked torn, her brow deeply furrowed.

'What's the big deal?' Ben impatiently prodded. 'It's not like you're going to run into a grizzly.' This last remark made him feel guilty, however, after his own wild imaginings. 'And, anyway,' he sheepishly added, 'you put on enough Bug-Off to scare off a moose. Come on, Sarah, for crying out loud. Can't you see that Mom's worried? We're trying to find Dad.'

'Ben, that's enough,' their mother broke in. 'I can handle this.'

'You think I'm not worried, too?' Sarah's pout began trembling. 'You think I don't care about Daddy or Gus?' Her voice cracked and her puffy face pulled into a knot. 'How do you think – ' she stammered, 'how do you think *I* feel!' And as always, Ben thought, she would now turn the crisis at hand into hers alone. 'You think you know everything! You think you know what it means to be sick! You think you know what it feels like getting kept back while everyone else goes to high school! *"You'll make new friends, you'll see!"*' she bitterly mimicked something her father once said, and Ben saw his mother's face go gray at the outburst. This wasn't the time, he angrily thought as Sarah carried on, 'Well, you're wrong! You don't know a thing! Nobody knows how I feel!'

'We know how hard it is, sweetheart,' he heard his mother struggling to rein in impatience while his own continued straining right out of control 'It's just . . .' Her voice sounded hollow and helpless. 'It's just, right now . . .'

'What does getting kept back have to do with finding Dad?' Ben broke in with sarcasm then, glowering at his sister and missing his mother's 'let's not make it worse' look. 'Can't you see how bad Mom's feeling? Can't you think about anyone else?' Then Sarah was suddenly stumbling back down the path, and his mother was turning to follow when Ben added anxiously, 'Mom, she'll be OK. Come on. We gotta find Dad.' Again she looked torn, but after a moment of frowning indecision, she finally turned, her face full of more worry than Ben had seen since Sarah first got sick.

As the two of them went on in silence, Ben started regretting what he'd said. It was true that Sarah was too wrapped up in herself, and now of all times was the worst for their mother, but he couldn't imagine himself in his sister's shoes, to be that sick, and then to be kept back a grade to boot. And now, with all her old friends starting high school next year he supposed she'd be branded a dummy by all the kids younger than her who'd be in the grade she'd have to repeat. It *was* a rotten deal, he had to admit, and as the slope they were on grew steeper, Ben resolved to swallow his pride and tell her he was sorry when they got back.

It wasn't that she didn't care about anyone else, Sarah miserably thought, it was just sometimes everything went wrong at once and nothing she did seemed to help. First and worst, of course, was getting sick, and not something like mumps or the measles that went away and left you pretty much the way you were before. No, this one was for keeps, and it not only turned you into a freak, making your hair fall out in clumps and swelling your face up like a balloon, it also made you tired all the time and had everyone fussing around you, or like most of the kids at school, avoiding you, not knowing what to say or scared that they might catch it, and being so silly about it they even gave a leukemia lesson in homeroom, which, thank God, they held on a day that she was too sick to go to school. But she knew about it, just like she never missed all the stares in the halls between classes, just like she knew why her two best friends — former best friends, she amended — had gotten so sugary sweet and so careful about what they said that it made her want to scream. It wasn't because they liked her more than before, but because she was going to die, and now they treated her like some special project like 'Help The Elderly Week'. Why couldn't anyone see that all the special attention was just as bad as acting like those kids who treated her like she had the plague? Couldn't they see that being so disgustingly nice all the time, always fussing around her, even always letting her have her way was just a constant reminder that things were only different now because everyone knew she was dying. All she really wanted was for everything to be like before, to look like she did so the kids wouldn't stare, to be able to do a few things for herself, to forget that she had this awful disease so she wouldn't feel so damn scared all the time. Which was why she insisted on going along on the search for her father, because nothing scared her so much right now as being left alone. That's what dying was like, she imagined, being left completely alone.

But then, she tired very easily. In fact, she was just about to collapse, and after less than half an hour of walking. And she couldn't even tell them that was the reason she couldn't go on, because then her mother would get that horrible look which she thought that no one could see, but she saw it, every time she so much as sneezed, that look of panic, and she knew what her mother was thinking then, she knew she was wondering, 'Is it time?' And because there was no way to stop it coming, at least till it did she could try and forget. That is, if everyone would only let her.

Reaching the end of the path, now feeling more tired than anything else, she glimpsed the van that Gus and her father drove down in and felt a twinge of guilt. Ben had been right, she'd done it again, she'd just managed to make her mother feel worse. And it didn't help any to know that she hadn't been able to help herself. She should have just done what her mother suggested and stayed behind to begin with. Oh, why, she wondered, did everything keep going from bad to worse? It just made everything harder without her father and Uncle Gus. And this, she wryly, miserably mused, was supposed to be getting away from it all, away from the trips to the hospital every two weeks, away from everyone's stares, a whole summer, or at least as long as it lasted, of being just a regular family. But the only thing that was regular was the fighting between her and Ben, which upset her just like it always did from even before the time she got sick. But in an odd way, it also somehow comforted her, to be treated the same.

A paradox, she thought it was called, when one thing

made you feel both awful and good. Not good, exactly, because she didn't really like fighting with him, but it did help to make her feel not so scared, because it was like the old days. Without even knowing it, her brother with his constant pestering was the only person she was able to be with and forget. But lately, she could not even appreciate this, not with Gus and her father gone, not with even more stuff going wrong to the point that she didn't think she could stand it. Not even the Walkman helped the way it had before this trip, when it kept her from hearing what people were saying and stopped her from thinking about her problems so much.

Now, while it blared away in her ears, her mind was still running a mile a minute. And not with the sort of self-pitying things Ben thought, but with worry for Gus and her father, and such deep concern for her mother that she had in fact been concealing her greatest fear. The remission her doctor had seen was far more fleeting than he'd guessed, but Sarah resolved not to let on that she'd started a relapse driving down. A relapse so severe that even she knew she should be in the hospital. Her one wish, walking toward the house, was that Gus and her father would soon return and that the five of them might really be just a regular family again . . . if only till her visit with her doctor's Arkansas colleague, at which time, she had a fairly strong sense, she'd be hospitalized for the final time.

After climbing the stoop, she stopped for a moment to lean by the door, exerted from hiking and suddenly feeling slightly woozy, as if she might even pass out. With no one around to see her, she made no pretense of how she felt, her whole frame sagging as though it were carrying a terrible weight. When the moment of dizziness passed, she dragged her head upright and reached for the latch. Then her hand simply hovered a second or two when she saw that the door was ajar. She had been the last to leave and was certain that she had closed it. Perhaps, she thought, too tired to dwell on the matter, the molding was warped or a hinge was loose or the latch was defective and hadn't caught. Pushing it wider and stepping inside, she found the room just as she left it, but brighter with the late morning sun glaring through the windows.

Crossing to the counter by the sink, she worked at the handpump until the spout coughed up several splashes of cold river water which she thirstily drank. After the night, which had got chilly, the day was becoming another scorcher. But today, with a bit of a fever now blooming, she still felt a little chilled. Well, at least any fevered perspirings would pass for the sweat of another hot day, she told herself, grateful for anything that would keep the others from knowing. She pumped another splash of icy river water to pat on her brow, the music from the earphones of her Walkman blocking the groan of the pump, along with every other sound in the house, like the creak of an opening door and the squeak of the floorboards behind her.

Oblivious to a presence in the house, Sarah stared over the sink through the window where the shadow of the little house spread over the yard. It wasn't all that bad for a summer cottage, tiny but cozy, and she was sure she'd have found it more pleasant to be there if only she wasn't feeling so rotten. That's what made it so hard not to be cranky, that and the struggle of trying to hide at least how physically uncomfortable she felt all the time. She'd far rather have them all think she was just an old sourpuss than see her parents anguish over all the pains her illness caused her. Like the one in her back which was steadily growing worse, 'Because the bones expand and grow brittle when the marrow turns fibrous,' her doctor had said, though he'd promised to keep it their secret. There was nothing one could do, after all, but grin and bear it. Or bear it, at least, she thought when something caught the corner of her eye.

A slowly widening path of brilliant sunlight spread over the stove to her left, which was odd, because there wasn't a window across from it on that side of the room. Turning then, her hand clapped over her mouth, catching a startled cry as her squinting gaze caught sight of the silhouette stepping through the opening door. The sun pouring in all around it was nearly blinding, leaving the silhouette black, till it tiptoed out to the stoop, then glancing back, it froze in the blazing light. The two of them gawked at each other for one interminable moment before she managed to pull off her earphones and ask:

'What are you doing here?' Cotter's son managed a smile in return, but it looked both embarrassed and sheepish. In fact, everything about him at that moment made him look like a thief. 'Well?' Sarah persisted. Then the boy made a sound as if clearing his throat.

'I came to see if your pa got back.' She thought he sounded nervous, but then, he'd had that peculiar warble the first time she heard him speak. Still, she eyed him accusingly as she started across to the door.

'Then why, if no one was here, did you let yourself in?' She stopped at the threshold and glared.

'There *wasn't* nobody here. *You* was here.' He smiled more confidently, but something about his voice, the purring edge, even his choice of words, sounded unnatural somehow, not like a real rustic out of the Ozarks, she thought, but more like someone mimicking an accent. She'd done it herself when she used to act in the plays at the Peabody School, but just as she and her classmates still sounded American, putting on accents, she had the oddest feeling this boy was a foreigner faking his Arkansas speech. 'I knocked on the door and hollered in but it seemed like you couldn't hear. So then I just came in and I was gonna tap your shoulder.' She couldn't see his eyes behind the dark glasses, but felt them, on her neck. Her hand moved to her throat where the Walkman headset hung.

'It looked to me like you were sneaking out.' Her gaze went to the bedroom door, and though it stood wide open, she couldn't recall if it had been closed when they left.

'I was,' he quickly answered with his eerie, warbly purr. 'I mean, I started in, but then I got to thinking I might scare you, so I changed my mind and started out again. And then, you turned around.' The quickness of his answer and his smile, which merely looked shy to her now, started Sarah doubting her own suspicions.

'But I just got here myself,' she pointed out. 'So why didn't I see *you* coming?'

'Which way you come from?' he asked, still smiling, and when she said from the path through the woods, his smile turned into a loopy, victorious grin. 'Well, that's why. You could see the field and the river, but I walked down from the falls.' She half expected his hands to come clapping up with this flawless answer, except, she now noticed, he'd had them behind his back the whole time they'd been talking.

'What were you doing at the falls?' Her suspicions were swelling again as she stared at his arms, crossed behind his back as if they held something. 'Ausable's *that* way.' She pointed in the other direction. This time the youth did not have a hasty reply and his smile went flat.

'Just hanging out,' he answered somewhat awkwardly. 'I like it up there.'

'What are you hiding behind your back?' She took a step out to the stoop.

'Why, nothin',' he mumbled, stepping back with that clumsy shuffling way he had, which had made her think he was lame when she saw him yesterday, working around the car.

'Then hold out your hands.' She held out her own with the challenge, almost certain now that whatever he held, he'd taken from the house.

'I told you, it's nothin',' he answered, now seeming nervous. 'I just stopped to ask after your pa.'

'Let me see what you have,' she persisted. But when she reached toward him, he lurched away, nearly falling off the stoop with his arms flailing out like wings in his baggy shirt. But this she scarcely noticed, her gaze snagged on one of the youth's gloved hands. It took a moment to realize the thing that it held was just an odd-looking jar. Shaped like an oversized test tube, the dark blue glass seemed almost to glitter, although it was not from the sun beaming down, but from wriggling things inside that glowed, and strongly enough that their light was shed right through the nearly opaque container. 'What do you have in there? Fireflies?' She studied him curiously, for collecting bugs was a thing kids did, not a boy his age. He looked tongue-tied a moment, and then very slowly, a smile crept back to his face.

'I caught 'um up by the falls. I was going to give 'um to Danny. On account of he's sick.' Sarah remembered Ben and her mother discussing the boy. The one who'd been bit. 'It keeps your mind off things, if you're stuck in bed. They're real pretty to watch.' Sort of like her Walkman helped to take her mind off things, she supposed, finally believing the boy had been telling the truth – or wanting to believe, for she wished someone brought her a dark blue jar full of fireflies when she was stuck in bed, instead of make-up work for school and cards with corny little prayers and all the other things that only reminded her of how sick she was.

'That's nice.' She smiled at the boy, deciding that what she mistook for suspicious was shyness. And then she self-consciously lowered her gaze, for she realized she had been staring, trying to make out the features of his pale face, buried under those scraggly white bangs. She bet he knew just what it felt like being gawked at all the time. It couldn't be much better, being an albino, except that couldn't make you die. Maybe she and this boy had a lot more in common than both of them looking like freaks. Then shyly bringing her gaze back up, she decided she actually liked his strange looks. In fact, she thought, he sort of resembled a rock star, what with his glasses and hair.

'So, did he ever show up?' It took her a moment to recall what he came for.

'No,' she replied, the spell of the moment broken by thoughts of her father and Gus. 'And we've all been worried sick about it. It doesn't make sense, with the van right there.'

'I'm sorry.' His smile appropriately faded and he sounded as sad as she felt. 'Maybe you ought to go look for his friend down in Reedsville and see if he knows where he went.'

'Mom said we're going to as soon as she gets back, if she doesn't find anything here. Her and Ben are out looking for him right now.' This seemed to make him frown. 'Is something wrong?'

'Where are they looking?' Now he sounded as concerned as she felt.

'That hill back there. They took the same path I came back on.' She gestured away from the falls.

'Hope they know to head back in time so as not to get caught in the dark.'

'It's barely one. They have plenty of time.' And as if to contradict her, a great dark cloud slipped over the roof of the house and directly across the sun. Watching the shadow spread over the field like a stain, she felt the air turn cool. It felt a bit the way it does before a big storm breaks. She turned to the boy, still watching the spreading gray sweep over the van and the forest. In a matter of seconds, the blazing day suddenly looked like dusk.

'You won't need those glasses now,' Sarah said offhandedly, but she saw the boy stiffen a bit and she worried he took it in the wrong way. 'I mean, if the sun really bothers your eyes . . .' Then she realized she was making it worse, for if he did have albino-pink eyes, all her talk would just make him more self-conscious. Then she saw that it already had. Face bowed and turned away from her, he stepped awkwardly down from the stoop.

'Guess I better be moving on,' he said in a warbly mumble.

'Maybe you should wait, if it's going to start raining.' She mentally kicked herself for now she felt sure the glasses weren't just to shield his eyes from the sun, and that she had made him uncomfortable calling attention to his affliction.

'Rain don't bother me none,' he murmured back, starting across the field, his gangly, bundled-up form wading clumsily on through the rippling grass.

'Thanks for coming by!' She hugged her arms to her chest as the breeze picked up and the dark cloud overhead continued to swell, blotting out the last bit of blue sky. She watched him, his baggy shirt flapping, his snow-white mane whipped back by the wind, till he turned past the trees at the edge of the road and she felt the first drop of rain hit her cheek. It was only then that it passed through her mind that fireflies only came out in the dark, and she wondered for a moment how on earth he managed to catch some by day. But only for a moment, for the wooziness returned, and her back was still aching and she felt like the shadow which spread through the valley had crept into her. Missing her parents and Gus and even Ben, half wishing the boy had stayed, if only so she wouldn't feel quite so alone, she stepped into the now darkened house and painfully and unsteadily lowered herself into the rocker to wait.

8
Things of the Present Lost in the Past

'There's a hut or something down there!' Ben had climbed to the top of a boulder that jutted up from a cluster of silver birch at one side of a steep winding road. The path they had followed met the continuation of the road they drove up on, though past the Marsden turnoff, it looked like it hadn't been used in years. Waist-high ferns sprung out of mossy ruts which were rapidly turning to rivers as the black cloud above unleashed a torrent of rain.

'Does it look like anyone's there?' His mother was huddled beneath an enormous old pine, its sheltering furry-green arms shivering under the weight of the storm.

'Can't see anyone!' Ben shouted, slipping and sliding back to the ground. 'Should we keep on going?' he breathlessly asked after sprinting across the road to her side.

'Whoever lives there may have seen your father.' Blinking against the rain, she pushed her dripping bangs back from her brow. 'Maybe they'll let us come in till the storm breaks. It can't last long, coming down this hard.' Then taking a tentative step from under the pine, wincing up at the pummeling downpour, she said, 'Thank God your sister went back before this started. Come on, let's run.' And the two of them went dashing down the shrub-entangled trail, feet skidding across the rain-slickened moss and stumbling around each sloping bend until they reached a gully like the one around the Marsden house, except here there was no open field, just woods not quite as old and tall as the rest, as if it had been cleared away at one time and then left for the forest to creep in again. 'Is that it?' his mother asked in surprise when she spotted an odd-looking structure ahead. With a roof made of metal which arched like a bubble, it nestled snugly between the trees, looking more like a monstrous rust-spotted mushroom than anything like an abode.

'Wow, it looks just like a spaceship!' Ben exclaimed as he hurried ahead of her, working his way from the side of the road through the brambles and bracken surrounding the thing. Closer up, he thought it looked more like a doll house on wheels, or on what were once wheels and were now only rusted spindles that rested on crumbly black hills that must once have been tires. And the funny domed roof, he discovered, was rounded only on two sides. The side he stood before, where the windows were, was perfectly flat. 'What is it?' he asked as his mother straggled up through the rain beside him.

'It looks like a very old trailer.' His mother sounded as awed as he by their find. 'Very, very old. In fact this thing should be in a museum. I once saw a picture of one like this when I was – I couldn't have been more than ten, and the picture was in an old magazine that I found in my grandmother's attic.' While Ben ogled the outside, his mother was trying to peer through a grimy window. Then she picked her way through the shrubs springing up all around it and vanished around one side. 'I can't believe this!' he heard her say above a metallic creak, and scrabbling through the rain-soaked brush he found her, her head sticking through a small door. The door itself looked as though it hadn't been opened in years, for the outside was rusted while inside the metal was still a silvery-blue. Again the door creaked when his mother pulled it wider and cautiously stepped up inside. 'I just can't believe this!' he heard her exclaim again. 'There's a calendar on the wall, and would you believe, it's actually dated 1939!'

Then Ben was scrambling past the door and in from the pummelling rain, which drummed on the arched metal roof, filling the stuffy insides with plunking sounds. The light coming through the door and the grimy windows was thin, but enough to see that the narrow space had three sleeping bunks at one end and the tiniest galley kitchen. But most intriguing, Ben thought, was the hinged formica table that hung from one wall, or rather, the assortment of things set across it. Wiping the dust from a square tin box, the label read Scotch Rolled Oats, and another tin, which he opened, appeared to be half filled with coffee beans. As he picked one out between his thumb and forefinger, it burst into dust. Brushing his fingers off on his jeans, his eye roamed over the rest of the table. A bottle of something called Cod Liver Oil stood beside a bottle of vitamins which apparently had disintegrated, for the bottle held nothing but pinkish-white powder. And then there were two cups stained black at the bottom and three juice-size glasses and a larger one that might have held milk and three cereal bowls with some hard looking flecks on the sides. Whoever the owners had been, if looked like they left in the middle of eating, and as best he could tell from the things on the table, there'd been two adults and one kid.

'It was a family of three.' His mother confirmed this as if she had just read his mind, and turning, he found her looking inside a small narrow closet back by the bunks. 'The girl looks like she might have been . . .' she was thinking aloud as she pulled something out. 'Let me see.' To Ben's embarrassment, she then held a frilly dress up to his shoulders. 'She'd probably be about your age.' He sniffed at the moldy odor it held. Then, as she poked in the closet again, he sidled around her toward the bunks. 'And just look at this dress of the mother's. Gram would call it a church-going dress. And there's slacks and a matching vest. The man's Sunday best, I bet, but I can't find the jacket.' His mother was utterly taken with the quaint wardrobe, for a moment forgetting their mission.

'Mom,' Ben started, no longer listening, for something on one rumpled bunk caught his eye.

'And this hat's positively Smithsonian. People haven't worn anything like this for decades.'

'Mom, the hat.' Ben tried again as she continued to rummage around.

'And suspenders so wide you could use them for a hammock!' She was actually enjoying their find. And Ben regretted spoiling this break from the somber, worrying state she had been in.

'Mom, the hat that – '

'Here it is.' She turned to him, misunderstanding. Then the hat she was holding, wide-brimmed with fake cherries and big ruffled flowers, fell from her hands. It hit the floor in a cloud of dust as Ben gave her what he'd found.

'It's the hat Uncle Gus gave Dad when he gave me mine,' he said as she clutched the thing, a cap like his own, only bigger and black with felt letters which spelled out BRUINS. Though his father wasn't nearly as big a fanatic for hockey as Gus was, the cap made him look more like a jock than some stuffy old history teacher, and it covered his bald spot, and if that wasn't reason enough for his father to wear the thing out, perhaps, like Ben, he practically lived in his cap because it was a gift from Gus.

'What's it doing here?' his mother asked anxiously, glancing around them.

'I found it on one of the beds.' As soon as he said this she jostled around him. After fumbling a hand through the rumpled blankets, her fist came away with a jingling sound.

'It's the keys to the van!' She did not sound excited, but panicked. 'He must have been sleeping here.'

'But why would he sleep in a dusty old camper instead of back at the house?' Ben asked. 'And why would he leave his cap, and the keys – '

'They must have slipped out of his pocket.' Then something crunched under her foot, and stooping over, she came back up with a pair of shattered glasses.

'Mom, Dad wouldn't forget his glasses. He never does.' Ben felt sure of that much. Forgetting his glasses would be like forgetting his head. He was never without them. He'd have to be *out* of his head, Ben thought, now feeling more worried than ever before.

'I wish this damn rain would stop,' his mother mumbled, now starting back toward the door.

'It never rains this hard for long.' He echoed what she had said earlier. Then the two of them listened in silence to the relentless hammering overhead.

A ground fog steamed up through the soggy moss when hours later, they finally started back. The going was harder than coming, between the slippery slopes and the shadows of dusk, which made the trail through the woods, so easy to follow by morning, now all but obscured. They should have just stuck to the overgrown road, Ben thought, but his mother thought this way was shorter. She was soon to regret it, however, when Ben heard the river and ran ahead, thinking they were no more than perhaps twenty yards from the Marsden house. But the louder the sounds of the river became, the thicker the forest seemed, until it finally dawned that he'd lost the trail, and his mother, as night hurried closer.

'Mom!' he shouted several times, but each time he strained to hear her call back, he heard only the rumble of water, so close and so loud now it shook the forest like thunder. Barely able to see all of three feet in front of him, he groped along, assuring himself that he couldn't go wrong if he kept toward the river. They'd never be able to start on plan two, and drive down to Reedsville, not now, he thought. The Ausable road had been bad enough by day, but at night, and after the rain . . . then the thought broke away as something flapped by his head, then another, and then there were more, till all at once, a wind rushed down through the trees as hundreds of wings beat the air. And then he heard it, scarcely a whisper beneath the thundering water nearby, the tiny rodent squealing of the bats. He threw himself down on the ground, feeling something slimy squish beneath one hand. A slug, he guessed, and a big one at that, but he'd rather a slug than bats stuck in his hair. Or worse, if Sarah was right and they did carry rabies and that was what bit the boy. Better not to take chances, he told himself, hoping his mother had reached the house. Then squinting up through the misty dark, he watched them pass, like shadowy phantoms, rustling the leaves, fluttering off through the night like a swarm of fat black moths. He pushed himself up again, wiped the slime on his jeans with a squeamish shiver, then headed again toward the deafening rush of water just ahead.

'You found him?' Sarah excitedly asked, awakened by the creak of the door and in spite of the dusk, recognizing the white-lettered cap her mother clutched. Though her stomach had been grumbling with hunger for hours, she hadn't budged from the rocker. Till now, when she rushed expectantly past her mother and out to the stoop. 'Where are they? Did he and Ben go somewhere?' She heard a match strike behind her and turned.

'Why didn't you light the lamp?' her mother asked as she held the flame to the wick. 'It couldn't have been very pleasant sitting alone here in the dark.'

'Mom!' Sarah shouted impatiently. 'Are you going to tell

me where everyone is?' Then she watched her mother collapse in the rocker, her blonde hair hanging in stringy damp strands while rain still trickled down her pale, wan face. But then Sarah realized the storm had been over a while now and what she saw were tears. Anxious then, she walked up beside her mother and reached out a tentative hand.

'I lost Ben in the woods.' Her mother's voice was faint, exhausted, empty. 'He ran ahead. He thought we were almost here. When I called, all I heard was the river. I thought he'd get here before me. I thought – ' Then struggling and failing to hold it back, she wept as she told of the trailer they'd found and how she believed their father had stayed there. And as Sarah felt her mother's shaking swell beneath her hand, she felt a swelling urge to cry herself, but knew she wouldn't.

The fear that had started over a year ago, when she really thought hard about death, and whether or not there was really a God or if everything ended in nothing, that fear had been so potent that it literally made her heart stop cold and with it all her tears dried up for good. Oh, there was a lot that upset her, like every last detail of her life, and she grumbled a lot, if only to show she did not go along with her miserable plight. In fact, getting angry over it all, getting hopping mad, helped to wear out the hurt, and not only the physical hurt, but the hurt from watching her life fall to pieces. But the fear she quietly carried inside was too great to be spent in anger or tears. Nothing she could do would change a thing, whatever would follow would follow. Whether she passed or whether she failed or whether she put on a smile or a frown, anger and tears could no more bring back her father than they could save her life.

'They'll show up,' she said with conviction, to comfort her mother, while filling with doubt. 'You'll see, they'll be back.' And if Ben were there, he'd doubtless think she was just brushing things off, which she wasn't at all, for trying to give hope was a far different thing than not caring. But how could he know about hiding fear behind anger or aloofness, and what it felt like to always be gritting your teeth at the pain not to worry your parents. How would he know how much she really cared and how bad it made her feel to see them all constantly watching her, and to always be putting up a tough front. Better coming across as a grouch then letting on how she really felt. Which was scared, and it got a lot scarier when she did show it and saw how it scared them too.

'They'll be back.' She rubbed her mother's shoulder, praying it was true, not sure that she could put the tough act on for too much longer.

9
The Stairway Beneath the Falls

Even through the dark and the smouldering mist, Ben could see the falls. Ghostly white, they tumbled down from the cliff with a deafening roar. On the riverbank, leaning between the trees, he could even feel its spray, exploding up from the head of the river, roiling with its crashing weight. The clearing by the Marsden house, he knew, would be through the trees to his left. But the lure of the falls, like a pale, mysterious veil concealing some secret, was not the only thing that held him fixed to the spot. Barely discernible through the thundering water, he heard the eerie cry, faint as tinkling glass yet as full of life as the cry of an infant at birth. Why it gave him that sense, of a new life first awakening, Ben could not understand, for he'd never actually heard a baby's first cry, yet it seemed to project that impression. Straining to listen, it seemed to him that it came from behind the falls themselves. Then abruptly it changed to the musical, song-like sound he'd heard with his mother. Mesmerized by the melody, he moved as if in a trance through the trees.

Below him, through the swelling mist, he could see the river's violent currents, ripping through one another in foamy explosions that spun ever wider, then downward, swirling away through the sucking, spiraling, inky-black eyes of dozens of whirlpools. At least there was one thing Cotter was truthful about. The water looked treacherous, and Ben kept clear of the river's eroding bank and close to the edge of the forest. It was a wise idea, for nearer the falls, the drenching spray was near blinding and he had to grope his way so not to take a false step off the crumbling slope.

Finally, when the sound of the falls was so loud it seemed to roar through his head, he found one groping hand had not touched bark but damp and icy rock. Squinting, he sorted the grays of mist from stone and found a space through the boulders. About half the width of a door, his shoulders brushed the sides as he started through. Once inside, he found the narrow space ran up like a passageway, the rock walls stretching high overhead and opening up to the inky sky. Although he could still just see one edge of the falls slipping over the cliff high above, its sound was muted here, and he heard his own footsteps scraping the pebbly ground. Feeling his way, he listened to the scrape of his feet and squinted ahead where the mist was so dense, it looked like solid rock till he found he could keep stepping through it. Then something underfoot made him stumble and flying forward, he banged both knees and his hands slammed down on a shelf of rock that formed a shallow step.

'Dammit!' Wincing and rubbing his knees, he eased himself on to the rocky seat and continued to curse the mist and the dark and the rocks and his own clumsiness. That is, till he heard a scuffing sound, as if something was scaling the face of the cliff – or descending toward the base of it, he thought, for the sound moved steadily closer. Soaked to the bone from the spray, his teeth starting to chatter, he twisted around in his seat and saw there were other step-like shelves behind him and that they appeared to wind up in a crude sort of staircase leading behind the falls. Against his own best judgment, for the angle looked steep and precarious, and the spray from the falls was so dense that it made the rocks slippery, curiosity nonetheless won. After all, he told himself, starting to climb, perhaps it was here that his father had come. At least, whoever was making those musical sounds, and so close to the Marsden house, was the most likely person to know what had become of his father. But Ben had only gone three steps, however, before starting to lose his nerve.

While the scraping sounds grew nearer, he finally saw what it was moving down through the mist, a dim bluish glow, drifting almost vertically down the face of the cliff. Creeping back a step as it came ever closer, the shape of it grew more distinct. The glowing did not come from one thing, but many, like fireflies in a spherical swarm. It seemed to him odd, if that's what they were, that they'd all mass together so close to the falls, where surely the heavy spray would have made it impossible for an insect to fly. But as the swarm swam toward him – and it did seem more like swimming now, the way they drifted lazily down in a globe as wide as he was tall – the scuffing sound grew steadily louder and finally he was able to see the shape of the thing they surrounded, climbing down the slippery stairs of rock. Taking another step backward, Ben nervously watched the figure approach, till he finally saw the familiar face, looking eerily death-like, haloed in blue, and dripping with some slimy jelly-like substance that had a glow of its own. Then the boy named Daniel saw him, too, and the deathly-blue mouth formed a wisp of a smile, till Ben backed further away and the boy's smile widened around gleaming white teeth.

Reeling around, Ben clambered back through the passage, and just as he reached the end, something flapped at the back of his neck and he yelped and plunged through the woods.

'Ben!' His mother's voice carried across the night, and he tried to holler back, but he barely could gasp for breath as he battered his way through the trees running back from the river. 'Ben!' She sounded alarmed and he prayed that he'd make it, just a bit further, he thought, struggling to drag enough air in his lungs to keep running, his heart pounding up in his throat. Twigs reached out like fingers snagging his shirt and scratching his sweat-soaked face. He'd never do anything wrong in his life again, he promised, if he'd just make it back. Then he couldn't tell if the flapping around him was leaves and if the pricks at his back were nothing but branches, or something else, something he'd shrugged off to nightmares till now. And suddenly, mercifully, there was the dim, distant light of a kerosene lamp, and the next thing he knew he was crashing out of the woods, looking wild as a bear, and lumbering over that last stretch of field toward the house and his mother, he started to giggle, a jittery, breathless, uncontrollably giddy release from his narrow escape.

'Where were you?' His mother's voice switched abruptly from panic to something harsher, and hauling himself the last few yards, lungs bursting, he scarcely managed to pant:

'The falls.' Winded, he caught his breath and looked back. There was nothing behind him. Nothing would dare come after him with his mother right there. Or so he hoped. 'When I lost you I went to the river and then when I got there, I saw the falls, and I heard that sound again, and I wanted to see what it was so I hiked back up and – '

'You deliberately went to the falls?' Her tone grew sharper. 'You knew the way back and you – '

'Mom, I didn't know till I got to the river. *That's* when I decided to look – '

'You decided to look? While I thought you were lost? While I waited here at my wit's end for worry?'

It was going all wrong, Ben thought as she scolded him. She was supposed to be so glad to see him she'd practically swoop him up in her arms, and he would then tell her about the boy with the bite mark who yesterday looked half dead. Only he wasn't half dead any more, instead he looked like he was totally dead, with those glassy eyes and that blue cast to his face and those bugs swarming all around him. He looked, as it was called in movies and books and his nightmares, like the *un*dead. 'Don't you think I've been worried enough with your father gone?' she ranted on. 'And then with Gus, not to mention your sister, as though all I needed now was for you – '

'But, Mom, the reason I – ' He was cut off by something she'd never done before. Her slap startled him more than it hurt, and he stared at her, speechless, as she in turn stared at her hand, as if she were even more startled and hurt than he by what she'd done. Then she looked at him with more pain and regret in her eyes than he'd ever seen, and she pulled him into her arms and sobbed in great racking heaves that shook them both. 'Mom, the only reason I went was to look for Dad. When I heard that sound – '

'I know.' She wept over his cap as she held him so close he could scarcely breathe. 'It's just – it's already too much with your father and Gus and just never knowing about Sarah.' He wanted so much to blurt out what he saw, both last night and now, up at the falls, but even more, he didn't want to frighten her more than she already was. And perhaps it was better he missed the chance to blurt it all out, for thinking about it, it wasn't too likely she would have believed him anyway, not if he'd jabbered away about the undead and some of his other wild theories.

'Promise me,' she barely whispered now, her sobbing

subsiding, 'that you won't go near the falls or river again. And try to be nicer to Sarah.'

Before he could answer, however, he heard Sarah asking behind them if they were all right. Then his mother let him go with a tug of his visor, pretending at playfulness, and swinging the kerosene lamp up from the grass, the light fell on his sister. Something about her face, caught in the glow of the lamp with its eerie blue cast, made her look a bit like the boy, and it made him sense, like his mother, just how sick she was.

'Tomorrow,' his mother had wrapped her arms around both of them, 'we're driving to Reedsville. I'm sure if we can just find Gus, he'll know what's become of your father.' Impulsively glancing back over his shoulder before following them through the door, Ben saw the mist drifting up from the river and with it came dozens of glowing specks. Overhead, like a reflection, pinpoint stars fringed the edge of a massive cloud. Then a light flickered through the cloud's belly like a rock skipping over a vast black lake, and the handful of stars sprinkled beyond it blinked out as the blackness filled the whole sky. A long, grumbling volley of thunder echoed over the valley then, heralding a storm, Ben feared, that would be far worse than the last. Reluctantly starting into the house, he wished they were leaving for Reedsville tonight, but it wasn't because of a fear of thunder and lightning.

10
The Seeding

When Ben woke the following morning, it was not to the lulling rush of the river and falls, but to a steady drizzle pelting the windows and tapping the roof. The big storm either passed them by or still was on its way. Whichever, he just hoped it didn't get worse than a drizzle until they reached Reedsville

How he'd even managed to doze off at all now amazed him, particularly after Sarah's description the night before of young Cotter's visit. He was now convinced the Cotters knew far more than they had told, especially after hearing young Cotter had not only been at the falls, but that he'd lied about the boy named Daniel, implying that he was home sick. Still entertaining the notion that Daniel might now be some sort of a vampire, what with the way he had looked that first day, and then the talk of a 'bite mark', not to mention those pale winged creatures that looked nearly human in size, Ben had tried his darndest not to fall asleep before the dawn. Rolling up on one side, he saw that the door to his mother's room was still closed and his sister looked as if she were sleeping soundly, huddled up in her bag. Still drowsy and feeling the damp, chilly air on his face, he'd like to have snuggled far down in his bag and gone back to sleep himself, if he hadn't needed the outhouse. Just as well, he thought, unzipping his bag and then shivering into his clothes, for the stove had gone out and he had to fetch wood if he wanted the room to be toasty by breakfast. Hobbling about in his socks, trying to hunt down his boots, he stepped into something wet. Only then did he see the muddy tracks leading right to the half-open door.

Dammit, he thought, he was sure he'd slid the bolt before crawling into his bag, and he'd lain awake most of the night and until he dozed off at least, no one went near it. Then his gaze traced the footprints back from the door to the side of the stove where Sarah now slept, where he spotted her muddied sneakers and realized that she must have been the one to go out. She probably had to use the privy, too, then forgotten to slide the bolt, though neither she nor his mother had much reason to worry about it here. After all, what did they know of those things he'd seen gliding up to the falls? Or of Daniel?

Half wishing now that he'd told them, if only to make them more cautious, he tried to determine how long the door was left open, which wasn't particularly hard. The unvarnished planks would have drawn off all the moisture from the mud by now if Sarah made her tracks much before dawn. So, she must have just come back, and the light in the sky, if dim, was still sufficient to ward off any vampires, if in fact that's what they were dealing with. This brought to mind the Cotters again, the way they'd been all bundled up despite the blazing heat the day they arrived. And now, Ben thought he knew why. If they had been bitten, too, and were vampires themselves, it would make perfect sense. Everyone knew that vampires couldn't tolerate the sun. But then he recalled Sarah saying albinos had to watch out for the sun as well, and the Cotters certainly looked a lot like albinos. Thinking about this, he changed his mind, for no vampire he'd ever read about was able to move about in the daytime, even if all covered up like the Cotters. Unless . . . if the Cotters were *recently* bitten, perhaps they were still in the process of changing, and maybe, until they were fully transformed, they could get by in the day bundled up. Deciding that they were still suspect, he went back to hunting down his boots, which he found right under the table where he left them the night before. Sitting down to pull them on, his gaze was drawn back to the half-open door where something suddenly snagged his peripheral vision. Drifting in with the wan gray light through the doorway was a glowing speck.

'A firefly?' he murmured curiously, for these insects, like moths, shied away from the day, which made him think again of the story young Cotter told his sister. It made no sense that he'd find them by day, and especially up by the falls with that spray. Yet even he had seen them swarming, albeit at dusk, and in spite of the spray. Except that they weren't swarming exactly, but rather, they'd enveloped the boy, following him just as if they were bees and the boy had been honey. And watching this one hover over the threshold as if it were taking its bearings, Ben also recalled the few he'd seen by the woodpile, and how they'd kept coming at him. Somehow, this didn't seem like shy and retiring, nocturnal firefly behavior.

Forgetting his need for the privy for now, he watched it. It seemed to take stock of the room. First it drifted a bit toward the bedroom door, then dropped lower as it veered toward the stove. Maybe it felt a bit of lingering warmth there, he thought, for it hovered again, and the light it exuded seemed to deepen, the color now silvery-blue, and it throbbed. Then standing, moving quietly closer, he saw it drifting downward again, although it looked more like swimming now, for this near he could just make out an odd wriggle. Then, too late, he saw just what the thing was heading for.

'Pink eyes aren't so bad.' He scarcely heard Sarah murmur out of her sleep just as the throbbing speck alighted in her feathery hair. Suddenly the light was pulsing faster, like a quickening heartbeat, and stooping by her head to flick it away, he saw it for just what it was. It wasn't even remotely like a firefly, it didn't even have wings, just a delicate ruffling along either side of its transparent body, like fins. And the body itself was elongated, more like the larva of something instead of a bug, and now it was crawling up a strand of hair toward her ear, moving along like an inchworm. On touching the lobe, its throbbing light deepened again, now turning a rich reddish-purple, almost as if it were suddenly blazing with heat or flushed with blood. But Ben's fascination abruptly gave way to fear as it inched toward the inner ear, and his fingers frantically fumbled through Sarah's fine hair.

Gasping in her sleep, she came bolt upright, batting Ben's hands away.

'What are you doing?' she indignantly grumbled, now groggily pawing the sleep from her eyes.

'There was a bug in your hair.' Ben stared at the side of her head, but the thing was gone.

'A bug? Like a spider?' Panicked all over again, she frantically shook out her hair.

'It must have dropped off.' He watched her squeamishly hunting about her bag for the thing. It should have been easy to spot with its glow in the dim gray light of the drizzly dawn, unless it had slipped to the floor and crawled into a crack between boards or beneath her air mattress, or so Ben thought as his eyes combed the bag with his sister's. Then their eyes met, and Sarah's narrowed down suspiciously.

'Is this some kind of a joke?'

'No! I saw it, honest! A glowing thing, like a worm, with these wrinkly things on its sides, and it – '

'What's the commotion?' The door to their mother's room opened and Mrs Liebling emerged looking, Ben thought, worse than he'd ever seen her. Between her wildly tangled hair and puffy, bloodshot eyes, it was obvious that she had spent a good part of the night restlessly tossing and weeping. Then Sarah sneezed, and her mother asked with a worried glance, 'Are you all right?'

'It was only a sneeze,' Sarah drolly replied, though she sounded unusually stuffy.

'It's freezing in here,' their mother observed, sashing her thick flannel robe with a shiver. 'I'll bring in some wood and get the fire started.' She picked up her boots from the floor.

'That's all right.' Ben grabbed up his sweat-shirt from the back of a chair. 'I was just going to get some.' Then, pulling up the zipper and hood, he went out the door.

He slogged through the soggy yard and the drizzle, making his way toward the outhouse. The muddy field steamed and the forest was still full of shadows in the misty dawn. Behind the house, the craggy cliff rising over the trees gushed furiously, the falls seeming even wilder and heavier now from a night of rain. Feeling braver by day, his curiosity burned to know what was behind them, but he'd promised his mother he wouldn't go back and anyway, they'd all be driving to Reedsville.

On reaching the outhouse door, he found it open. This made him annoyed with Sarah all over again, for inside, he found the tissue roll shredded all over the floor. He guessed this mischievous mess had been made by a racoon or some such creature who'd wandered inside after his sister had left the outhouse door ajar. It would serve her right if that weird-looking worm had crawled right into her ear, like an earwig, although his father once told him that business about the earwigs was only a myth. Probably no bug would really do a thing like that anyway, and if one had, it would regret it as soon as she blasted the thing with her Walkman.

Stepping up to the hopper, he felt something brush the

top of his head and glancing up to the ceiling, he all but bolted right back out the door. A fat brown bat hung upside down, preening itself while it swung like a pendulum. Apart from some squeaky chatter, it seemed less disturbed than Ben by their bumping of heads.

'They eat insects,' he calmed himself in a nervous whisper. 'They're just like that mouse John Antonellis used to carry around in his shirt.' But his old friend's pet was raised in his uncle Mel's lab in a university, and this bat was the size of a well-fed rat, and with its pugnacious nose and preening fangs and veined and fleshy ears and wings with long, curling claws, it was the furthest thing from that cuddly mouse that Ben could imagine. Still, he made himself do what he had come in for, if quickly and with one eye on the ceiling and repeating aloud every harmless thing he'd ever heard about bats.

It was only while slogging back through the mud and the rain to the house with an armload of logs that he thought again of what Sarah had said about rabies, which brought that strange boy back to mind. If Meg had seen a bite mark on Daniel, after last night, Ben still couldn't help thinking that whatever it was that bit the boy might be far worse than a rabid bat.

11
Tales of Travelers Lost

'I'm Clare Liebling. My husband was here a few days ago with a friend.' Ben and Sarah's mother stood on the porch of a big old colonial house in dire need of a paint job. Huge white strips curled from the wall like birch bark and flakes from the ceiling littered the floor as if there'd just been a flurry of snow.

'Miz' Liebling?' The short withered man looking through the screen door used his shirt-tail to wipe his fogged glasses. When he pushed them back over his red, lumpy nose, they magnified his squinty eyes to a startling proportion that made them look as if they bulged from his head like a toad's.

'Yes, Mrs Liebling,' she echoed, hugging herself to stop shaking against the damp cold. By the time she reached Reedsville, the rains had become torrential, the chill reaching down to the bone. 'My husband's name's Ray. His friend's name is Gus. It would have been two nights ago.' Trying not to seem too impatient, she struggled to smile over chattering teeth while praying he asked her in before she went and caught her death of pneumonia. She also prayed that Ben remembered to keep the fire going at the Marsden house.

She'd felt guilty leaving them there, but by the time she'd gotten their breakfast, Sarah was coughing and sneezing fit to bring down the roof and she'd thought it better to keep her in bed. As susceptible as the girl was it made no sense to drag her out in this rain, and the long drive down the mountain could only have made the girl's cold worse. Particularly since what should have taken two hours turned out to be more like three, what with the flooding she'd hit when she reached the lowlands at Four Corners Junction.

'You *must* remember, a bearded man with glasses, and Gus you couldn't forget. A big fellow, built like a bear, with curly red hair.'

'Talk like you, with that funny accent?' The toady-eyed man ogled her through the screen. She might have found this amusing, after thinking that Arkansas accents were odd and now realizing that her own accent would sound every bit as strange to them. But she was too cold and too concerned for her husband and Gus to feel much but impatience.

'Yes, they have the same accent,' she chattered through her teeth. 'And they would have gotten here pretty late. Mr Cotter in Ausable said – '

'Cotter? In Ausable?' He cut her off with a frown, as if the mere mention of Cotter and Ausable disturbed him somehow.

'Yes, we stopped to fill our tank at the station Cotter runs with his son. My husband, Ray, was supposed to meet us there but – '

'Cotter's boy would be my age by now.' His toady-eyes skeptically narrowed. 'And Cotter, why, he'd be dead for years.' There wasn't a hint of nostalgia in his observations, only scorn.

'Well, maybe the son you knew grew up and had a son of his own,' she suggested, to which the old man replied:

'Don't know who he'd marry. Only girl there near his age

was taken. And they don't take to outsiders, not up in Ausable.' Nor, from his tone, did they here.

'Look!' Her patience had come to an end. 'I'm just trying to locate my husband, and they told me in Ausable he was last seen on his way with his friend to see you.'

'Me?' The toady eyes blinked in surprise.

'They said Sam Whittaker, and you are the only physician in Reedsville.' To underscore this she glanced back at the fence where a sign that read 'Dr S. Whittaker' hung. 'And if Gus, that's my husband's friend, if he was sick or had some sort of accident, I don't know who else Ray would have brought him to.'

'You city folks are all alike.' His withered mouth wrinkled up in a grin. 'The way you get one notion in your head and you think you know every darn thing.'

'You are Sam Whittaker, aren't you?' Although he'd said yes when he answered the door, his odd remarks and peculiar grin now had her doubting everything. 'And the sign did say Dr Whittaker.' She looked back again to be sure. 'And I did hear you're the only MD in Reedsville – '

'Hogwash. You city folk, think you know every darn thing,' he repeated, then to her amazement, he turned, clucking his tongue and shaking his head as he shuffled back down the hall, leaving her standing there, shaking from the cold, bewildered, heart sinking, near tears. Not knowing where to turn next, she stared through the screen at the bald-headed, hobbling man, then, with her eyes beginning to brim, she turned to the stairs feeling helpless and lost. It was just as if she had fallen into a nightmare and couldn't wake up, and now, on top of her husband and Gus vanishing from the face of the earth, Sarah, who'd been looking none too well since arriving had a cold, which could easily turn into something much worse if she relapsed. Starting down the puddled walk, she did not even feel the downpour. She could scarcely see through the blurring of tears in her eyes as she opened the white picket gate.

'*Hello!*' a voice called from behind, and when she kept going, lost in her own frantic thoughts, the screen door creaked on its hinges and the voice called again, '*Can I help you?*' With her hair plastered over her skull and the rain running down her bangs into her eyes, she squinted back over the roof of the car at the woman now crossing the porch to the stairs.

'That's all right!' she called back hoarsely while the woman, young, with a round, plain face, peered down at her while absently wiping her hands on an apron tied over her jeans. 'I made a mistake! Sorry if I disturbed you!' And then she yanked the car door while the woman on the porch shouted back to her:

'Are you from Boston?'

'I suppose you can tell from my funny accent,' she bitterly answered without looking up, still tugging at the door to the car till she realized it was locked. Shaking with the cold and rain, she rifled through her pockets.

'Oh, I didn't mean to insult you,' the woman quickly replied. 'It's just that you sound so much like the patient I had, and it's rare to see any outsiders.'

'The patient *you* had!' She stopped searching for the keys and peered up through the rain at the woman.

'Why, yes. I'm Dr Whittaker. Sure I can't help? Grandpa said you were asking for me.'

'You'll have to pardon Grandpa.' The woman poured out a hot kettle of tea and Mrs Liebling, still shivering, clung to the cup with both hands, trying to warm up by the stove. 'It's so rare he sees anyone not from here, and those he does usually look down their noses. And one thing he can't help taunting outsiders about is that business of who has the accent.' Ben and Sarah's mother watched her bustle around the big country kitchen filled with the fragrance of something she had baking in the old cast-iron stove. 'Another thing,' the woman went on as she started to clean off a rolling pin, 'is being mistaken for me. Get's a kick out of that. Always has to rub it in.' With her round flushed face and wheat-coloured hair caught back in a single thick braid, Samantha Whittaker looked like she'd be more at home milking cows than examining patients. And though she was not what you'd call a pretty girl, Mrs Liebling observed, her smile was full of warmth and her clear blue eyes looked as wise as an owl's.

'I guess I had it coming.' Mrs Liebling blew into her steaming cup. 'It was a rather sexist conclusion, assuming that he was the doctor.'

'Well, we're both S. Whittakers,' Samantha good-naturedly pointed out. 'And to make it more confusing, folks hereabouts all call me Sam and him Samuel.' She took a chair at the table and poured another cup of tea for herself. 'If it makes you feel any better, your husband made the same mistake. When I came to the door in my night-gown,' she blushed and grinned, 'he asked if the doctor was in. You can imagine the look on his face when I let him know that I was she.'

'You said Ray told you he'd be back the following day to see how Gus was doing?' Clare Liebling somberly brought the discussion back to the question of where he was.

'But it wasn't till the next morning I realized Gus really should be in a hospital. When your husband left, his friend was still somewhat coherent. I thought I could handle him here. So he might have come back while I was driving Gus to Watersville General. Grandpa was out playing penuckle all afternoon so Ray couldn't have known where we went.'

'I don't think he ever left Ausable once he got back

there,' Mrs Liebling said grimly, to which Sam Whittaker quietly murmured, as if she were thinking aloud:

'He should have just stayed the night, like I asked him.'

'Why didn't he?' Mrs Liebling asked.

'Gus had calmed down some. Ray didn't want to impose.' The doctor met her gaze, and after a moment of silence, with solemn set eyes, she quietly added, 'He also said he had to meet someone early the next afternoon.' And that someone, Mrs Liebling sadly thought, was herself and the children, of course. Only something prevented her husband from ever leaving the farm by the falls again.

'Do you think Gus might have any idea where he went to?' she hopefully asked. 'Maybe if I drove to – where is he? Watersville? If I drove down there and asked. I'd want to see him anyway, of course, and if he can shed any light – '

'Mrs Liebling. Clare. The last time I saw Gus he couldn't follow a thought of his own let alone understand the simplest question.' Sam Whittaker's tone underscored the deepening crease in her brow. 'I wish,' her voice now sounded as full of unease as Mrs Liebling felt, 'that he'd just spent the night when I asked. It was nearly three in the morning when he finally drove back to Ausable.'

'Is there something,' Mrs Liebling uncertainly started, seeing the grave look on Sam's face, 'something about Ausable itself, or am I just imaging things?' When Sam Whittaker evasively lowered her gaze to her cup, Mrs Liebling persisted, 'Why is it I get the feeling you and your grandfather don't much like the place? Is there something to worry about, just being in Ausable?'

'Clare,' she at last replied, but proceeding slowly, as if she were weighing each word, 'Ausable isn't a place even people from Reedsville would want to visit. There's something – ' she cut herself off, then after a moment, uneasily started again. 'They're different from us. They deliberately cut themselves off from the rest of the world long ago. Not that much of the outside world intrudes in Reedsville either, but at least we're part of this century, and though there aren't many outsiders through here, we're not unfriendly, and we certainly don't run them off.'

'Run them off?' she anxiously echoed.

'They even make it uncomfortable for people like us to go up there. Not that anyone here's all that eager to go up the mountain anyway. At least, not now, though there was a time when Grandpa and some of his friends fished Lost River. Back when he was a boy. But no one's been foolish enough to go up there in decades.'

'Why foolish?' Mrs Liebling apprehensively asked, no longer thinking just of her husband, but also of Sarah and Ben, stuck by themselves back up on the mountains.

'I tried to drive up there myself a few years ago. I'd just finished Med school, and I had this idea that the place I could do the most good was right here, at the foot of the mountain. The closest doctor before I moved back was all the way over in Watersville, and if folks ever had a real serious problem here, by the time they got help, it was often too late. So the first thing I did was let folks in Wee Pausamet and Four Corners know I'd set up practice, and it took a while, but now they're all glad to have a doctor of their own. Except up in Ausable. Folks around Four Corners told me I was the first 'down-mountainer' – that's what they call us – to go up there in almost fifty years. That is, except for the fellows who drive the fuel trucks up to fill the pump, which I hear doesn't happen more than a few times a year. They're very frugal up there. Apparently they use horses to get around with the roads in such terrible shape and save the trucks for heavy work and emergencies. But to make a long story short, I never quite made it to Ausable Center. A tree the size of a utilities pylon was laid out across the road.'

'I didn't have any trouble getting up,' Mrs Liebling pointed out. 'The roads were bad, of course, but they weren't blocked up.'

'Maybe they were expecting the boys who drive fuel up to the filling station. Folks in Four Corners say that road's blocked up year round, as sort of a warning. In any case, I asked them the next time the fuel truck went through to leave word up there that I was open for practice if anyone ever needed a doctor. But if anyone gets sick in Ausable, believe me, they don't call for help. Unless the folks up there just never get sick.' Sam Whittaker wistfully smiled at some private thought, then seeing Mrs Liebling's questioning gaze, she explained.

'There's been stories for years about how Lost River has some sort of magical powers, how drinking the water keeps everyone healthy and even prolongs their lives. Like it was some sort of fountain of youth, and that's why they won't let anyone up there, because they want to keep it all to themselves.'

This made Mrs Liebling remember Samuel Whittaker's comment about the Cotters, how the son would be his age and the father long dead by now. Since no one had been up there in years, she supposed the man Samuel knew was dead, and that the son, grown-up now, had a son of his own, just as she'd told him. Still, she would never have guessed Mr Cotter to be Mr Whittaker's age. In fact, she'd be hard pressed to guess at any age for the strange-looking man. But this train of thought broke off with another, regarding their so-called magical waters.

'They must be having trouble in paradise, then,' she said with some sarcasm. 'The day I arrived I saw a young boy who looked more dead than alive. A woman brought him down to the Cotters. She said something about a bite mark.'

'The Cotters?' Sam Whittaker said with a frown.

'Your grandfather didn't seem too fond of them either. What is it about them, anyway? There is something odd about that boy and his father.'

'I don't even know them.' Sam looked thoughtful. 'I never met anyone up there. I just remember Grandpa talking about them, but that was years ago. It just surprised me to hear you mention the name. The old man couldn't still be alive.'

'That's what your grandfather said. But I'm sure this must be the next generation. And the next generation looks just like the one before it. The boy's an albino.' This brought another look of surprise from Sam Whittaker.

'But the man Grandpa knew was too.'

'But isn't it passed on genetically?' Mrs Liebling asked.

'It's determined by a chromosome for albinism,' the young doctor acknowledged. 'But I've never heard of it showing up in three successive generations. In fact, when I was studying genetics in Med school, I remembered Grandpa's story about the father and son both being albinos, which I later found out was quite rare. And to have it recur in all three generations – ' The young woman looked thoughtful. 'Every time I hear about people up there, which isn't too often these days, I always feel like trying once more to go up. And I probably should after what you told me about that boy being sick. Not that I'm all that sure they'd let me see him. If they're not used to doctors, and Grandpa of course would make a big fuss, and not just because he's afraid it's not safe.'

Carried along on her own train of thought, she missed the effect her last comment had on Mrs Liebling, who, now on top of everything else, was concerned for her children's safety. 'Grandpa's sour on Ausable for more reason than losing a good fishing spot. In fact, he probably bears a bigger grudge than anyone else down here. You see, before he met Grandma, there was a girl up there he fancied.

Grandma used to tease him about it whenever he'd badmouth Ausable folk. They never took to outsiders, but at least before Grandpa met Meg – that was her name – they still let down-mountainers fish up there even if they didn't like it much. Then just when Grandpa was getting serious about this girl Meg, everything changed, and they started doing just about everything to keep folks here away. Grandma used to kid him that that was the real reason people up there stopped letting us in, because one of their own fellows had his eye on Meg and the clans around there joined together to keep the girl from running off with an outsider. Almost like Romeo and Juliet, only Grandpa got Grandma instead.' Sam Whittaker smiled nostalgically as Mrs Liebling quietly said:

'That was her name, too. That woman with the sick boy. They called her Meg.'

'It's a common name hereabouts.' Then seeing Mrs Liebling's worrying frown, she asked, 'You said the boy was bitten by something?'

'They talked about some sort of bite mark.'

'I wonder what they could have meant. There aren't any poisonous snakes in the region.'

'Could it be something like encephalitis, carried by ticks, or mosquitoes?' Mrs Liebling's face was full of concern for her children again. 'Or Spotted Fever?'

'We've never had anything like that here.' Sam put her mind at ease. 'Or rabies either, if they meant some sort of animal bite.' Then, after a long thoughtful moment, she added, 'Unless the boy had something like Gus.'

'I thought you said earlier Gus had some sort of amnesia.'

'But I don't know what's causing it. And though it was reasonably mild when Ray first brought him down, it's gotten much worse, so bad now he can't even remember from one day to the next. At least,' she sighed, 'it wasn't because of some trauma to the head. At first, I thought he'd been beaten up, because of the way his ear – '

But before she could finish the thought, Mrs Liebling apprehensively cut her off:

'How would Gus have gotten into a fight? Who with?'

'Clare, I told you,' she gently replied. 'They don't take to outsiders up there, and years ago, when they started to keep people out, there was all sorts of trouble. Of course, no one's actually disappeared in years – '

'Disappeared?' Mrs Liebling turned white. Sam appeared to regret her remark, but the damage was done. At Mrs Liebling's pleading insistence, she reluctantly went on.

'It's all speculation. Nobody knows for sure what really happened. And each of these cases was so many years ago, well before I was even born.'

'What cases? What happened?' she prodded when Sam paused again, clearly reluctant to finish.

'Remember, I said this happened nearly fifty years ago,' she repeated, as if to reassure Mrs Liebling it couldn't happen again. Then she told her, 'First a pair of hunters from Little Rock were thought to have wandered up there. A boy from Four Corners found their abandoned camp at the foot of the Ausable road. Then there was this fellow from Baton Rouge who had a cousin in Reedsville, and the last time they were heard from they were planning to motorboat up to Lost Falls. You can take the Pausamet River up to something called Midnite Lagoon, which is really more of a swamp where the Pausamet and Lost rivers meet. Grandpa says it's easy going, because the currents don't get all that bad except when the rain floods the rivers, and up around Lost Falls. Anyway, their boat came back empty, but most folks thought they got swamped at the falls. There're whirlpools if you get too close. But their bodies were never found.

'And then there was one other incident, some family

from Tennessee. But it's not even sure they went up there, mind you, that's just what some folks in Wee Pausamet think, and considering Ausable's not even on the map, it could be they just took back roads right through the lowlands and disappeared some place else, maybe found some place they liked better than where they were from, settled down and started all over. Who knows what reasons folks might have for picking up and vanishing. Maybe they were in some sort of trouble back where they came from. But God knows, they weren't all swallowed up by the earth. And the way the stories go, when the state police finally made their investigations – I guess they had family, or friends, who last got postcards mailed from Wee Pausamet – they never turned up a thing to prove any of them had even made it up to Ausable. Which wouldn't make much sense to start with, given it's so off the beaten path. And anyway, it's one thing for people to go disappearing without a trace, but I really don't see how it's possible the police could miss a whole trailer.'

'A trailer?'

'Did I say trailer?' Sam Whittaker, after just talking a blue streak, recalling the rumours heard years before, looked suddenly stumped, as if trying to remember some detail a little more clearly. 'Yes, I'm sure that's what Grandpa said. I can ask, but I'm sure I heard there was a trailer. That family from Tennesse was last seen with – '

'I found it.' Ben's mother broke in, and her voice was none too steady.

'What in tarnation you baking in that oven, girl?' a voice called down the hall, jarring both Sam and Clare Liebling out of their shared preoccupation. Then both of them sniffed at the air and winced, for something indeed was burning. Sam Whittaker jumped from her chair, grabbed up a dishcloth and rushed for the stove.

'Darn it!' she muttered as smoke billowed up the moment

she opened the oven door. 'Oh, *darn!*' Using the dishcloth, she gingerly pulled out a smouldering pan.

'Your grandma would turn in her grave if she saw what you do in her kitchen,' the old man clucked as he shuffled into the room with both hands dramatically cupped to his mouth. 'I don't mean to hurt your feelings, Sam, but if that's what we're having for lunch, I'm afraid we're both gonna be needing some of your doctoring up. Why don't you stop tryin' to fiddle in here and just stick to your medicine, girl. I can manage the kitchen OK. I managed before you moved in on me.'

'If I didn't "fiddle" in here, we'd both be dead of malnutrition right now. The way you were eating, you're lucky I moved in here when I did.' Then she dismally frowned at the embers and murmured, 'And anyway, this wasn't for you.'

'Do you hear me complaining?' the man chortled back.

'I was making it for Gus.' Sam sighed.

'Made a mess is all I can see. Looks like a blizzard, the way you spilt flour all around.' It might have amused Clare Liebling to hear them sparring over the charred remains with Sam pouting like a young girl at her first kitchen failure while her grandfather bustled about, throwing up windows to air the smoke out and swabbing up spills like a vexed, fussy mother. But she couldn't let go of her swelling concern for her husband, for Gus, and now for her children.

'It *was* supposed to be Shoo Fly Pie.' Sam disconsolately set the pan in the sink. 'The one thing Gus didn't lose with his amnesia was his appetite. Or should I say his sweet tooth.' She glanced at Ben's mother as she continued, 'At Watersville General they say he won't touch anything but the desserts. Not that I blame him. I did my residency there and I'm lucky the food didn't kill me.'

'You should talk,' her grandfather muttered, still cleaning up around them, but Mrs Liebling was blinking at Sam, as though she'd been only half listening till now. In all the years her husband and the High School coach were friends, for all the meals that Gus had shared with her family, not once had he touched a dessert. On the contrary, a near fanatical health-nut, Gus had lectured her kids more than once on the reasons *not* to eat sweets, considering sugar all but a poison.

Just one more baffling piece of a puzzle where none of the parts appeared to fit and all of them, scattered between the mountains of Ausable down to Watersville General, were growing ever more ominous as the meaning behind them pushed further from reach.

12
The Elusive Quark

'I wish there was hot running water.' Sarah shivered by the wood-burning stove in spite of the sleeping-bag pulled like a shawl round her shoulders, and the fire, which she gloomily watched. It made the stove less efficient, with the oven door left open that way. It accelerated the burning of the wood, which Ben had to fetch in the rain, and though it made things look cozier, it prevented an adequate build-up of heat. If she'd just leave it shut, she would not have to sit so close to it, Ben broodingly thought, but he bit his tongue rather than set them off on another fight. Anyway, Sarah looked miserable as it was, sniffling and coughing and sneezing, and Ben for his part was preoccupied with something far more pressing.

Browsing through a bookcase, he found a journal belonging to Matthew Marsden. Gus's great uncle had not only been a black sheep, forgotten by family, but Ben now discovered that he must have been remarkably old at his death. Nearly a century earlier Marsden had been a promising student of physics. That was until he was laughed out of the Massachusetts Institute of Technology for a theory he founded called 'Intra-dimensional Biotic Conduction'. It seemed Marsden believed that the universe was made up of countless dimensions, on the lines of parallel worlds, or realms, that shared the same space but different planes. In his theory, he also held that all realms were contained within some sort of maze-like wall, like the many-layered walls of a beehive, but made of an energy field that defied all perception. He also believed that while it divided countless unseen dimensions from ours that, with the right conditions, it could be traveled through, just as we travel through space.

As the journal was written for a general audience, it was not too hard to follow. And although it was written a long time ago, and apparently never published, some aspects of the theory which made Matthew Marsden a laughing stock in his own time were not really all that far-fetched in light of more recent discoveries. Even Ben knew about the black holes which modern astronomers found in space.

In school he had learned they were also called worm holes, believed to have strong gravitational pulls that sucked everything near them in toward their centers, and eventually right through them to vanish from one part of the universe to reappear in another. His teacher once demonstrated the theory, which worked a bit like a whirlpool. He took a large piece of paper and crumpled it up in a ball. Then he asked the class to suppose that the ball was the universe, all folded up on itself, and on one side he drew a small circle to represent all space now known to man. In this circle, he then put a dot to represent the nearest black hole. Then taking a needle and thread, he pushed it into the dot and through the ball and out the other side. When he smoothed the ball out on the blackboard, the thread made a zig-zagging path across the page. This path, he told the class, represented a single black hole running through space, and everywhere it pierced the page represented an entrance or exit.

Reading Matthew Marsden's theory ninety years after he thought of it, Ben did not see much difference between a piece of paper crumpled up in a ball and Marsden using the many-layered walls of a beehive as a model. But he still found it hard to grasp Marsden's theory of worlds that occupied the same space, invisible to one another only because they existed in separate dimensions. It would mean that trillions or more other beings could be walking right through him, just like ghosts, only he couldn't feel them or see them because it was happening in different dimensions. But hardest of all to believe was his theory of Intra-dimensional Biotic Conduction, or the thought that one could actually slip through this wall from one dimension into another. Then suddenly, something else came to mind that made Marsden's whole theory seem plausible.

On the TV show Star Trek, the crew was always getting beamed somewhere or other. They'd just step in the spaceship's teleport, dematerialize, then show up on some planet. And it seemed to him that if people could be beamed through the walls of a spaceship, and if a black hole could be in one place while connecting two distant parts of the universe, then maybe Marsden wasn't all that crazy after all. And then, he thought again of ghosts, passing right through things, like walls and closed doors. Not that he really believed in ghosts, though he couldn't help wondering why some people did. There must have been something to start the superstition, it couldn't have come out of nowhere. Unless . . . he uneasily thought of Marsden's wall and what might live in other dimensions.

As if something outside of himself were trying to make him believe, drive the point home, he suddenly stiffened on feeling as if something cold were passing right through him. The ghost of Matthew Marsden, he nervously thought as the sweat broke out on his brow and he anxiously glanced through the room, at the walls full of eerie undersea creatures. They all seemed to waver a bit with the flickering light from the stove and the lengthening shadows that had begun to creep into the room through the rain-spattered windows.

Either it was getting darker sooner, with all of the storm clouds, or his mother was taking a long time getting back. He wished that the room had a clock. Then he felt the cold pass through him again and nearly leapt from his chair, till he realized that it was merely a damp, chilly breeze slipping through the window behind him. Had to be, he assured himself, for what else could rattle the pane in its molding.

Then he turned again to the journal, picking up where he'd left off, where Marsden talked of the Intra-dimensional Biotic Conductor machine he was building. He also refered to it simply as a 'cyclotron', and it seemed that all it did was move electrical particles through a hollow ring. Not just move them, but spin them, terrifically fast and in opposite directions so that they'd collide. This required a very powerful magnetic field, which was why Marsden moved here, for he'd somehow discovered these mountains contained an ore with a strong magnetic charge. It seemed that Marsden thought that by forcing electrical particles to collide, he could break through his Intra-dimensional wall and get to the other side. Then picturing this hollow ring with electric sparks racing through it, Ben realized he wasn't imagining something, but that he'd actually seen it before.

Pushing out of his chair he went back to the shelf where he found the journal. It did not take long to find what he wanted. It was the only new book on the shelf. And the picture on the cover of *The Elusive Quark* showed a cyclotron, and inside, a diagram of the same thing was labeled 'The Super Collider', and it wasn't used to make electrical sparks fly into each other, but to make atomic particles, like electrons and protons, collide and break up. Its purpose was to look for this thing the book took its title from, called a 'quark', which was now believed to be the tiniest unit from which all things were made. So, Ben thought, even Marsden's cyclotron was way ahead of its time. Only Marsden did not want to simply split atoms, but the Intra-dimensional wall. And what if one really existed, Ben wondered, recalling that ball of crumpled-up paper and imagining what it might mean if it could be pierced with the ease of a needle and thread.

'You'd probably have to boil up tons of water on the stove first, then carry it all outside to pour into that pail full of holes he used for a shower.' Hearing her mumbling, Ben glanced at his sister, still huddled up by the stove. As if hypnotized, she still gazed at the dancing flames while absently scratching one ear.

'Gallons, not tons,' Ben corrected. Here he was working out worm holes through space and parallel worlds while Sarah still whined about how hard it was just to take a dumb shower. If ever there were parallel worlds, Sarah, he thought, was a perfect example. She only appeared to exist in this world while really being off in one of her own. And he didn't mean he found her otherworldly so much as out-to-lunch. 'And *I* wouldn't have to boil up gallons of water first, *you* would.'

'I didn't *mean* you. I meant you as in *one* would have to boil – oh, forget it.' Then she reached for the earphones slung at her neck and adjusted them over her head. As she fidgeted with the Walkman, she pushed herself up and started across the room. Ben thought she looked a bit wobbly, but perhaps it was just from squatting so long by the stove. Returning to his seat at the table and picking up the journal again, his eye repeatedly roamed her way as she noisily poked through the shelves by the sink. When she picked up a big jar of honey and glanced his way, he dropped his gaze, and the next thing he heard was the clinking of metal on glass as Sarah trudged back to the stove. When he looked again, it surprised him to see her eating the honey right out of the jar, and not just a dab on a fingertip, but great gobs of the stuff scooped up on a spoon. The only times he'd ever seen her eat honey was sparingly on toast, and then only if they were out of jam, and even that, she'd not eat with a spoon. Ever since her medications started making her face and her belly puff up, she'd been careful of anything that might add to her general appearance of bloatedness.

Looking at her, however, the thought of the pains she took with her diet seemed foolish, for apart from her face and distended belly, Sarah was built like a rail. In fact, he'd seen pictures of starving kids in an Oxfam booklet at school, and all of them looked just like she did, like skeletons with round tummys. It did not seem to make much difference when their mother explained that it was the drugs which made her stomach and face swell up with something called 'fluid retention'. It did not matter to Sarah that none of this had to do with how much she ate, or that starving herself, as she did, wouldn't change the way her medicines made her look.

Watching her crouched by the stove, now gulping down spoon after spoon from the amber jar, Ben felt sorry for her, thinking how hungry she must always feel with her pointless diet. So hungry that she had finally broken down and was now making up for lost time. Then, as if she knew he was watching, she sheepishly glanced his way. Ben instantly dropped his gaze to the journal again and pretended he hadn't noticed. He was reading about all the trouble Marsden had getting supplies up the mountain when Sarah returned to being her usual self, which began by complaining.

'There's something wrong with this.' He knew when she griped that she couldn't care less who was listening, and most of the time, he thought she simply liked to hear herself complain. Like at home, in his room, he could frequently hear her right through the wall, grumbling away about every little thing that came into her mind, as though everything was a problem. Sometimes he even thought her griping was sort of like being plugged into her Walkman, just something to do, the way some people bite at their nails or keep cracking their knuckles. Little nervous habits, like sucking a thumb, that make people feel more secure. If she didn't have something to gripe about, Ben sometimes doubted she'd know what to do with herself.

'Now I can hardly hear anything!' Sarah was shaking the plastic Walkman case.

'You don't have to shout!' Ben shouted. '*My* ears aren't plugged up!' And at last, she looked up.

'I wasn't talking to you!' she irksomely shouted back.

'Well, I don't know who else you expect to hear you! I'm the only one here!' But Sarah did not respond this time, still shaking the Walkman and playing with the volume. Watching her angry fumbling about with the thing, he could not help shouting again, 'Did it ever occur to you maybe we're too far away to get decent reception?'

'It's not the reception, know-it-all!' Sarah scowled at him, lifting one earphone. 'It so happens I'm playing a tape, not the radio, and it's just this one earphone that's broken!' But even as she spoke, Ben could clearly hear music blaring out of the ear-piece. Either Sarah had mixed up her sides or she'd finally made herself deaf, which wouldn't surprise him at all, for it sounded like the volume was all the way up. Shaking his head in disgust, he turned back to the journal, deciding that parallel worlds and quarks and going through dimensional walls made a heck more sense than his sister. But he hadn't read two sentences before she was at it all over again, banging the base of the Walkman against the rug and muttering furiously.

'What good does it do to keep banging the thing?' he hollered. 'You're just going to make it worse!'

'Because – ' Her voice was trembling, and in the light from the stove, he could see she was flushed. 'Because – ' she sniffled and cleared her throat while repeatedly banging the thing on the rug. But her banging grew steadily weaker, and she kept sniffling back a runny nose as she muttered, over and over again, like an echo, 'Because . . . because . . .' Then she dropped the Walkman and started to batter her fist against her knee instead.

'*Because of what?*' Ben all but screamed, feeling as if his head would explode. Then Sarah sobbed:

''Cause of everything!' Nothing, not even seeing her wolf down the honey, surprised him so much as seeing his sister actually start to cry. All he could do was stare at her bobbing head with its wispy, moth-eaten hair, at her runny nose and the torrent of tears splashing over her flushed, puffy cheeks, and while she continued to beat at her knees with her fist, her body began to rock, pitching forward and backward like a small boat being battered about by that storm within. And while the storm outside continued to build, the wind raging, the rain sheeting down, Ben somehow knew Sarah's 'everything' meant much more than the effort involved in a shower, or even the frustration of having the Walkman not work, or failing a grade. It had always been easier taking her constant crankiness at face value. Easier, because to look at what was behind it was scary. It was scary to think of Sarah in pain, and they all pretended she wasn't, because her doctor told them all that she wanted it that way. And Ben had gotten so good at it, he'd convinced himself Sarah was just like she acted, a whiny, spoiled, inconsiderate, self-centered brat.

He didn't know when it started, being angry at her for getting sick, for worsening in spite of all the attention, which made them all feel so damn helpless. And Sarah, for her part, seemed to prefer their anger to their pity, and Ben had been as willing to play along with her front than see what was behind it. But now, he could not escape the thing that started it all, that terrible fear which Sarah and he and their parents had felt at her very first trip to the hospital. It had been easier, being mad, and not just because she preferred it that way, but because it was scary to think of her dying, and much scarier thinking how scared *she* must be.

With a sinking sensation that made him feel almost as if his heart had dropped in his shoe and his stomach had filled with helium, flying up to his mouth and clogging his throat, he forced himself up and clumsily started toward her with no idea what to do.

13
A Trickling of Light

'Sarah?' his voice squeaked out as he knelt by her side. Still, she rocked inconsolably. He tried her name again, but this time it barely scraped past the clog in his throat. He doubted she would have heard anyway, between raucous sobs and the faint tinny racket that sounded as if it came from not one, but both of the Walkman earphones. Either all the banging had fixed the thing or it hadn't been broken to start with, and Sarah actually was losing her hearing. That thought made him think of her illness and all of the various unpleasant symptoms involved, and though he could not recall deafness being one, he now dreaded that maybe it was. Still feeling clumsy and helpless, he moved a tentative hand toward her shoulder, remembering how his parents held one another on first hearing what Sarah had. He felt awkward trying to hug her, but he wanted to make her know he was there, that he cared and it scared him too, and touching seemed somehow better than words. But just before his fingers reached the sleeping-bag over her shoulders, her sobbing abruptly broke off and her face grew suddenly pale in the firelight.

'Sarah?' His voice cracked. Something about her expression had changed and it frightened him. It had gone from being flushed and contorted from weeping to blank as stone in the bat of an eye. 'Sarah, you OK?' He gave her shoulder a squeeze, then a gentle shake, but he might as well have been off in the other room for all the notice she took.

Scrabbling around till he knelt right before her, he found her gaze frozen, in pain, or surprise, hanging in the middle distance, between them, as if she'd gone suddenly blind. 'Sarah, come on,' he said, anxiously now, terrified at the thought of a relapse, for once overhearing his parents discuss this, he'd sensed it meant the start of the end. 'Please, Sarah.' His hands fumbled up to her head and yanked off the earphones. The tinny music blared from both of the speakers. 'Please, don't be sick.'

Then he saw a shiver run through her, as if she'd been touched by an icy wind, and the next thing he knew her eyes rolled up to white and she started to slump. Then all at once, she crumpled toward him, all the air in her lungs sighing out and her body going so limp it was just like her bones had all dissolved. His arms frantically grappled with the sagging heap at his chest. 'Oh, please . . .' he pleaded, feeling sick as her head lolled lifelessly back from one shoulder. 'Wake up, Sarah, please God, make her . . .'

Something trickled across his hand, something so warm he thought it was her tears still falling, or so he hoped, for if she could cry, then she must still be – but the hope dissolved as he dragged up her head and saw that her eyes were still rolled back and that the trickle he'd felt on his hand was something blue and luminous. Still bracing her up, he shivered, breathing in short anxious gasps, too panicked to move. He could not even get his mind moving beyond the paralyzing fear she was dead. Then his heart felt as if it were going to burst right through his chest, the way it was beating so fast, and just as he thought he was going to be trapped in this horrible moment forever, he realized the throbbing was not only inside his chest, but against it.

It was then that he heard her weakly inhale and shift slightly, like someone about to wake up.

'Ben?' Her voice came feebly when at last she dragged her head back up. 'What happened?' She groggily wiped the damp from her cheeks.

Something else trickled down one side of her neck and just as Ben noticed it, she absently wiped at that too. 'Did I faint or something?' Ben scarcely heard her question, now distractedly watching another trickle of iridescent blue creep down one side of her jaw. Exactly like the drop of shimmery wetness he'd found on his hand, he suddenly realized where he'd seen it before and the memory made him shiver. 'What's the matter?' Sarah asked as he continued to stare at her, tracing the path of the substance up from her throat to the ear it oozed from. And then he saw the ear was red and scratched, much like the Ausable boy's. 'Why are you looking at me like that?' She began to sound alarmed.

'It's nothing,' he nervously mumbled, avoiding her questioning gaze by averting his own, then spotting the box of tissues she used for her cold on the floor by his knees, he snatched one up and wiped at the stuff still trickling down her jaw. More of it smeared on his fingertips, and it tingled, like tiny electric shocks. A warm, glowing, bluish jelly-like substance, it felt almost alive to the touch.

'What is that?' She squirmed as he swabbed at her ear. 'What are you doing? What's wrong? Am I cut?'

'Just some gunky stuff, like jelly.' Trying his best not to sound too concerned, he balled the tissue up in his hand and tossed it into the woodburning stove.

'Jelly?' Sarah's hand groped at her ear, but the oozing had finally stopped.

'Or honey,' Ben fibbed. 'When you fainted you must've got some on your hand and then your hand must have gotten it on to your ear.'

But he knew it was not honey or jelly or anything of the kind, and his head was swimming with words like electrons and protons and quarks and Matthew Marsden's theory about Intra-dimensional Walls and Biotic Conduction. And in the eye of his mind was an image, a death-white face, but smiling serenely. And glistening with the same luminous substance. But he couldn't tell her the truth, at least not the little he thought he now understood – that those things he'd mistaken for fireflies, first at the woodpile, swimming about his head, then up at the falls swarming around that boy whose face literally dripped with the stuff, and the last time, just after awaking – he was sure that the thing he'd tried flicking away from her ear that morning had not scurried down between the floorboards, but that it had gotten inside her. And he couldn't tell her, because in spite of all their differences, seeing the state she was in just before she passed out, having glimpsed all her pain and her fear, he suddenly wanted only to protect her from being more frightened or hurt.

How many kids, after all, have to think about dying twenty-four hours a day? That alone, he now shamefully thought, had been reason enough to be patient with her, and watching her pick up the Walkman and eye it curiously, he firmly resolved to try to be more understanding no matter how bad a mood she was in.

'It's working,' he heard her say with some surprise as she held up the headset with music still pouring out of both tiny earphones. Of course, it had never been broken to start with, Ben thought, biting his tongue. The worm-like thing that had been in her ear had blocked her from hearing, and now it was out. At least, he hoped it was out. The luminouse ooze had looked like the very same substance that made the worm glow, and all Ben could think was the music blaring into her ears had destroyed it. And none too soon, he suspected, for the ooze had been quite a bit more than might come from one worm, and while wiping it off her, some of it dripped on his hand and he'd had the unnerving sense that it came from something the worm had been changing into. It was like some sort of an egg sac that had ruptured, the ooze giving off a weak, flickering current, conveying that eerie sensation he'd had of life fading away with the discharge.

In any case, he now looked at Sarah's Walkman in a whole new light. Not only had it destroyed the thing, but if she continued to wear it, like earplugs, it would protect her from more of those flying glow-worms getting in. But his sister now flicked off the volume, slinging the earphones around her neck, not seeming particularly interested in why it now worked or in using the thing. The reason for this was because her mind was stuck on something else.

'I did faint, didn't I?' She seemed more embarrassed than anxious at first. Then anxiety swiftly kicked in, but it wasn't over the fainting itself. 'Please, don't tell Mom. It's nothing. I just didn't eat much, that's all.' Except for about a fifth of a pound of honey, he thought, and right from the jar. But other than that, it was true, neither of them had felt much like eating since breakfast. Nonetheless, he knew she did not faint from hunger. 'Please, promise me, Ben,' she persisted, now squeezing his hands, her eyes pleading. 'They'll just put me back in the hospital and they can't do anything for it. Please, don't tell.' Her eyes misted over. 'I don't want to be left in a room by myself when . . . when . . .' her voice trailed off to nothing, and that nothing held all that she most deeply feared.

But it wasn't that awful thing with her blood that made her faint, Ben told himself, it was that thing that had crawled into her ear. And as for the leukemia, hadn't her doctor said she was doing much better? That's what his parents had said, at least, when discussing the prospects of summering here. But he'd also overheard his father telling

105

Gus that Sarah's remission could last anywhere from several months to as little as several weeks. And she wasn't looking too well, he had to admit, even if her fainting had nothing at all to do with the thing that was wrong with her blood.

In hindsight, he now had the uneasy feeling she'd gotten much worse on the long drive from Cambridge, which might explain why she'd been in such a bad mood. In fact, she'd been looking increasingly sicker just since their mother left, and he wondered, apprehensively now, if this maybe had nothing to do with either the thing that had gotten inside of her *or* her cold, if maybe it *was* her blood. And this terrified him, to think of her getting sicker, so sick that nothing would help. And looking into her eyes filling with tears, he saw what she meant by 'alone', and it scared him to think of her going to the hospital and being by herself and maybe – the thought made him cold inside – maybe not coming out again. He reluctantly nodded.

'I promise.' His voice was a hoarse-sounding whisper that echoed his sister's fear, plus the fear that it might do her more harm than good, by not letting their mother know. What if she was wrong, what if there was something else the doctors could do if they caught it in time, if some kind of cure was being found at that very moment. It's a terrible thing, to live without hope, at least that's what Gus told his father one day driving them home while his mother remained at the hospital with his sister. And when Gus pulled the car in the drive, his father started to cry, forgetting all about him being in the back as he banged his fist on the dashboard and angrily said how unfair it was, that parents should outlive a child. To which Gus had said the thing about hope, and how it was important to keep it, and not just for themselves but for Sarah's sake. But now, Ben realized that none of his parents' hoping had done her a bit of good, for it was painfully clear at that moment that

Sarah herself had none. But there had to be hope, he told himself, already regretting his promise. But he'd given his word, and as much as he wished he hadn't, he couldn't take it back. And then, as if she knew just what he was thinking, Sarah did something else she hadn't done since they were much younger. She went to hug him. She opened her skinny arms and wrapped them around him and held him as tight as he'd so often seen his father do with his mother when he caught them discussing Sarah.

'It'll be our secret,' she whispered in such a way that he almost cried, too, for it somehow made his promise feel like the most important thing in the world which he couldn't break even if he were suddenly sure it *had* been a mistake. But it wasn't only sadness he felt in her thin, weary hug, but an odd sort of closeness, as if he could feel all the hurt and the fear in her growing a little bit dimmer, as if sharing it with him somehow made it not quite so hard to bear. 'Ben.' She let him go and sat straighter, her tears sinking back where they came from. 'I'm sorry I've been such a witch. I don't mean to be, really. It's just when everything get's so . . . so – '

'I know,' he told her, and he did, he now understood perfectly. 'But maybe if you just said how you felt instead of keeping it all inside. Like . . . you could tell me if it got really bad.' Then she leaned forward and kissed him flat on the cheek, and he felt his own face blaze and he started to mumble inanely, 'I better bring in more wood for the fire.' He awkwardly pushed to his feet. But glancing back as he slipped on his jacket, he saw her gazing into the fire, and he saw something else that was very rare for his sister. Her pale and puffy face actually held the trace of a smile.

While Ben braved the torrents to fetch more wood and Sarah tried to stay warm by the fire, their mother was leaving the Whittaker house to drive back through the storm before nightfall.

'If you'd wait at least till the rain lets up a little, I'd drive up there with you!' Samantha Whittaker called from the porch through the steady downpour. 'I'd like to have a look at that boy in Ausable, anyway! Please wait! When it rains this hard, the roads up the mountain usually wash out, and it's not going to do any good if you're stuck in your car somewhere!'

'I can't just sit around and do nothing!' Clare Liebling shouted back, already drenched to the bone again just running down from the porch to her car. Blinking through the rain, her fears peaked by Sam's tales of unsolved disappearances, Clare Liebling yanked at the door on the driver's side and found it locked. 'Damn!' She'd forgotten she'd locked it, not that there'd been any need in so quiet a town, but coming from Cambridge, where car thefts were common, she often locked it on reflex.

'Matthew Marsden lost the road in a storm like this.' Sam came through the gate as Mrs Liebling frantically searched her pockets for the keys. 'He was on his way down from Ausable when it happened, it was in the paper here, and I'd lay ten to one the Four Corners crossing's already knee-high in water.'

As had happened before, when she rushed herself, like those days when Sarah was due for a check-up, Clare realized she must have left the keys in the car when she hit the lock on the door. Sprinting around to the passenger side, praying she hadn't locked that door as well, she nearly collided with Sam, still trying to convince her to wait till the rain stopped. 'Last time we had a storm this bad, Wee Pausamet looked like a lake for a week, what with the overflowing of the Pausamet and Lost rivers.'

'But my children!' Clare yanked at the passenger door,

the thought of flooding rivers only adding to her already burgeoning fears.

'You wouldn't do them much good with your car washed down a ravine, now would you?' The young woman doctor gently grasped her arm. 'Come back inside. It won't flood on the high ground like here. And from what you told me, your boy's a smart fellow, right? He'll handle things.'

'I can't leave them alone up there!' Mrs Liebling was in a frenzy now, but she found that the passanger door was locked as well. There was nothing that she could do. 'I *have* to get back!' She banged her fist ineffectually over the window, oblivious to the stream in the gutter swilling over her shoes.

'Maybe we can work a wire hanger in through the edge of the window. One time, I locked my keys in, too, and Grandpa got it open that way.' Sam's firm but gentle hand on her arm gave a squeeze. 'Come back inside. I promise, as soon as it lets up a little, I'll have him try.' And Clare, defeated and soaked to the bone, let Sam lead her back up the puddled walk, littered with writhing worms driven out of the earth by the flooding rains.

14
The Swarm

The wood Ben fetched had kept the fire going till night fell over the mountain, and after a day full of rain, which still fell in torrents, the evening came on with a chill.

Sarah had fallen asleep by the stove where the last dying embers glowed weakly. Ben tried not to wake her, quietly pulling on boots and his slicker to head to the woodpile. Because it was dark now, he took a flashlight with him and used the wheelbarrow, intending to bring enough back to last them through the night.

Foremost in his mind when he splashed through the puddled yard was his mother. He had expected her back before nightfall and worried now for her safety. The storm would have turned the dirt road going down to a mud slick if not a river by now, and he hated to think of her car getting stuck and then trying to hike back through the dark and the rain. Particularly with the air now literally swimming with those glowing worms.

Perhaps it was the storm that brought them out in such vast numbers for they no longer drifted sluggishly but dove and swirled, quite at home in the rain, now looking more like darting schools of minnows – or a frenzy of feeding piranhas, he thought as he stopped every few feet to wave them away from his head. Maybe they only congregated here, by the river, he thought. At least, he hoped this was the case if his mother was forced to abandon the car. Then he thought of the luminous discharge from Sarah's ear and shuddered to think what might have happened if her Walkman hadn't somehow destroyed the thing. And he had no doubt of the seriousness of being implanted with one, for Marsden's journal ended abruptly, switching from talk of his cyclotron to a final, brief entry that mentioned 'worm-like spores' and a thing called a 'Brilliade', and whatever this was, his last words outlined a plan to blow up a cave where it nested.

Pushing the wheelbarrow under the overhang sheltering the wood from the rain, Ben went over the unsettling bits and pieces he'd read as he loaded the logs. The man had talked about purchasing a substantial amount of explosives and setting them up in the cliff around something which he called 'the chink in the falls'. He did this because, as he wrote, he thought he saw 'a bat pass through, and if the weave was unravelling once again, they could slip back through the wall between worlds.'

Though Ben had a good idea that 'they' were these odd glowing worms and the great, pale creatures he'd glimpsed gliding up to the falls his first night in Ausable, he was not at all sure what was meant by a 'chink' in the falls. Perhaps some sort of tear in Marsden's Intra-dimensional Weave, he thought, wondering if Marsden had tampered with something better left alone.

One thing, however, which Marsden's journal clarified was the business of 'bite marks', which Ben till now had imagined came of encounters with the kite-like creatures. In fact, he'd heard correctly when Meg told the Cotters she thought the boy had 'the bright mark'. 'Soon, everyone living in Ausable could end up with the bright mark,' Marsden had written, and when Ben had read this, he'd thought of the boy by the falls, in a cloud of worms. But his face had held a light of its own, and even that day back in Ausable Center, it seemed almost to radiate light rather than merely reflect the sun.

Having filled the wheelbarrow, Ben started pushing it back through the mud while his mind struggled with the weight of all he'd discovered. He still had no idea what sort of a change the 'bright mark' made in a person, apart from leaving them looking like death, like the boy, with his eerie, glowing smile. He also had no idea just what the kite-like creatures were, or what made this 'chink' in the falls reopen, though he guessed Marsden's cyclotron started it all. One of the closing entries in the journal referred to the 'weave' breaking down, creating 'a rent in the wall between worlds' over fifty years ago. And that event, as best he could understand, had been an accident which required countless tries before just the right number of quarks in collision could open the weave. It was also clear that whatever explosives Marsden set in the cave he had mentioned had either been insufficient to close up the chink and the Brilliade's nesting place, or perhaps his plan had been sabotaged and the charge was never set off. Ben suspected it was the latter after his trip to the falls, for there'd been no sign of the rubble which would follow that sort of explosion, and then, there was the ever-swelling swarm of worms, and the kite-like things, which meant that 'they' indeed had been able to 'slip back through the wall between worlds'.

Perhaps the car accident Gus had been told his great uncle had had on the Ausable road was actually caused by one of those great winged creatures forcing him off the road. Perhaps, Ben thought, his father and Gus had also read the journal, maybe they'd even gone up to the falls to detonate Marsden's charge. Maybe Gus had been hurt on the climb, or invaded by one of those glowing things, and that was why his father had had to take him to a doctor. Then Ben was suddenly all but convinced that after his father returned, he'd gone back to the falls to set off the charge meant to seal the 'chink'. Only his father, like Marsden, had failed, he thought dismally. With a lump in his throat, he remembered the Bruins' cap found in the camper and the mystery of what had become of his father grew ever more ominous.

He stopped to wave away a thick swarm of the air-borne worms with his flashlight, but it seemed to have the reverse effect, drawing them like moths. As he batted them back from his face, his lopsided hold on the wheelbarrow sent it awry, pitching off to one side and sending the whole load of logs rolling into the mud.

'Darn it!' Ben swung the light like a sword, his other hand pulling his slicker hood tighter to keep the swirling mass of worms from getting into his ears. 'Get away!' The feel of them bouncing off the back of his hand made him shudder. Just like the luminous ooze, each fleshy speck emitted a ticklish current, and in no time, the air was so thick with worms that he soon lost sight of the house. Panicking, Ben reeled around in circles, both arms flailing out, but the shimmering bodies just seemed to be drawn by these protests, and in no time they smothered both arms.

Horrified as others lit on his face, inching over his chin and his mouth which he kept clenched shut for fear of their crawling inside, he finally broke into a run. For several minutes, with one hand clutching his hood so it pulled snugly over his head while pinching his nose with a finger and thumb from the other, as if he were now underwater, he scrambled blindly about, eyes clamped shut as more lit on his eyelids, inching right through his lashes and over the crease of his lids, trying to find a way in.

It felt as if every last molecule of air had been replaced by worms. Until something hard slammed against his shoulder, knocking him down to the ground. It was only then that he cracked an eye open to find that he'd finally outrun the swarm while running himself right into the woods in the process. And far enough not to know where he was. It might have helped, he realised, to have the flashlight, which he'd dropped, for apart from the worms which covered the slicker he frantically yanked up over his head, the stormy night looming all around him was utterly black. Then, tossing the infested slicker aside, he heard the eerie song, weaving down through the sheeting rain, the trees and the deafening roar of the falls.

'Ben?' Sarah groggily murmured, shivering hard against the cold damp air as it hit every feverish pore like needles of ice. 'Where are you?' She'd pried her eyes apart to take in the room in one sweeping squint, and though it seemed brighter, bright as day, in fact, she could not find her brother. 'Ben!'

Still squinting against the eerie light, she pushed up to a sitting position and pulled her down bag tight around her, for despite the room's brightness, it felt like winter. For a moment, she almost imagined it really *was* winter, between the cold and the bright bluish light, much like the bluish glare from snow on the ground on a clear winter's day.

Then, the disorientation from fever and having just awakened passed, and blinking at the brightness, her eyes slowly adjusting, she now guessed she slept right through to morning. After rubbing the last of sleep from her eyes, however, she was startled to find that it *still* looked like the bluish glare of snow stretching off through the windows. Which made her think she might still be asleep, lost in some dream about winter, but the room itself was too vivid for a dream, and much too cold, and all at once she thought that she had died, and that death had brought her into some wintry version of the world of the living. An empty wintry world, and her terror of being alone brought her scrabbling up to her knees, then less steadily to her feet.

Feeling woozy, weak and frightened, she shivered across to the nearest window. Before she reached it, however, she felt an odd warmth pouring forth with the light. Bewildered, moving closer, she brought her fingers up to the pane, then jerked them back again when she found that the glass was so warm it was almost hot. Resting her hands instead on the sill, she leaned forward again, squinting out through the glare. Like some movie version of heaven, the blue-tinged light seemed to permeate everything. But her gaze was unable to penetrate the light, to see the landscape within it, and it took another few moments before her focus adjusted to see why this was. With a single astonished gasp, followed by uncontrollable trembling, she saw that the glass was covered with thousands of tiny flat worms, and that each of them glowed. And turning about the room, feeling suddenly faint, she found that thousands more were crushed to every window in the house, like a vast swarm of bees peering in.

'Ben!' she shouted, near hysterical now as she stumbled across to the bedroom. Swinging open the door, finding the room dark and empty, she turned away – then stopped and turned back again, staring at her own shadow cast out before her, over the floor and up the wall to a window that looked out on blackest night. For some reason, there were no worms at this side of the house. At least, there were none for a moment, but the longer the light of the worms and the kerosene lamp spilled in through the door at her back, specks of light began to appear at this window as well. It came to her then that the worms must be attracted to the light, like moths.

Reeling around, she rushed to the table behind her and fumbled about with the lamp till her shaking hands finally managed to turn back the wick. Still shaking, with the room now solely lit by the light of the glow-worms themselves, she reached for the blind to the nearest window – the one just over the sink – and yanking it down, she moved on to the next, then the others, till every blind in the room was drawn. Then she went to the door and threw the bolt, and unable to think of what else to do, she curled back up in her sleeping-bag feeling shaky and cold and drenched with sweat, and much too distraught over what had become of her mother and Ben and being left all alone to notice just how terribly sick she was getting.

To Ben's left, the falls gushed out in an arch that dropped to the roiling river below where black funnels spun out through the ghostly foam and away with the oily black rapids. The heavy spray from the water pounding the rocks swirled up like a gossamer mist, thinner than on his first visit, less blinding, because of the rain that pounded it back. But the rain made the face of the cliff a good deal more slippery than the spray alone, and Ben had to climb the sharply rising steps with both hands, taking one at a time. He could not have stood free for a moment between the rivulets running over the rocks and the strong, buffeting winds that battered the rainswept face of the cliff. But staunch and scruffy shrubs with roots that tenaciously clung to cracks in the rocks provided him with indispensable handgrips along the way.

It was crazy, he knew, climbing up here alone on the hunch that he'd find his father when it was far more likely the only things he might find here were just what he hoped to avoid. Like the glow-worms, of which he had already spotted a few, not to mention the Ausable boy and those gliding creatures and whatever else Marsden's invention let in through the wall between worlds. But then, there was also the matter of closing the chink, which someone would have to do. If only he could find the charge Marsden set and figure out how it worked – and then, only if it did not involve blowing himself to bits in the process. But mostly, it was the hope of finding his father that egged him on. At least, that's what he told himself, scarcely aware of the hypnotic pull of the faint, ethereal song drifting down through the thunderous roar of the falls. And then there were the crude, chiseled steps which held an allure of their own, the way they wound up and appeared to vanish directly under the bow of the falls.

Ben was barely ten or twelve yards from the top when, clinging to one scrappy shrub, he took another glance at the dizzying rush of water crashing below. One false step and he'd find himself slipping right over the edge and through the spray where the crushing weight of the falls and bone-shattering boulders met in a boiling foam. But there was something hypnotic about this, too, and it took an act of will to drag his gaze back up from the tug of this plummeting, treacherous view. It was then that he saw he had cleared the tops of the towering pines that skirted the field, and rising up from the nearest edge, like a miniature blizzard lit from within, an amorphous, ever-changing pale blue cloud swirled where the house should have been.

'Sarah!' he cried against the storm, his stomach knotting up in a fist and tears burning like fire against his eyes as he helplessly watched the swarm. It had swallowed the house entirely, and if there were any hope at all it was not in a pair of Walkman earphones, but only in prayer. And he prayed with a fury the house was secure, which, although it was old, it might well be, as Marsden had known of the worms and most likely had sealed every drafty crevice and crack. Otherwise, they'd have gotten him long before he abandoned his journal, Ben reasoned, for the entries outlining his plan to blow up the chink and the Brilliade's nest spanned weeks. But none of Marsden's safeguards, if they held up, would do Sarah a wit of good if she should awaken and, finding him gone, leave the house herself to search for him. And there may be another flaw, he anxiously realized, thinking then of the stove. The stove-pipe opened up right through the roof, and unless the fire was kept going, what was there to prevent the worms from swarming in that way? But Marsden would have thought of that, too, he tried to reassure himself, perhaps he'd covered the chimney-pot with a durable fine-mesh screen. In any event, there was nothing he could do to help Sarah now, and the rage he felt at the thought of her being harmed drove him up through the hammering rain. Scrabbling over the slippery rock, blindly groping at every stray shrub, he finally came to the topmost step, which appeared, in fact, to lead nowhere.

The cliff face held no opening, it just arched a dozen feet overhead, forming a sort of tunnel under the falls, scooped out by erosion. About to give up, for there seemed nowhere to go, he sighted one of the worms. Then another, gliding under the falls through the hollow, followed by a few more. These were joined by several dozen others, drifting over the ledge, and together they shed enough light to cast a glow on that part of the cliff face.

Squinting off that way, Ben saw that the step he was on was once part of the shelf which appeared to run the length of the scooped-out hollow beneath the falls. But erosion had worn away the chunk of ledge that should have run out to the step, which left a gap of two or three feet between them. Still squinting about for a handhold, Ben found a hank of moss hanging above from a branch sweeping down from one of the trees sprouting out from the crest of the cliff. Tugging it gently, he managed to bring the end of the branch within reach. Tugging this too, he found it sturdy enough to pull himself across. Moving hand over hand as his feet fumbled over the break in the ledge, he managed to reach the other side, which put him right under one edge of the falls. Letting go of the branch, he saw the cluster of worms slipping over the ledge to get caught in the falls and carried downriver – right by the house, he imagined with anger. And fear, for more kept appearing ahead, drifting lazily out to the falls. Wondering how long it would be before they sensed his presence, he continued to grope for handholds over the shelf, just to be on the safe side. Then his fingertips touched something in the craggy shadows alongside the ledge, something fleshy and warm that wriggled and jabbed just before he could jerk his hand back. It stung, as if he'd been bitten, and faltering, Ben nearly lost his balance.

In fact, he had been bitten. By a small bat, clinging upside down to the rock. Heart pounding, he squinted and found that the whole upward scoop of the cliff was rustling with bats. So this was where they roosted, he anxiously realized, caught between the flock and the falls, wondering why they weren't feeding when he saw a glowing fleck and guessed that the ones that still hung here were either content to stay put and feed on the worms, or were themselves infested and in some state of advanced incubation.

With his legs now feeling like jello at the thought of both worms and bats all around him and the treacherous drop to the river below, he lost nerve and turned back the way he'd come. Then he realized, too late, that by letting go of the branch sweeping over the gap, it sprung back, and was now too high to reach from this side, so he had no means of getting back – unless he was foolish enough to risk leaping several feet on to slippery rock.

'Stupid!' he reproached himself, beginning to shake against the cold, already drenched to the bone between the rain and the spray from the falls. Now he had no choice but to follow the ledge and just hope it led downward again, and starting under the falls, he'd gone all of five feet when he found what he thought was a railing.

The tubular pipe bowed out from the cliff and away from the ledge like a giant hoop, and pulling himself beneath it he saw that it intersected the falls. It couldn't have been intended for a railing, but it made no other sense. Unless, he suddenly thought, it was part of Marsden's cyclatron. And no sooner had he thought this when he spotted a figure ahead. The height of a man, it seemed to be wearing a cape as one arm reached over the ledge directly above the point where the hoop-like pipe curved into the falls. But whoever it was, all Ben saw was a silhouette backed by the ghostly rush of water thundering out from the crest of the cliff in a great pale arc. Hesitating, not daring to call for his father in case it was someone else, he squinted ahead through the spray while holding fast to the tubular pipe.

It was then that he felt the faint thrumming like a pulse running through the pipe, not water exactly, but something that made the pipe warm and tingly beneath his hands. But all sense of its warmth was lost as he saw something else that chilled him right to the bone. As the figure ahead stood right at the edge of the ledge reaching out toward the falls, another arm stretched from the water itself, as if someone were standing inside it. But this, of course, was impossible, for the ledge didn't reach that far, and the crushing weight of the water alone would have instantly swept them away if it had. Nonetheless, the disembodied arm continued to reach from the falls as the arm of the figure ahead stretched out to meet it till their fingertips touched. And in that instant of touching, a spark shot out between the two, and from this, a rosy warmth began to bloom beneath the falls. Then the figure vanished, lost in a sudden flood of worms through some hole in the cliff, pouring directly into the glistening falls, as if caught on some powerful downdraft. The bats that hung from the overhang started to scrabble higher, out of the way, many dropping from their roost and flapping frantically into the night.

Ben, in a panic, reeled from the chaos of wings flooding out from the hollow. Lurching blindly out toward the falls, he just managed to scramble back from the edge. But to no avail, for between the slippery rock and his frenzied footwork, he skidded. With a backward kick and a twisting, terrified lunge, he thrust himself back toward the cliff. Then a searing pain, like a burning poker, stabbed at the back of his head.

In heaving himself away from the falls, he had hit his head on the overhang. Unconscious, he crumpled into a heap on the ledge and began an inexorable slide toward the edge of the sloping shelf and the thundering falls below.

15
A Bat in the Privy

Peering out of her sleeping-bag, Sarah saw nothing but darkness. There wasn't even the faintest glow seeping in at the edge of the blinds. Straining to listen, there was no sound but the rain and the chattering of her own teeth. She was freezing, and damp right through from the sweat of her fever, and achy and nauseous and just to make matters worse, in dire need of the privy, which she'd tried to put off till now. But now it was hurting, and sending a funny sensation up into her chattering teeth, as it always did when she put it off too long. Still, she felt so miserable that she even half thought of staying where she was and just praying she managed to keep from soiling herself, and if not, well, when she felt a bit better, she could always wash her things out in the sink. But then, of course, they'd know how sick she really was, she tearfully thought, and even more than this the indignity of it all appalled her. It would be like that very first hospital stay, when she had had to use a bedpan, and the thought of being that helpless again distressed her so, she resolved to get up and at least find an empty jar if only to prove she was not *that* ill.

But she was that ill, and shivering madly, struggling to pull herself up, every bone in her body felt like a brittle stick about to snap.

'You're not sick,' she told herself firmly, as if this alone could correct her bad blood, but she knew that could only be done by another one of those awful transfusions, and then, if the chemo was losing its effect, the new batch wouldn't last very long, in fact, nothing would last much longer, not even the constant, nagging pain. At least there was that, she told herself. But swallowing hard, feeling hollow inside, she knew if given the choice, she'd even choose the pain over feeling nothing at all. Then the tears began to well again. 'Stop it,' she admonished herself, sucking them back, determined not to give in. 'You're not – you're not going to – ' Still, she could not bring herself to say the thing that frightened her so. 'You'll be all right,' she chatted away to herself so as not to feel so alone. 'You just need to find an empty jar, and everything else will be all right.'

It was not the first time she had played this game, making deals with herself – endure this pain, get over that hurdle, and then you'll fly right over the next. And the next, and the next, till there were no more hurdles to leap. Only thing was, there always were, even for people who had their health, there was always something, only because that was life. That's what Gus told her that very first hospital stay when her parents had left the room so she wouldn't see them crying, although she knew they were. He'd said these things were even harder for people around the one who was ill, because there's nothing harder than feeling helpless when someone you love is in pain. And if anyone knew this, Gus did. He'd watched his own wife die from something just as bad as what she had, and he said the hardest thing of all was being left behind. And that was when Sarah decided no matter how frightened she was, or how much it hurt, she could not show her parents, because it just made it all much worse.

But more importantly, Gus had said that death itself was not a bad thing, that the only cruel part of it all was the suffering some people felt before it came. But death, he told her, was only one more part of life, and it came to all things, and if people just remembered that it was as natural as birth, they might not be so frightened. After all, he'd said, babies cry when they're born only because they don't know just how wondrous the life they're about to begin really is. And all our fears of dying are just as unfounded, for whatever death is, he'd said, it's part of the natural order of things, and can't be any worse than life. In fact, for all anyone knew, just as babies come into this world kicking and screaming, only to find themselves in the loving care of those who preceded them here, perhaps, Gus told her, it might be the same when we leave this world, ushered into what follows with every bit as much love and care from those who preceded us there.

Still, it was hard to believe in these things when she felt so bad, when she felt so alone, and she worried that pain and aloneness was what dying was all about. But like Gus said, the pain and feeling lonely were parts of life, not death, and it was just plain silly to sit around making up terrible thoughts about death when in all probability it would be just as mysterious and wondrous as life, and in any case, every moment of life was too precious to waste trying to figure out death just as a baby can't possibly know what life is about till it's born. But the most important thing of all that Gus told her, the thing she clung to now, was that no one could ever predict what tomorrow would bring. Perhaps they *will* find a cure, or maybe she'd just wake up and find herself well – it did happen sometimes, though no one understood how – and then she'd have wasted all that time worrying over nothing when she could have been studying harder at school and graduating with everyone else in her class. Life was to live, Gus said, as best as you can, and the worst thing a person could do was to give up hope when there's no way of possibly knowing what lies ahead, any more than anyone living could possibly tell her what death was about. And thinking this, she did feel a little stronger, and turned her thoughts instead to matters outside of herself, like her parents and brother, who might be in worse shape than she. Particularly after seeing those horrid things that had swarmed at the windows, the thought of Ben being outdoors soon refocused her worry. Sucking back her tears then, turning her mind from the pain, she crept to the windows.

Lifting the blind away from the glass just far enough to see out, she found the window clear and could even make out the field and trees beyond. The reason for this was, despite the rain, something like moonlight filtered down through the woods that ran up from the back of the house to the falls. She let the blind fall back. The first thing of order, she told herself, was to bundle herself up warmly then get herself to the privy before her bladder burst. That is, after carefully checking the windows once more and then opening the door just a crack to be certain that none of those worm-like things were still about.

The only disturbing thing she found, however, was the wheelbarrow, turned on its side a few feet from the stoop by a heap of logs. Ben must have been bringing them in just before the worms came, she anxiously thought, wondering where he had gone to, fervently hoping that he was all right. By themselves, she couldn't imagine what harm the worms could do, but then, there'd been thousands, and not even knowing what they were, the thought of Ben caught in a swarm was alarming. She scanned the field and the edge of the forest running along the drive in vain. All she could see through the sheeting rain was the van, and that eerie moon-like glow seeping down through the woods behind the house. Shivering with the rain pelting over her hood, she looked off toward the outhouse. Then drawing a breath, she slowly slogged her way across the soggy yard.

The door to the privy hung open, the shadowy space inside looking far from inviting. Between the cold and the thought of going in, she half wished she'd just looked in the house for a jar. But now she was here, she stepped inside and shivered out of her rain-spattered slicker, hanging it from a hook on the back of the door. Pulling it all but a crack so she could see what she was doing, she reluctantly eased herself down to the icy wooden seat. It was then that she spotted the glowing specks on the paper by her elbow, then on either side of her on the shelf-like seat and over the floor. Before she could leap from the seat in a panic, she felt something drop on her head, and praying it was the rain leaking in through the roof, she queasily dragged her gaze upward.

That fat brown bat her brother had seen that morning still hung from the ceiling, only now, it looked dead, with a phosphorescent ooze dripping down from the tips of its ears. In fact, the entire head appeared to be smothered under the luminous gel, and the eyes, staring blankly down, seemed to hold the faintest flicker of light. Then, all at once, the head dissolved into nothing more than a transparent husk, and within it, a writhing mass began to unfurl, sending tendrils of light through the skull, and then it was suddenly bursting out with a sound like shattering glass and a terrible clicking, so shrill that Sarah, breaking at last through her numbing fear, could not even hear her own cry as she rushed back through the door into the blinding rain.

Racing back to the tiny house, she had only one thought in her terrified mind. A similar gel had trickled down from her own ear only that afternoon, and though at the time, coming out of her faint, she'd accepted Ben's explanation, in hindsight, she now knew it hadn't been simply a honey smear glistening with light from the fire, but that it was in fact the same eerie substance that dripped from the ears of the bat. A substance that had glowed with a light of its own, just like the worms. Reaching the door to the house, she remembered Ben waking her, just before dawn, and she now knew that it was no prank when he said he'd seen something about to crawl into her ear. And that something, she realized, glancing back just before she slammed the door, had been one of the glow-worms that smothered the house and which somehow, once inside something living, metamorphosed and hatched into what she now glimpsed slipping out through the privy door.

While Sarah was bolting herself in the house, desperately wishing she weren't alone, on the other side of the mountain, Clare Liebling desperately wished she were back with her children. But unbearable as it was to imagine Ben and Sarah alone in the storm, the rain had been far worse in the lowlands, flooding the streets of Reedsville.

'How long do you think it will last?' she asked, bleakly staring at the dining-room window where everything beyond it was lost in the blurry miasma of night and rain.

'No way of knowing,' Sam Whittaker said as she set a tureen of stew on the table. 'But your children should be fine. Remember, they're on higher ground.' Then Sam returned to the kitchen, leaving Clare alone at the table while Mr Whittaker fussed at the fireplace, rearranging the logs with a poker.

'Darn shield on the chimney-pot must have got loose,' he muttered while errant drops from the downpour found their way down the flue to make the flames sputter. Outside, the wind howled. 'Always get these gales this time o' the year. Last time, it flooded the cellar and blew so many shingles off the roof you couldn't see the damn lawn.' Then Sam returned with a bowl of salad and a basket of rolls that looked more like coals.

'They don't look like much, but the inside's OK.' She set

the basket and bowl on the table. 'At least they weren't as disastrous as my poor pie.' She started serving the meal. 'I still can't get over your saying Gus hates sweets. The night he stayed over here, I baked four dozen oatmeal cookies and he polished every one of them off.'

'No wonder he had to be taken off to the hospital.' Sam's grandfather sat down. With a sigh at this dig at her cooking, Sam added:

'He ate a big breakfast, too, before I took him, if you don't remember.'

'Oh, I remember all right.' He sniffed at the plate of stew Sam handed him. 'Told him he ought to have a pancake or two with his maple syrup.'

'He really was practically drinking that syrup,' Sam recollected on passing Clare's plate. Then, still trying to draw Clare out of herself, she attempted to joke, 'I think your gym teacher's a sweet-addict on the sly, and just wants you to think he's a health-nut.'

'Gus avoided sweets like the plague for as long as I've known him,' Clare distractedly answered. 'He's even lectured my children on it. He practically tells them that sugar's a poison.' Sam was thoughtful a moment, then said:

'Maybe it's a symptom of whatever it is that's wrong with him.' Her hand still poised with the serving spoon full of stew, she asked, 'That boy you saw – the one the woman brought down to the Cotters – '

'Cotter called her Meg, and the boy, I think his name was Daniel.'

'Apart from hearing something about a bite mark,' Sam completed her question, 'was there anything else you overheard or saw that was wrong with the boy?'

'Just that he had no color at all.' Even less than Sarah, she thought. 'And his ear.'

'His ear?' Sam sounded surprised.

'I thought I already told you.' She then saw Sam looking

nearly as troubled as she. 'It was scratched up pretty badly, but that young woman – Meg – said he did it himself.'

'Meg Gallagher's my age if she's a day,' the old man spoke through a mouthful of stew. 'Just like Cotter's son. And Cotter, I tell you, he'd have been dead for years.'

'Oh, Grandpa.' Sam shook her head at the man. 'It's probably Cotter's grandson, and Clare didn't even say this woman's last name was – '

'What's she look like?' He cut Sam off and turned to Clare. And as Clare did her best to recall, his gaze went a bit dreamy, and when she was finished he said with wonder, 'Ain't possible for a person not to age in fifty years.'

'Honestly, Grandpa,' Sam broke in. 'Just because her name's Meg and she has long black hair – '

'Who does he think she is?' Clare asked.

'That woman I mentioned this afternoon. The one Grandpa was courting before they started keeping any outsiders away.' Then Sam turned back to her original question. 'Besides the scratched-up ear, did you notice anything else unusual about the boy?'

'No,' Clare answered thoughtfully, 'just that she said she found him lost in the woods and acting as if he were out of his head. Until she got him back to her truck. Then she said,' Clare struggled to recollect, 'she was delivering honey when she found him, and he got into it, eating it like he was starved, until . . . he went into a sort of trance. Something about the sun . . . yes, that's it, she said he kept staring up at the sun and it seemed to calm him right down.' Then, seeing the young physician's brow crinkle up with concern, she asked, 'Why, do you think you know what was wrong with him?' Sam was silent a moment. Then softly, as if she were thinking aloud, she replied:

'Gus's ear was badly scratched. And I told you about his acting confused, except when it came to food, and only then if it happened to be something sweet. And when I examined him, when I looked at his pupils, I used a penlight, and as soon as I shined it into his eyes, he became . . . well, it seemed to make him subdued. Even at Watersville General, they said the only things that kept his attention were food, sweet foods, and when he was in a bright room, he would stare at the sun, or a light. But whenever he wasn't being fed or at night, when they tried to turn out the light in his room he grew agitated all over again, as if nothing else could pacify him.'

'Then you think that whatever it was that bit the boy bit Gus as well?' Clare asked, but before Sam could answer, the phone in the hallway was ringing and Sam left the table to get it.

'There weren't no other Megs up there,' the old man mumbled once she'd gone. 'And even then, Meg was sellin' honey from the family hives.'

'Maybe it's her daughter,' Clare suggested, but his gaze looked far away, and together they sat in silence, caught in their own private thoughts, neither touching their supper, while wind and rain battered the blackened windows as the storm raged on. Then Sam quietly reappeared at the door, and something about her expression – or rather, the lack of one – brought Clare uneasily up from her seat. 'Is something wrong?' For one interminable moment, Sam's wooden gaze seemed to hang in the distance between them, then finally it reached to Clare and she quietly said with a voice that was leaden:

'It was Watersville General. They said that Gus . . .' Clare saw the woman's eyes grow moist. 'They said,' Sam tried again, 'they said they lost him during a brain scan.'

16
The Cry of the Chrysalis

With the door bolted and the blinds still drawn, Sarah turned the wick on the lamp up high. Unable to stand the cold any longer but far too frightened to go out again, she used books to build a fire in the stove, by which she now anxiously huddled. And she ached, not in her body alone, but in her thoughts for her mother and brother, who now had joined her father and Gus in the ranks of the missing. But what hurt even more than not knowing where everyone was, was feeling so utterly helpless. At last she had some idea of what her parents had felt since her diagnosis. And now, to make matters worse, the gauzy light from the falls had faded away and the worms were returning, slowly but surely, attracted, she guessed, by the kerosene lamp. In fact at least several dozen had come down the flue before she got the fire going.

'Stop it!' She slapped a book down on one inching its way out from under the stove. Already the floor all around her was spotted with dimly glowing stains. At least they were no longer swimming around the room, which made them harder to hit. But they seemed to keep coming, creeping out of the shadows, two for every one hit, and it made her wonder if Cotter's son had indeed been collecting the things, for she now had no doubt what he'd actually had in his jar, and she'd even begun to suspect the strange youth had been planting rather than gathering them when she caught him there. But then, there were too many even to fit inside young Cotter's jar, and she thought, with a thread of hope, that perhaps he *had* been collecting them after all. Maybe he knew that some might have slipped in overnight and knowing the danger they posed, he'd come to clear them out during a possible dormant stage during the day. At least, she hoped it was true, for if he could be trusted, she might even ask him for help. If she bundled up and if only she could make it back to Ausable Center . . . but then she remembered the thing slipping out of the privy, and that horrible bat, and she wasn't all that sure she had the courage to hike through the storm and the woods. Or the strength, for that matter, she thought as she weakly pushed herself up from the floor by the stove. But then, she told herself firmly, her brother could be in serious danger, and how did she know whether or not she could do it until she tried?

Her mind made up, for failing while trying was better than not even trying at all, she pulled on several layers of the warmest clothing she could find. She still did not have the nerve to return to the privy for her hooded slicker, but then her gaze fell on the coatrack by the door where her father's was hanging. Pulling it over her head, she found the hem of it trailed on the floor. All the better, she thought, to shield herself if she ran into more of the worms. Then, glancing back at the stove, reluctant to leave the warmth of the fire, she spotted her Walkman and thought of another thing that might help on the way.

The worms, or whatever they were, entered the head through the ears. Wearing the Walkman, the earplugs would prevent that from happening to her again. Then something else occurred to her, something that might be a help, if Ben was in trouble. The Walkman headset was not only one way to keep the worms from getting in, but if someone had already been invaded by one, it could be a way to destroy it. Somehow, she now understood, by having the earphones on and the volume way up, the noise or the sound waves had shattered the one that implanted itself in her. Perhaps it was only at a particularly fragile phase in their transformation that the Walkman could stop these things before they matured enough to hatch from their hosts. In any case, it was a good thing to have, she thought as she picked it up. Then, clipping it on to her belt beneath the slicker, she turned to leave, then froze.

Her ears pricked at a sound like a creak from the wooden stoop beyond the door. Then she saw the latch jiggle up and the door give a jerk as if nudged from the other side. Her heart skipped a beat when whatever was on the outside shoved at the door again, harder, but the bolt she slid on coming back from the privy held it firmly shut.

'Ben!' she called apprehensively, straining to hear a reply through the wind and the rain. 'Mom, is that you?' she anxiously asked when the only reply was the jiggling latch. 'It's locked and you're not getting in till I know who it is!' she finally shouted, but pressing her ear to the door, she heard only the creak again, then nothing but rain, as though whoever it was had stepped down from the stoop and started away. Unless, she uncertainly thought, it was Ben, so badly hurt and shaking with cold, he'd collapsed in a heap on the other side of the door. Flooding with guilt, Sarah rushed to the nearest window and peeked behind the blind. Staring back through the rain-spattered glass were eyes so wild they seemed on fire. Even the face seemed to hold a faint light of its own, seeping through the gaunt white flesh. But while the bony fingers clawed at the window, trying to force it up, Sarah felt only relief and rushed to the door to slide back the bolt.

'Daddy!' she shouted out as she yanked the door wide. 'We've been worried sick since we got here!' She swept out to the puddled stoop. 'Mom went to Reedsville to see if Gus knew where you were!' As he moved stiffly back toward the stoop, she reached out through the rain and clasped her arms at his neck. 'Oh, Daddy, we've all been so worried.' Half sobbing into his rain-drenched coat, she clung to him, too lost in the flood of emotion to notice he wasn't hugging her back. 'Where were you? What's the matter with Gus? Why didn't you leave us a note?' she rushed on, till an icy trickle of rain down the back of her neck brought her drawing contritely away. 'Oh, Daddy, you must be freezing.' She grabbed at one of her father's hands and tugged him up the stoop and into the light of the lamp and the warmth from the stove. 'We better get you out of those clothes before you catch your death of pneumonia.'

She shut the door and bustled off into the bedroom, then returned with the quilt to find him staring glassy-eyed at the flames licking up in the stove. 'I had to use some old books to build the fire,' she sheepishly told him, then, without stopping to breathe, she lunged ahead with all that had happened since her arrival while struggling to get him out of his sopping clothes. Caught up in her task and her chatter, she never noticed how stiffly he stood, or that he did not even shiver, and that his face was as wooden and white against his thick dark beard as a plaster bust. She did notice, however, that the suit coat she dragged from his rigid, drenched form was not his. A very old style, with wide lapels and ragged with moth holes and covered with dirt, it looked, in fact, as if it had come from a corpse that had clawed its way up from a grave. But then her attention was drawn from this odd-looking suit coat to something more pressing. As she tossed it to the floor, she caught sight of another one of the worms. It was inching along the floor at the edge of the rug where her father stood dripping.

'There!' she exclaimed. 'That's one of those things I just told you about!' Although, if he'd heard one word of her rapid-fire chatter, he gave no sign. But it did draw his near-hypnotic gaze from the fire when she stomped on the thing. In fact, it made the flickering in his eyes grow suddenly wilder and it brought an angry-looking twitch to his mouth, till he seemed almost to snarl. But Sarah, getting right back to work, unbuttoning his soaking shirt and dragging it off, then pushing the quilt up around his broad shoulders was too busy to notice. And by the time she was prodding him back toward a chair by the table, still prattling on, his gaze returned to the flickering light from the stove and his face again grew subdued.

'I'll make you something hot to drink.' She now yanked the slicker up over her head. 'The kettle on the stove will be hot any minute.' She bustled across to the shelves and fumbled over the various jars and boxes until she found the instant coffee which she quickly spooned into a mug. Filling a second mug from the pump with cold water then stirring in powdered milk, feeling energized in the role her parents usually had with her, she continued to talk about Ben and her fears and how she had planned to hike down to find Cotter. She also felt her strength continue to swell as if from some unknown reserve, tapped in some magical way simply by virtue of being needed. But then, no one had ever really needed her before now, and perhaps it was that, she thought, as much as her illness, that made her feel so lethargic. After all, there wasn't much call to summon up one's hidden reserve, or even to know one existed, when everyone treated her like she was helpless.

'But now, if we could drive the van – that is, after you've warmed up a bit – we could be down at the Cotters' in no time, and if they know what's going on, and they'll help us find Ben – ' But the thought died away when she glanced back over one shoulder and took a hard look at her father, who appeared to be there in body alone, his mind clearly elsewhere. 'Dad? Are you OK?' she asked, growing anxious all over again. Then seeing the steam drifting up from the spout of the kettle on the stove, she said, 'Maybe you just need to warm up a little.' But she finally sensed he'd need far more than warmth, for no one doted on her like her father, even before she'd been ill, and for him to not give her so much as a glance or a word, let alone a hug, was starting to make her feel like she might as well be speaking to a corpse. It was then that she noticed the blankness of his stare, so vacant he looked almost blind. He looked, she finally realized, more dead than alive. With that thought her strength and her confidence started to wane. She tried to refocus herself on the simple task of getting the coffee made. She set the mugs on the table then fetched the kettle and filled the one with the coffee. Then she went to the shelves again to get a spoon and a bag of sugar. Something seemed to stir behind that flatness in her father's eyes. He leaned forward a bit as Sarah returned, but not to drink from his cup. The moment she set the sugar bag on the table, he snatched it up.

'Daddy? What are you doing?' She stared in bewilderment as he ripped it apart. Then the sugar was spilling out everywhere as he held the torn bag over his head, pouring it into his mouth just like it was water, as if he were dying of thirst. For a moment, he actually started to gag on the stuff, his throat bulging, his mouth overflowing, and Sarah, dumbstruck between the way he devoured it and panicked he'd choke on it now, gaped at him across the small table, still trying to make sense of it all. Then her father's head arched all the way back and his neck extended, the muscles all rippling much the way a snake's might if it were swallowing something whole. Horrified, she watched the bulge in his throat slowly moving down, then he straightened his head, his tongue sliding over his sugar-coated lips, and with an odd little smile of contentment, he turned his gaze again to the fire. It was then that she saw the scabbed-over scratches around one ear and understood.

Like a wave, fear and her fever broke over her, bringing back all the nausea and pain and helplessness she'd felt before, only now it was nearly crushing. The books she'd used for the fire burned quickly, and now it was almost out, and with the damp chill spreading out through the room once more and the rapidly dwindling flames, the worms, she knew with grim resignation, would soon drift down the flue again. Even the storm, still raging around the house, seemed insurmountable now. The surge of strength she'd felt on first seeing her father and all of her hopes slipped away. She could barely move one foot in front of the other let alone hike to the Cotters'. Staring at her father's stony face gazing off at the stove, her hands let go their anxious grip on the table and helplessly fell by her sides. And it took an endless minute of standing there, feeling as if she were going to fall, when her fingertips registered the thin cord at her waist and Sarah glanced down.

The Walkman! Of course! She'd been ready to give up too soon. Her hands groped at her one last hope, slipping the earphones up over her head and quietly starting around toward her father. If it had worked for her, it might work for him, if the thing wasn't too far along, if she managed to get it in place and turn up the volume before he could stop her. Treading softly behind him, keeping her eyes on the back of his head, her hands frantically loosened the headband then pulled the two ear-pieces out to the side. She would have to be very quick about it, she calculated, raising her arms, aligning the foam-padded earplugs and praying he didn't budge till she turned the thing on. Then she carefully brought the headphones around his ears and let the band gently clamp down. Her father shifted slightly, but her fingers were already flying down to the switches of the tiny Walkman cassette player clipped to her belt.

She'd already had the volume turned high before she hit the play button, and the instant the raucous music began, a quiver ran over her father's scalp. Then a glow appeared at the spot where his hair was thinning, shining right through the skin. Then it deepened to show every capillary and jagged joint at the top of his skull. In the fraction of a second, it was as if he were actually turning to glass, his fine hair turning to transparent threads, then his skull began turning translucent as well till the wriggling shape inside shone through, like a tentacled sphere of jelly. Then the arms of the thing were all slithering like a mass of luminous snakes, rolling itself around till the part that was turned toward her father's face slipped up. Then finer tendrils parted around a throbbing golden orb with a slit that widened and blazed like some monstrous blood-red eye glaring back.

The sound she then heard was every bit as frightening, like thousands of crickets at once. And it swelled through the room in an ear-splitting rapid-fire clicking, the pitch growing steadily shriller, till all at once, it shattered the hood on the kerosene lamp and the jars on the shelves and the windows exploded in a shower of splinters, raining over the room like hail. Then she saw her father's hands fly to his head, ripping the earphones away, and she stepped apprehensively backward as he pitched violently out of his chair. With the earphones trailing down by her feet from the cord running up to the Walkman, she continued creeping backwards while watching her father groveling over the floor. Then a board beneath her creaked and his head swung around, his whole face glowing while tiny tendrils of light darted right through his eyes like flickering tongues of fire. He – or it – was looking for her now, and all around him, specks of light flowed in around the blinds flapping up at the broken windows. Outside, another swarm was forming and swiftly flooding into the room.

Blind with tears, Sarah fled to the little bedroom and threw her whole weight on the door. There was no lock, but there was a heavy oak dresser against the adjacent wall. Kneeling, keeping one foot to the door, she grasped the legs of the dresser than dragged it inch by inch till it slid past the edge of the molding and blocked the door. Sagging back on her heels from the exertion, sucking the air in her lungs, she dared hope she'd be safe for the moment at least, till she spotted a thin thread of light. By moving the dresser, she'd uncovered a crack in the wall where light seeped through, and if light could slip into the room, so could the worms. Pushing herself shakily back to her feet, she eased open a drawer of the dresser and pulled out what looked like long johns – Matthew Marsden's – and worked part of them into the crack. Then she went to the bed and wrapped herself up in the heap of blankets draped over the foot, then she lay there, shivering wildly, as much from fear as from the damp cold. There was nothing else that she could do, but wait, and pray that help would come . . . and to take one last precaution. She slipped on the Walkman earphones.

After a while, her eyes grew heavy from searching for worms through the dark and her tears, and insidiously, her fever, combined with exhaustion, finally took its toll. Sleep crept up and dragged her down to deep, disturbing dreams. During one of these, thrashing about, she inadvertently pulled off the headset. But Sarah was well beyond noticing this, or the patter of rain that now wove through her dreams, just as she was well beyond seeing the crack of light reappear in the wall. The cloth she had stuffed there was poked away by a finger prodding the hole, and this in turn was followed by a single eye peering through.

After a moment, the eye disappeared, replaced by a stream of glowing specks, swimming through the crack and across the darkened room to the bed.

17
The Chink in the Falls

The jolt of utter blackness slowly faded back to grays as Ben came to with a thunderous roar in his ears and a crushing ache across his chest. An upward jut of rock from the sloping ledge had kept him from sliding right over, still it took him several long minutes of feeling the icy spray on his face before he pried his eyes apart to the dizzying drop below. Just inches away from a fatal plunge through the falls, numb from the cold and his fear, he closed his eyes and tried to sort out the various parts of himself. One arm tingled, pinned beneath his side, and it felt like his legs had dropped off, slung as he was like a sack from the outcrop of rock with his feet dangling over the edge. Despite his sudden panic, he was too stiff and sore to scramble back up, which served him well, for pinned as he was by the weight of his body alone, any sudden movement would have sent him plummeting over the ledge.

Carefully easing one arm up between his chest and the rock he was pinned against, his free hand blindly groped behind his back till it found a crack in the ledge. With his fingers anchored securely in the crevice, he slowly drew up his knees. With the lower part of his legs numb from hanging so long, he could not feel his feet hit the rim. He waited another long minute before the sensation returned like a prickling of pins, then he carefully slid his feet a little further back on the ledge.

Drawing one shuddery breath, he began to slowly push himself up from his chest while the fingers anchored behind him carefully pulled till he rolled to his back. He rested a moment, staring up to the top of the cliff and the arch of the falls, then he groped for another handhold and managed to roll himself on to his belly. Clawing and kicking, he inched his way back underneath the cyclotron ring, then, panting from the effort, he wriggled all the way back to the top of the shelf.

His legs still felt too rubbery to stand with the rock as slick as it was, so he sat for a moment, catching his breath and scanning the length of the ledge. It was then, with the danger of falling now past, that his mind made room for a new observation. With a skip of the heart, his gaze followed a trail of glowing specks on the ledge. Like some tiny procession of ants, they led down to the upward jut of rock where he'd hung. He'd come to just in time, he thought as he absently scratched an itch at one ear. Then his heart stopped cold on glimpsing one of the worms slowly inching along his sleeve.

With an anxious guttural sound, Ben ripped off his sweat-shirt. Worms covered the hood of the thing. Then he frantically raked his fingers through his hair and again his heart stopped dead as a flurry of glowing specks sifted over his lap like wriggling flakes of snow. But worst of all, the vague itch he felt deep in one ear now began in the other as well. In a frenzy, he gouged at both ears in a vain attempt to scrape the itching out, his head swimming with thoughts of the cloud of worms at the house with Sarah trapped inside, and of Gus off in some hospital and his father now missing for several days, and he suddenly had a terrible sinking sensation, believing that they were all doomed to some horrible fate at the hands of these creatures, and then his fear gave way to rage. Bringing both hands slamming down to the ledge, he pushed himself up to his feet. He had no Walkman to blast in his ears and force the things out, he was stuck on the ledge, but so long as he could still reason, there was one thing he could do.

Off to his right, where before he'd seen a figure reaching out to the falls, Ben saw the trail of worms wind off toward a barely perceptible glow from the cliff. Somewhere ahead, he thought with grim purpose, he'd not only find the source of these things, but also the explosives which he'd read about in the journal. Whatever it was they did to a person, whatever lay in store for him now, he'd at least try his best to stop them from getting at anyone ever again.

Groping his way further along the ledge, his gaze fixed to the faint glow ahead, he realized that it was seeping out through some crack or hole in the cliff. Most of the bats which had clung to the wall to his right had flown away, but a few still hung there, their faces encased in a luminous gel, their eyes seeming to flicker. Then nearing the very middle of the ledge, where the glow from the cliff hit the water, Ben saw one of these bats drop away from its roost and flap right into the falls. Or rather, he saw with his next stumbling step, it had flown through a part in that curtain of water, and squinting through the heavy spray at its small glowing shape still flapping away, he did not see the river below winding off through the wooded hills, but absolute blackness, as if the narrow slit in the falls were a portal into an infinite void. But there *had* to be something below. Even at night, through the rain, he'd see *something*, he thought. Then he spotted the rail-like ring of what he supposed was Marsden's cyclotron. But it didn't continue through the split in the falls, but stopped at either edge. It was as if, on hitting that blackness, it faded into nothing. And then Ben recalled the arm reaching through, stretching out to the figure he'd seen before falling.

His gaze soared up to the top of the falls for some outcrop that might have obstructed the flow, but that break in the curtain of water did not extend to the crest of the cliff. Yet, there was no logic for why the water should suddenly part on its own, creating this narrow, elongated hole wide enough for a bat or an arm to fit through. There was even less logic in how an arm might have reached through this hole from the other side, for beyond the hole there would be nothing but a sheer drop to the river below. Nonetheless, he had seen it reach out to the figure, as if in some greeting, and then there was the bat, and even now, as he gaped at the split in the falls, he saw it grow a bit wider, the ends of the cyclotron ring and the water around it wavering then fading like mist.

'Of course!' It finally dawned on him. 'This must be Marsden's "chink" in the falls!' Then, realizing it was through this that the worms, and God knew what else, found their way into this world, Ben, reeling with his discovery, turned toward the glowing and made yet another.

Almost directly across from this split in the falls, a tunnel sloped down through the cliff. And no ordinary tunnel, but one with walls as smooth as glass. It was clear it began as a natural formation, perhaps, at one time, no more than a crack, for down by the ledge and up at the top two gashes aligned, as if they once connected. Probably over time erosion widened the crack to a hole, but erosion alone would have left the surface as rough as the crude stone steps. And even if Marsden's cyclotron had been built in some cavern below, explosives could not have rendered the walls so evenly round and smooth. No, he thought, it would have to have been something else. Maybe even the worms. If they nested below, perhaps decades of swarming up through the tunnel had worn down the walls, polishing them to their current mirror-like sheen. Unless, he thought uneasily, a single massive worm burrowed through, for the shape of it was as regular as the hole of an earthworm, if vastly enlarged.

But no earthly creature could possibly have gouged its way through sheer rock. And with that thought, Ben started apprehensively in with one arm overhead, for the reason the tunnel was glowing was because of the clusters of worms on the walls. Not that it mattered much now, he thought, feeling the nagging itch in his ears. Then he stopped himself short as a deep oboe tone followed by a high-pitched trill echoed up through the tunnel, coming from somewhere far below.

18
Sweet Cravings

The heavy rains at last eased off to a gentle if steady drizzle and the dark outside the window began to fade to a velvety gray. Then, a little before the dawn, Sarah abruptly awoke with the strangest sensation, almost as if some powerful clock inside her had just struck the hour. She felt none of the usual grogginess when climbing from the bed, and though she was still very anxious over the fate of her father and Ben, she also felt the most peculiar craving for something – anything – sweet.

In addition, she felt remarkably alert in spite of her fever, so much so that all of her senses felt uncannily keener than ever before. She could hear right through the door a faint, steady breathing – her father, she thought to herself – but even more surprising, she thought she could actually smell the honey and jams right through their containers on the shelves on the other side of the wall. But of course such a thing wasn't possible and more likely, she thought, after going to bed hungry, these sugary fragrances couldn't be anything more than a product of her own mind. But whether it came from her mind or her belly, the craving was driving her near to distraction, so much so that Sarah scarcely noticed her headset now trailed from the cord at her waist, and she did not notice at all that both her ears were scratched raw and encrusted with blood. But the itching had come and gone in the night, and the damage was done in her sleep, and the thing that had caused the itch had gone beyond the point of obstructing her hearing. In fact, it now enhanced this particular sense just as it enhanced all the others. But Sarah had no way of knowing how badly she had scratched at herself in her sleep, or how one of the worms that had crawled down her ear canal had appended itself to her brain. She had no way of knowing her senses were heightened because she was joined to the thing, or that the uncharacteristic craving for sweets was not her own.

Then, hearing the breathing again, the night before came rushing back. Her heart quickened with each dreaded memory – her father's head glowing under the Walkman, then suddenly turning transparent as glass and the hideous thing that it held staring back, and then, that terrible wounded cry, so shrill that it shattered the windows. And now there was only that soft, steady breathing and all she could think was her father was hurt, and here she had let herself fall asleep and awoke thinking only of eating sweets. With miserable self-reproach, she rushed to the barricaded door. Once the heavy oak dresser was moved to the side, she opened the door just a crack and looked out. The thin gray light preceding the dawn lapped under the blinds that flapped at the windows, the window panes reduced to shattered scatterings over the floor. Still, she heard the breathing, yet she saw no one. She quietly started out.

The floor was so littered with glass, she had to tread carefully to the table where she turned up the wick in the kerosene lamp and lit it. The pre-dawn grays jumped back from the golden glow as she carried the lamp through the room. Then she found him, curled up on the rug by the stove, his pale, bearded face looking peaceful in sleep. The stove, however, was cold, as was the room without its windows. And the floor beneath the windows was puddled with rain, but at least all the worms had gone. Unless, like bats and moths, they'd crept off to the shadows to sleep through the day, she thought, looking down at her father, curled up like a child, and trying to decide what to do. She wasn't so sure she should wake him, not if that horrid thing was still growing inside, and she knew she did not have the nerve to use her Walkman again to see if it was.

But before she could give the matter more thought, her strange craving was back, and unbearable. She dragged her gaze across the room to the shelves and the counter cluttered with food. Maybe it would be wiser, she reasoned, now edging after her gaze, to simply let him sleep, and hope that help would arrive in the meantime. But once she reached the stock of food, all other thoughts gave way to the craving. Like someone obsessed, her hands moved uncontrollably over the shelves.

On finding a plastic container of apricot jam, she urgently twisted the lid off and dropping it to the floor, she began scooping jam in her mouth with two fingers. Never in her life had she felt so ravenous for sugary things. The moment she finished the jam she was drinking maple syrup right out of the can. And when she moved on to a plastic bottle of chocolate syrup for mixing with milk, something which Ben was addicted to but which she, till that morning, had always abhorred, the door to Matthew Marsden's house began to open slowly behind her. Despite her heightened senses, however, Sarah was so lost in her binge that she didn't quite register the footsteps crackling over the glass on the floor.

'He's in advanced chrysalis stage.' The warbly words seemed to come from inside of her head just as she'd taken a great greedy gulp from a cellophane bag of raisins. Then the first purry voice was replaced by another while Sarah nearly choked trying to swallow.

'But it's weak. The man's been without nourishment for

days. It can't possibly hatch in time, not without killing the host if it would survive. It still needs time to mature.' It no longer had the Arkansas accent, but even before Sarah turned from the shelves she recognized the warbly lilt to the words, though they still came like thoughts in her head. Or, more precisely, the thing that was growing inside her was picking up their thoughts while Sarah, gaping now at the Cotters stooped over her father, still thought they were speaking.

'The boy may be seeded as well.' It was the man's voice now, but his mouth wasn't moving.

'The only ones I found the day before yesterday were under the woodpile.' Neither was young Cotter's, she saw, and at last Sarah understood – they were projecting their thoughts, but just what they meant, she wasn't all too sure.

'It's not your fault. The Brilliade senses her home in the air through the chink in the falls, that's why she's begun another fertile cycle so soon.' The man's gaze rose from her father to take in the room full of glass with its flapping blinds. 'The house must have been crawling with Brilliade larvae. It's doubtful the boy was spared.'

'But then we would have to leave one behind. We can only carry two chrysalides back.' Young Cotter's snowy white head came up, and Sarah, her craving now smothered by fear, wondered if they were both blind behind their dark glasses, as neither yet noticed her there.

'Do we have any choice?' the man replied, then both their heads turned her way, and if she had felt invisible moments before, now she squirmed self-consciously, for this time she practically felt the eyes hidden behind their dark glasses boring right through her. 'At least we'll have these two Brilliades to take back. Get the girl. I'll deal with the father. Then we'll find the boy and see if he indeed has been seeded as well.' And as Sarah watched young Cotter approaching, she realized they'd known she was there all along. Which made it even more horrifying, knowing they found her so inconsequential, calmly discussing their business before her, driving it home just how helpless she was.

'Take us where?' She finally found her voice, now as trembly and strange as the Cotters. 'What are you going to do to us?' She backed away as young Cotter came closer.

'There's nothing to fear.' The white-haired youth began to pull his workgloves off, then Sarah felt the sink at her back and nearly screamed when she saw him reach out. Even his hands were like something out of a nightmare – skeletal-thin and webbed, the tip of each finger spread out in a broad, flat pad, each with a slit like a mouth. And as they drew nearer her throat, the slits quivered with soft, wet sucking sounds, and a pale blue light, like that in the worms, began to seep out with a dribbling gel. Then Sarah was flailing away at the youth, missing his arms and striking his face. The band on his glasses snapped and they fell. Sarah's heart flew up to her throat.

Where young Cotter's eyes should have been, there was only smooth white skin and a fine, ruffled line running across his face from ear to ear – or where ears might have been had he had them. 'No need to be frightened,' he told her again, his unmoving mouth fixed in a smile while the ruffled line on his brow began to quiver apart like the lid of an eye. Then his brow was opening up like a wound, revealing a moon-like, bone-white globe, and this spherical skull began spinning, emitting a web of crackling light. Sarah, still sinking, unable to draw a breath, fell into a sort of trance, and everything faded except for the flickering lines darting over the whirling orb and a deepening glow from within it as if it were lit with the same blue light of the worms. Then the lightning web swelled out like veins of fire from the throbbing orb at its core and she felt young Cotter's fingers probing her head with a sucking, prying sensation.

From a very great distance, she sensed that a part of her mind was being loosened and tugged like a tooth, and when it ripped free, all feeling and thought went hurtling into oblivion.

19
The Secret of Ausable Cavern

How much time had passed since he entered the tunnel, Ben could not even guess at. But already it seemed an eternity since the maddening itch faded off into deafness, followed by the return of his hearing and with it an urge that nagged more than the itch. He'd always had a weakness for sweets, but nothing so strong as this. And the strength of that craving brought with it a sharpened alertness that helped him to stay awake. And staying awake seemed critical now that he found himself trapped in the cavern.

Peering around the flowstone wall where he hid, some twenty yards from the tunnel, he searched again for some sign of another way out of his prison deep in the cliff. Stalactites hung from the ceiling of the vast cavern like great white fangs, and sprouting up from the floor like a forest of tree trunks which had lost all their branches and leaves were hundreds of stalagmites, formed by the calcified drippings from cousins above. And winding through this forest of stone was a shallow stream of hot steaming water. He knew the water was hot because he had slipped in it several times now, and he guessed that the reason why it was hot was because it was used to cool Marsden's equipment. The man's life's work had outlasted him, still humming inside its great metal jacket, rising out of the floor in the shape of a dome intercepted by a great ring. The ring, cutting high through the wall where the tunnel was, was the same he'd seen out by the falls. And the falls, he guessed, were what powered the thing, running like a perpetual motion machine. But nothing he saw – the great hooded shell of the cyclotron, the forest of stone and the sweeping curve of the ring running right through the cavern – looked in any way solid. All of it swirled with flickering lights that danced through the shadows, dissolving hard edges, reflected in the stream and caught in the steam like a galaxy whirling with stars. And the source of that light was more frightening – and beautiful – than anything he'd ever seen.

Hovering under the roof of the cave, the great hump of its head formed a sort of umbrella. The height and width of this alone, he guessed, was far greater than Marsden's house. But it was the anatomy under this sprawling 'cap' that intrigued him most, with ruffles, like the underside of a mushroom, that rippled as if with some breeze – or breath, for this great, translucent husk was very much alive.

Through what looked like a very thin membrane, as clear as glass, shone an intricate web of light that spiraled up through the dome of its head and glittered like stars running down its long arms. And the arms, or tendrils, which hung from the heart of the thing all the way to the floor of the cave swept through the air with such delicacy, bringing up water like transparent elephant trunks, spraying it over itself with the gentlest hiss followed by a deep, oboe hum. And yet, in spite of its vastness, it looked like some buoyant, exquisite aquatic flower. Which wasn't unlike the pictures he'd found plastered all over Marsden's walls. Pictures of something almost as beautiful, in their own way, and quite dangerous, too. Oceanic hydrozoa, medusa, the Portuguese man-of-war. But the mammoth creature hovering overhead had something much worse than a sting. With every breath that rippled the ruffled gills running under the great husk above, thousands of glowing specks were released like spores, gliding off like milkweed pods, filling every square inch of the cavern with glimmering star-like worms.

He also thought he now understood why bats were crowding under the falls while the roof and walls of the cavern would have provided a far better roost. Here and there, he still saw a few who had chosen to stay behind. Hung upside down, their gaping snouts dripping a glistening ooze, they looked quite dead, as if whatever had grown in their heads had drained their life away. And that something had grown inside them was no longer theory, for Ben had seen several hatch, passing right through the skulls of the bats with the ease of a mist rising out of the ground. First had come the arms, slithering out like a nest of new-born snakes, the tip of each then attaching to anything near to pull out the bladder-like husk. And they came with that terrible cry, like shattering glass and thousands of crickets at once, and it awed him that they could have such horrible voices, like the beautiful peacock's shrieks. But he'd also heard the whale-like song of the vast one, which, by contrast, seemed nearly angelic. But even the delicacy of their form was in no way apparent just after hatching. Rather, they hung from the ceiling, ungainly as butterflies fresh from their cocoons, dripping wet and crinkled up like soggy, matted leaves. Then, gradually, the dim, throbbing glow they emitted grew steadily brighter and each wrinkled, bladder-like husk would begin to puff up like an opening parasol. And then, with their light swirling and pulsing in ever more dazzling hues, they'd drop from the ceiling and glide toward the great one that spawned them and orbit like tentacled moons.

Already, Ben had given up trying to count these orbiting offspring. He guessed there were close to a hundred, most of them small, but two or three dozen quite large. Either they grew very fast once they hatched, or some had been hatched a long time before. And though he did not have a clue as to what they were or where they were from, he didn't have much doubt about how they got here. And judging from one he'd seen squeezing itself through the tunnel, he sensed they would not be here long. At least, those small enough to slip out might have left if the first hadn't got itself stuck. And this was the reason that Ben had been trying to find another way out. Although, it did not seem too hopeful, as some of the others would surely have found it by now. But then, most seemed content just to hover above, slowly circling the great one that spawned them.

Ben could no longer see the one that had caught itself in the tunnel, but he heard it, with its creaking call and the squeaking its body made trying to squeeze through. If they hadn't frightened him so, he might have even found this amusing, the way it labored to push itself up toward the falls, its head like a water-balloon, sloshing and squealing between the walls while impatiently clicking away to itself. Ben wondered what it was that made it so eager to leave the cave – to wreak further havoc on Ausable, or to slip through the 'chink' in the falls?

Whichever it was, Ben doubted he'd ever find out, for soon after he entered the cave, he spotted Matthew Marsden's explosives, attached to hooks chiseled high on the walls. How Marsden had managed to get them so far out of reach, he couldn't imagine. Some of the wires ran all the way up to the top of the wall where the tunnel was. And over the tunnel, a small black box held the detonating device. Ben guessed this because of what looked like a digital clock on the box which was flashing red numbers.

Perhaps the thing was hooked up to the cyclotron, set to go off when the chink got too wide, or maybe it was already in the process of counting down the time. In any case, Ben couldn't make out the numbers themselves from this far away, and each time he tried to return to that side of the cave, the great one's arms drove him back. But one thing was clear. His trip down to the cavern had been an utter waste, for someone else had already set the detonator on Marsden's explosives.

About that same time, on the other side of the mountain, someone was pounding down the door and bellowing out through the drizzly dawn to rouse the Whittaker household. When the yawning and grumbling old man and his groggy granddaughter finally opened the door, what they found cleared their heads as effectively as a cold shower.

'Sorry to make such a ruckus.' The red-headed bear of a man on the porch smiled contritely, his clear blue eyes turning suddenly shy as a kitten's. 'But I did try the bell.'

'Bell's broke,' old Mr Whittaker muttered, rubbing his eyes, half-blind without glasses, and guessing that was why he imagined seeing what he knew shouldn't be. Samantha, on the other hand, had nothing wrong with her vision, and continued to gape at the man on the porch as if she were seeing a ghost.

'I tried driving back up to Ausable before coming here,' the man told them, 'but the roads out that way are so flooded, I couldn't get near the base of the mountain.' Then he turned and looked down at the Liebling family car parked in the puddled street. 'Fortunately, since I see they're down here.'

'But – ' Sam finally found her tongue, 'last night, they said that they'd lost you!' The burly man with the curly red hair turned back with a look of confusion. 'The hospital,' Sam clarified. 'They called and said – '

'Oh, that.' The man frowned. 'I don't know who was shaken up more. Them or me. When I walked out of the morgue, I nearly gave three people coronarys. Nearly had one myself when I learned I was scheduled for autopsy just about now.' The thought of Gus alive, and that close to going under the pathologist's knife sent a visible shudder through Sam as she managed to find her tongue through the shock once again.

'How did you get here?' Her shuddering didn't stop, but now the damp cold was at work. Behind her, her grandfather muttered about the ungodly hour and shuffled inside.

'I borrowed the car of the doc who pronounced me dead. It was the least he could do.'

'But – ' Sam's head was still spinning with questions, but Gus cut her off with a few of his own.

'Why are Clare and the kids down here? And where's Ray? I didn't see the van. He isn't still up in – '

'Clare's the only one here,' Sam interrupted. 'She drove down when she couldn't find her husband. But her children are still up in Ausable, and now that she's stuck with the flooding, she's been in such a state that I had to sedate her to help her sleep.'

'She couldn't find Ray?' Sam saw him turn a little pale at the news. Then old Mr Whittaker called down the hall from the kitchen:

'I got the coffee on! Now come in and close that door before we all catch our death of cold!'

While Mrs Liebling continued to sleep off the sedative, Sam and her grandfather sat by the warmth of the stove sipping coffee while Gus nervously paced and told them his tale.

'After a while, I got this feeling the craving wasn't mine at all. It sounds crazy, I know, but it was as if . . . as if there was something inside me.' As Gus went on, Sam tried to make sense of the things he recalled with the symptoms she'd seen: the deafness that followed the maddening itch might account for how distracted he'd been, but the craving he now spoke of made no sense to her at all. 'It was like I could actually sense this other awareness inside my head, and that's where the craving was coming from — this presence. And something else — I could tell it needed the sugar to survive. Or, it needed the energy rush I'd get from the sugar. Then this thing would siphon it off. It used me as a sort of power plant — my body converted the sugar to energy, then this thing would skim off the surplus to feed itself — to grow. But when I told that to the doctor in Watersville, he just thought I was out of my gourd.' And although Mr Whittaker studied Gus as if he might be prone to agree, Sam was recalling all that she knew about quick-burning carbohydrates like sugar and the impact excessive consumption had on the central nervous system. The increase of electrical impulses firing between the brain's neural synapses did create a sort of energy overload like Gus described. Still, the thought of some presence inside him siphoning off a pure energy surplus did seem more like the ravings of a madman than anything real. Yet there was something about Gus himself that kept making her want to believe — the earnestness in his voice, her own intuitive sense for truth, and on an even subtler level, Sam had a bit of a crush on the man. And then, there was also the boy Clare had told her about who had all Gus's symptoms, and all the other mysteries shrouding the mountain which she had been hearing since childhood, such as people vanishing into thin air and the mountain folks' powers to heal. Although she wasn't sure what to make of it all, at least she had little doubt that something very odd was going on up on Ausable mountain.

'And then it got so strong,' Gus continued, 'it started to

feel like a part of me. All its feelings and thoughts – it got so confusing, I couldn't tell where I left off and it started. I guess I was acting so crazy by then, the doctor had me in restraints. Then, yesterday, he put me in some machine that sends sound-waves through the brain, a sort of scanning device to see if I had a brain tumor or something like that. But this thing, it still wasn't fully developed, and then when they started the sound-waves – it's like the sound itself was actually breaking the thing apart.' The intensity of his expression grew more deeply troubled then. 'I could feel it . . . how it hurt.' And even the memory seemed to be hurting him. 'I could feel it trying to rip itself free from my mind, but it wasn't strong enough. And then, it cried out, and I guess I blacked out. That's when the doc said he lost me. At least, he's now convinced I was in some sort of sleep so deep all signs of life defied detection.' Sam had heard of rare cases like this, as with people found frozen in blizzards, where the cold slowed body functions to such a low rate that they only appeared to be dead.

'But the strangest thing,' Gus added, 'was that he said something . . . that something *did* come through my skull. Like a light, or streams of light, and he said it left a glowing gel on my skin. And when he touched it, he said that it tingled, as if it were alive, but when he looked at some under a microscope, there was nothing but the light. Like pure energy – as if that's what the thing had been made of. And then even the gel disappeared. Like ectoplasm – that's what he called it – appearing from nothing then vanishing.'

Ectoplasm usually meant the substance around a cell's nucleus, something like the white of an egg that nourishes the developing yoke, but Sam recalled another meaning for the term as well, one that was more like a matter for seances than science. It referred to the residue left when something passes between dimensions, and 'something', by this definition, generally meant some spiritual entity.

'If you don't believe me, I'll understand.' Gus studied their skeptical faces. 'Even the doctor said after it vanished, he couldn't see telling anyone else, not unless he wanted them thinking that he was as nutty as me.'

'This thing that you say was inside you,' Sam asked, still struggling to make some sense of it all, 'do you have any idea at all what it was or where it came from?' And then Gus drew a deep breath, sensing that she at least accepted his story, and he told her about a journal he'd found in the cabin beneath the falls.

'Did you ever actually find the thing?' old Mr Whittaker asked when Gus described the cyclotron – but it was clear from the question that Sam's grandfather believed him, too.

'I tried, but it was just about dusk when I found my way to the foot of the falls, and that's about the only place I could figure he might have built the thing. And I did see some sort of a path up the slope of the cliff, like steps. Not cut there, exactly. More like Uncle Matthew had a lot of help clearing the loose rock away, leaving a sort of crude natural staircase that looked like it ran up under the falls. As best I can figure, that had to be how he made the thing work – hydraulic power – using the force of the falls to run the generator. Had to be. There's no other power source. And that's the only way I can see how he'd keep the thing running non-stop all those years. And according to his journal, the type of collision he wanted occurred only once, about fifty years ago, and that sort of alignment was utterly random and rare.'

'Fifty years ago?' Old Mr Whittaker's thoughts turned to the past. 'It was just about fifty years ago I stopped calling on Meg Gallagher. That's when they started making it clear outsiders were no longer welcome up there.' And frowning, he added ominously, 'And that's when outsiders began disappearing.'

'*That's* what it's called,' Sam Whittaker exclaimed before Gus could reply to her grandfather. 'The Super Collider. They were building one not too long ago, out in Texas, I think.'

'A super collider?' Gus noticed a light in Sam's eye, as though something at last made some sense.

'What you described, what you read in his journal, I don't really think it's a cyclotron. I mean, he may have called it that, but there's something just like it that's been on the news. It's a high-energy proton-smasher. They call it a super collider. "Sixty Minutes" or "Twenty/Twenty" or one of those news shows did a piece on it. Apparently, the point of the thing is to break proton particles down to find quarks, pretty much the same way you said Matthew's invention worked. But they called it a super collider, and I think it was built way under ground.' She looked at Gus in amazement. 'Your uncle was way ahead of his time.'

'Great uncle,' Gus corrected, 'and I'm not all that sure how great he was at that. This thing may be best undiscovered.'

'Do you think he really managed to break some dimensional barrier?' Sam asked, alarmed.

'Well, whatever it was that got into me sure didn't come from this one,' Gus answered. 'And if Ray and the kids are still up there . . .' He looked at her gravely. 'I've got to find a way back.'

'You'll never make it past Wee Pausamet.' Sam touched his hand. 'Remember, you tried.'

'That was a couple of hours ago.' Gus glanced at the kitchen window. 'It isn't coming down as hard as it was the first time I tried.'

'Gus,' Sam persisted, 'just because it's not raining as hard won't make any difference. Whenever the roads flood as bad as they've been with this storm, they can take several days to clear. Sometimes longer,' she added reluctantly.

'And it's not even going to start to clear in a place like Wee Pausamet till the rain stops.'

'Well . . .' Gus looked thoughtful. 'If I can make it as far as Wee Pausamet, maybe I can hike it the rest of the way. I remember a ridge running up behind the town all the way to Four Corners. If I leave the car there, I might stand a good chance of making it up before dark.'

'Only thing you stand a chance of's getting lost,' Mr Whittaker told him. 'If you hike along the ridge, you'll be climbing the back of the mountain, away from the road, and I wouldn't even risk that, and I've lived here all my life.' Then, after dashing Gus's hopes, he raised them all over again. 'Unless, of course, we went by boat.' Both Gus and Sam looked at him quizzically.

'You mean, find a boat in Wee Pausamet to take over the flooded roads?' Gus asked.

'To take up the Pausamet River.' Sam's grandfather started to stuff the bowl of his pipe. 'It branches off Lost River, which starts at Lost Falls, where the Marsden place is.'

'Can you do that?' Gus asked doubtfully. 'I mean, go up river that far by boat?'

'Grandpa used to fish up there as a kid.' Sam excitedly pushed from her seat. 'And that was well before anyone drove a car in this neck of the woods. He still fishes Pausamet sometimes, but then he just drives out and sits on the bank.' Her excitement waned a bit as she stopped at the door to the hall and asked, 'Grandpa, you sure Aggie'll make it?'

'Who's Aggie?' Gus asked as he poured out more coffee.

'Grandpa's old boat. It's in the back of the house. Been there as far back as I can remember. When Grandpa got too old to deal with loading it on and off the trailer, he turned it upside down out back for me to use as a fort.'

When she saw Gus grin at this, she blushed and said shyly, 'I was just six at the time.'

'And the trailer's still under the crawlspace.' Her grandfather puffed on his pipe. The room filled with sweet smoke. 'And the outboard's still in the garage. Where are you going?' he called as she stepped from the room. 'We're all going to need a big breakfast. There's a few spots on that river you're going to be carrying that boat around.'

'Then *you* make breakfast. You threaten to often enough. And you can pack us a lunch as well. It's going to take a while to get Clare on her feet after that sedative.'

20
The Hatching

When Sarah came to, the craving had gone, and with it her heightened senses. She felt as sick and weak as she had before her father returned. She had none of the intimations which Gus had had – but then, his had been growing for a while – except for the disturbing recollection that prior to sleeping, she hadn't been feeling much like herself at all. It was a bit like a dream in her mind, her memories of that morning, like the craving and seeing the Cotters were somehow things she just imagined. She was not entirely sure that she was awake even now, for no matter how hard she tried, she couldn't recall having gone back to bed. Then groggily raising one hand to wipe her face, which felt damp and prickly with sweat, she found instead that her cheeks and brow and hair, in fact every square inch of her head, was smeared with a tingly substance the thickness of jelly. When she looked at her hand, it glowed.

'Oh, God.' She sat bolt upright, grabbing the sheet and swabbing it over her face. When she pulled it away, she found the cloth covered with glowing streaks of gel. In a rush of nightmare images, she remembered the morning it oozed from her ear, and only that day how it dripped from the bat in the privy before that thing crawled from its head – the same sort of thing she had seen a little bit later right through her father's skull. Then young Cotter's paddle-like, puckering fingers and face with its horrible slit filled her mind, and suddenly none of it seemed in the least like a dream. It was as real as the clicking and creaking sounds she now heard from the other room, and struggling up from bed, she anxiously wondered if one of those horrid things had hatched from her. Close to hysterics, expecting to find herself monstrously changed, and like the bat, more dead than alive, she stumbled across to the dresser and looked in the vanity mirror. She found herself looking no different than ever before, except that now she was glowing. For all of her wiping, her face was still blotchy with traces of luminous gel. And as for being more dead than alive, she did feel weaker than ever before, but somehow she knew this was not from some alien life-form but from the bad thing in her blood. Then all her concern was abruptly refocused when the clicking and creaking grew suddenly louder. The last time she'd seen her father, he'd been asleep in the other room on the floor. And she'd left him alone there. Alone, that is, with the Cotters.

Rushing to the door, she clasped the latch in both hands to steady her shaking and easing it up, she took a deep breath, then pulled the door open a crack. With the blinds still drawn and flapping against the wind and the rain, the room was quite dim. A thin hazy light hung over the table, but it was not from the kerosene lamp. With her heart beating under her ribs like a wild frightened bird trying to find a way out, she gaped at her father, stretched out on the table, his face so bright it looked on fire, and stooped over him like a pair of surgeons, the Cotters stood, now stripped of their clothes.

Though still vaguely human in form, all that was hidden before now made it quite clear why they moved about so awkwardly when they were masquerading as men. Their feet were like some aquatic bird's, broad and flat like flippers, and great ruffled folds of white skin hung between their arms and legs like the wings of a bat. Then she focused again on the eerie sounds and realized the creaking came from her father while all the clicking noises seemed to be coming from the Cotters. And although it wasn't unpleasant, sounding like the dolphins heard on an aquarium trip, it horrified her, hearing it pour from their mouths as their heads hung over her father's, as if they were trying to coax out that hideous thing she'd seen through his skull. And then, on hearing a delicate tinkling like tiny glass bells being rung, she saw that this was precisely what the Cotters were trying to do.

A slender strand of exquisitely colored light slithered out from her father's brow. Then another appeared, and then a third, slipping gracefully up toward the ceiling. Then several more slid over their heads, quivering in the air, and the creaking grew quicker and louder, as if an army of crickets swarmed over the room. Then all at once, her father's face went clear as ice, and more strands appeared, snaking out from the table and over the floor and up the walls. Then the glow from her father's head began pulsing, first blue, then violet, then violently red, as if the sun itself were about to burst through. Then her knuckles turned white on the door.

Like the cry of an infant, a terrible bleating exploded through the room, and beneath it, the sound like tiny glass bells grew as loud as if they were being rung till they shattered.

'Oh, Daddy!' she cried, but the ruckus absorbed her plea and all she could do was look on as the slit in the brow of old Cotter yawned back like a mouth, revealing the spinning blue orb. Then the nimbus of flickering lines all around it began whirling out like a ball of fire, sucking all the air up and whipping it into a crackling cyclone of lightning. And just as it swelled to fill the whole room, it began to close again like a net, tugging the tentacled arms of the creature until they dropped free of the ceiling and walls. Then the tendrils slithered wildly about till they found their way to Cotter himself, where one by one, they probed the spinning blue orb then began to coil snake-like around it. Then the light from the orb began to flow into the arms, as if the creature absorbed it, and gill-like slits along Cotter's ribs fluttered, as if with some great exertion, while the glow from the orb continued to fade and the arms all about it grew steadily brighter. The lightning net was all but closed when a slipping, sucking sound came from her father. Dragged by its arms, a quivering, bladder-like husk slipped out through his skull into Cotter's.

Cotter's slitted brow began to fold over the wrinkled, glistening husk, the pale blue light of the orb it enveloped pulsing through its glassy skin. And the same blue light now covered her father's face, looking lifeless and smothered beneath the very same luminous gel she had found on her own face when she awakened.

'Cotter?' a voice called from outside as the slit in his brow was sealed. Then the room was in shadow except for the fading light seeping under the flapping blinds and the luminous patches of gel all over the room on whatever the creature had touched. A board creaked from beyond the front door as someone climbed to the stoop. Her heart still pounding wildly, still peering out through the crack in the bedroom door, Sarah held her breath as a woman with long dark hair stepped into the house. 'Has a chrysalis hatched?' the woman asked while surveying the mess in the room, apparently guessing what had gone on just from the state things were in.

'It's in me,' the older Cotter explained in the same warbly voice Sarah heard before. 'It was not yet quite mature enough to hatch. And Rakkis has one from the girl.' The woman seemed to take this in with a moment of silent concern, her pretty face creasing up at the brow. 'It's all right,' the older Cotter added, seeming to guess her concern. 'The Brilliade cannot leave part of itself in the host when it's taken this way. It replenishes what it has used only when it is hatching. It has not worked the change on these two.' Cotter's eyeless face turned from the table toward the bedroom. Sarah, holding her breath, quickly stepped back from the door into darkness. 'The girl will be awaking soon. You will find her to be quite alarmed and confused. We did not have the time to alter her memory, but the others can help you do that when we're gone. In the meantime, just say that you came here to see how they fared through the storm, and until you have help, act bewildered by all that she tells you, say you found her father like this when you came. In any event, once we've gone and her memory's altered, our secret again will be safe.'

'Unless the boy is incubating a chrysalis,' Rakkis, the younger, put in. 'And if he's allowed to carry it to maturity after we've gone back to Nightsea.'

'Which is why we must leave you now,' the older Cotter turned back to Meg. 'It would be awkward if we left the boy behind in that state.'

'But what can you do?' the woman asked. 'Now you have two from this man and his daughter, you can't bring another one back with you – unless you brought the boy back too.'

'We will deal with that problem when we come to it,' Cotter replied. 'Although, I'm not so sure a human child would survive on the other side.'

'We don't even know how Brilliades hatched in this world will fare in the other.' Rakkis, the son, sounded very anxious over this prospect. 'Those born of your people – and so many more that have hatched from the bats – carry part of your world. A part of your life-force runs in the veins of these young, and they will be changed in some way, just as they have worked the change on you who have carried them through to their hatching. Only when we are home will we see how your strain in their blood affects them there, if it will be an asset or a disaster once they're in Nightsea.'

'At least there are those that we hatched ourselves from the Brilliade's first pollenation. Those, at least, we can be sure will thrive,' the senior Cotter remarked.

'It'd be a pity if they all don't survive.' The woman looked wistful. 'I like to think part of us goes with you, just like part of you lives on in us.'

'We too hope this, Meg. And now, if you would remain here, we will look for the boy. If he has been seeded, and if he is left behind . . .' his voice trailed off, but from the grave expression Sarah saw on the woman, it was clear she had caught Cotter's meaning. And whatever he meant, it would seem that Ben was in danger whether they found him or not, for if he was 'seeded', and carried the chrysalis through to its hatching, he'd be changed in some way.

''Course I'll stay,' the woman replied. 'But if she wakes soon, there's one thing I can't hide. That's what I came to tell you. Daniel's hatchling found its way to the chink. It managed somehow to work its way up from the cavern and now it's out by the falls.' This brought a look of what Sarah guessed was surprise from both of the Cotters. Their heads turned to face one another and the mane of white hair down their backs bristled slightly.

'Perhaps those hatched by bats do not have the instincts of those born in Nightsea,' Rakkis remarked, turning back to Meg, 'but those which are human-hatched have the homing instinct, it would appear, like the fish of your rivers who swim against the strong currents to reach their old waters to spawn.'

'This is good,' his father added, 'for it may mean their other instincts are intact. But if the lure of the world beyond is so strong it has summoned one of the earth-born, it means the chink in the falls is now nearly wide enough for our return. We must hurry.'

'Meg, if the boy returns before we can find him, if he carries the chrysalis . . . you know what you must do if a Brilliade hatches after we've gone.' The woman nodded to Rakkis, then Sarah watched the Cotters move past her, catching only a glimpse of the pair as they stepped to the stoop and raised their arms. Their wings flapped out like snow-white sails, and then there was only the woman, framed in the doorway, face raised to the sky full of rain, her long hair black and glistening, whipping back from her shoulders with a strong, damp gust of wind. Then she turned back to the room, and Sarah quickly and quietly latched the door, her mind rushing back with a frenzy over all she had just observed.

Whatever it was that the worms became, these things which the Cotters called Brilliades, apparently they could not change a person if they were removed before they could hatch. And this, as best she could understand, was what had happened to her and her father. But hers, they had said, was just starting to form, while her father's had been near maturity, and though she had recovered, her father had been so still on the table next door. Perhaps to take one out of a person when it had grown for that long could be fatal. With tears burning her eyes, she listened to the footsteps in the adjoining room. Whatever her father's state, she knew she could do nothing but wait and pray he'd recover. And then she thought of Ben, and Meg asking the Cotters if they would take the boy with them back to this place they called Nightsea, where they were not even sure that Ben could survive. And just to try and save one of their precious Brilliades, she thought, enraged, as if people were nothing more to them than some sort of disposable incubators.

Then the footsteps in the other room were moving toward the bedroom door, and panicked, Sarah rushed to the bed and burrowed back under the blankets. She held her breath at the sound of the door easing open, then hearing the woman step in, her heart began pounding so loudly that her pulse roared in her ears, and she froze, sure the woman could hear.

And she did feel frozen, not only with fear, but with the chill of the fever she ran, every pore pumping out beads of sweat that felt like ice in the cold, damp air. But she fought the urge to shiver and clenched her teeth to keep them from chattering, until she heard the footsteps retreat from the side of the bed and the door ease shut. Then she let herself yield to the fear and the cold, and it broke like a wave, and passed through her, and for several long moments she simply lay there, shaking, her eyes still burning with tears.

And the worst thing of all, a voice crept into her head, *is feeling so helpless*. The voice was her own, repeating a thought from last night, when she'd felt little better than now, and yet, by focusing not on herself but her family, she'd somehow managed to find a reserve of strength that might have carried her through the storm for help. And then her father had returned, and once again she'd yielded to fear, giving into that terrible feeling of being utterly helpless. But helplessness was, she now saw, just a state of mind, a giving up, and if only she focused outside of herself, on her brother this time, the strength might come back.

Clamping her eyes against the tears, she saw him, the morning before, by her side, his face so full of concern when she first recovered from blacking out. And now he was in danger, and the concern she felt began swelling inside her, and changing, like the Brilliade larva, into something else. It was then that she truly understood the source of this hidden reserve of strength, which was nothing more in fact than very deep caring. And it held an immeasurable power. If only she cared enough, she told herself, she might overcome anything. Picturing Ben with his sad, worrying eyes and his Red Sox cap, she threw off the blankets and crept from the bed to the window and quietly pushed it all the way up. Scarcely aware of the cold on her fevered skin or how hard her heart beat from the effort, she pulled herself over the sill and out into the drizzly late afternoon.

Shivering, Sarah sloshed through the mud to the back of the little house. Peeking under the edge of the blind that flapped at the window above the sink, she glimpsed Meg in the rocking chair by the stove, staring off toward the bedroom door. She saw her father, too, still sprawled on the table, unchanged, except for one thing. The luminous gel had vanished, leaving his gaunt, lifeless face looking paler than ever. Wrenching her eyes away, her heart near breaking, praying he'd be OK, she ducked her head below the sill and continued, hunched down, to the edge of the house. She could not cross the field without risking being spotted, and anyway, if she went by the road, someone else in Ausable might see her, and none of them could be trusted. *The Brilliades hatched by you and your people*, she'd heard Cotter say to Meg, which meant that probably everyone living here was in league with them. Perhaps the change that came when a Brilliade hatched turned them into some sort of slaves, unable to resist the commands of the bat-like father and son.

The only place Sarah could safely seek help was down at the base of the mountain, and to get there, she would have to find some other way than the road.

It was then that she remembered driving over the bridge at Four Corners. If she just followed the edge of the swollen river, it would lead her down. With her mind made up, she moved in through the trees at the back of the house and pushed on toward the river. When she reached the river bank, she would have to crouch below the waist-high grass, at least until she came to the forest that started again across the field. But several yards short of the river, she spotted something that made it hard to go on. Ben's Red Sox cap and his rainslicker were on the ground between the trees, and leading away from them, marked by trampled ferns and odd puddles like prints in the ground, was a track of sorts that ran in the other direction, off through the woods toward the falls.

Against her better judgment, for she could not think of what she could do on her own, she followed the path her brother had left hearing only the words of the woman and Cotter: *You can't bring another chrysalis back ... not unless you brought the boy with you ... I'm not so sure a human child would survive on the other side*. Almost certain now that Ben had been 'seeded' with one of their Brilliade larvae, and that he had lost his slicker and cap struggling against the Cotters, the thought of them taking him back with them fueled her purpose with a fury. She remembered their saying that there was little time, and that some of the Brilliades must have the homing instinct, for Meg had spotted one of them up by the falls. The way to 'the other side', as they called it, and to Ben, she decided, must be that way, too. Soaked to the bone and burning with rage, she strained to keep sight of her brother's tracks as she stumbled along through the rain and the darkening forest toward the roar of the falls.

21
Where Currents Collide

'Easy now.' The toady-eyed Mr Whittaker shuffled backward, his arms held out from his hunched, withered frame as if he were moving the boat by himself. But the only thing he held was a flashlight, the beam pointed up a slope at the three lifting the boat from a trailer parked by the road that ran into Wee Pausamet. 'You're walkin' right into a felled tree, Sam. A little more to your left. That's the ticket.'

His granddaughter managed to step past the uprooted tree as she carried her end down the banking, but both Gus and Clare lost their footing in the rain-eroded soil. The motor flipped up in the stern as the boat pitched forward, all three of them losing their hold. Then the gasoline can tumbled out, nearly hitting Sam's grandfather as it rolled to the water, splashing him just as the hull hit the ground with a crack that made them all wince. But old Mr Whittaker merely clucked his tongue and said, 'Just push the dang thing.' And they did, and it slid down the muddy bank to the swollen river below. 'You're all gonna have to do a lot better,' he muttered while grabbing the rope on the bow, ''cause there's four little falls before Ausable that we'll have to carry her up and around.'

'Sorry about that,' Gus said as the old man gingerly waded in, fishing out the gas can just before it could sink completely from sight.

'We're all gonna be a lot sorrier,' the man muttered while splashing back toward the boat, 'if you city folk are as bad with a bailing can as you are at launching a boat.' The beam of his flashlight fell on a puddle of water gurgling up from the bow where a pair of lima-bean cans bobbed about, already filling with water. But apparently he did not think the damage was bad enough to abort the excursion. 'You, in the bow.' He waved Mrs Liebling in first, for she was clearly the lightest. 'Red, in the middle with Sam,' he barked at the burly, red-headed coach. 'And don't mess with the oars. You lose them and we run out of gas, we'll be paddling back with our hands.'

Then, when they were all seated, he put one foot in the stern and pushed off from the bank. Then he hunkered over his seat, pushing the outboard back till the props were submerged, then he opened the choke and yanked the chord on the motor. It took several more yanks and a stream of grumbled curses before it choked into life, tossing him back in his seat in the stern as it sputtered away from the swollen bank. 'Hand that up to the lady in the bow.' He passed the flashlight to Gus. 'And keep your eyes sharp for drifting debris!' he called out to Clare. 'And you two best start bailing!'

'How long do you think it will take?' Gus asked as he grabbed up an empty lima bean can. However, most of the water that covered the floor was not from the leak, but the rain.

'You tell me what it's like up in the hereafter,' Sam's grandfather grumbled back, and when Gus looked back in bewilderment, Sam smiled at him and explained:

'That's Grandpa's way of saying there's no way of telling, not with the currents from flooding.'

'You mean sort of like a backwoods Zen koan.' Gus grinned back as he started to bail.

'It's no such thing,' the old man, overhearing, grumbled

back. 'It's just what Sam told you, something to make you think when you ask things that don't have an answer.'

'That's what I said, a Zen koan,' Gus replied, to which the old man harrumphed, giving the motor the gas as he steered them upriver, cross-cutting the strong, choppy current.

By the time Sarah neared the base of the falls, the last of the storm clouds had finally broken. A clear black night opened up overhead while the river, engorged from the rain, foamed white. At first, Sarah took the brilliant light sparking back from the rapids for moonlight. And without the lunar-like glow through the trees, she would, in fact, have lost her way. But pushing through the last several yards of dense underbrush and out through the forest, her heart skipped a beat and she caught herself short with her first full view of the source of that light.

Halfway up the cliff, its humpbacked husk as buoyant and clear as a bubble, a bladder-like creature splashed about through the falls with the grace and ease of an otter. A brilliant light pulsed through its transparent body and the dozens of tendrils it trailed. Although Sarah knew what it was, it seemed somehow less menacing. Rather, it seemed at play. Whirling about like a top, its long graceful arms entwined like a maypole, then several snaked out like elephant trunks, blowing water with a high gleeful clicking. It made her think more of a squealing puppy darting in and out of the surf than anything like the monster it seemed when she saw one, just hatched, slipping out from the privy, or later and far more horrifying, coiled inside her father's skull. Still, it was the same thing the Cotters had taken from her and her father, the same thing that left her father still as death and which now put her brother in danger. *You can't bring another chrysalis back*, Meg's words continued to nag, *Not unless you brought the boy back too*. And then they said he may not survive. Watching this thing that they'd sacrifice Ben for frolicking above, her hope of helping him faded along with the Brilliade's light as it plunged through the falls.

It was then she caught sight of a hollow of blackness that parted the backlit, watery wall, and the thing about it that snagged her attention, besides there being nothing to split the falls, was that even the light of the creature cavorting behind it did not shine through. Was this the portal to Nightsea, she wondered, the gateway to 'the other side'? And if it was, if that's where Ben was taken, how could she possibly follow? The Cotters had wings, but how could a human reach an opening at that height? Unless – she scanned the cliff as the Brilliade slipped through the water again.

Its brilliant light cast a series of step-like shadows that led to a ledge near the top. Her gaze traced them down the sheer wall and behind a pair of massive boulders, and between them, she could just make out a sort of corridor to the base of the cliff. She almost lost heart as her eye climbed back up the craggy, spray-slickened, soaring height. One false step, and . . . her eye plunged dizzily down to the roiling river and rocks. But then she thought of Ben kneeling beside her again, his face so full of concern, and the secret they shared, her secret – she did not have so much to lose, after all. Better lost trying to help her brother than waiting alone for the end, she thought. And at that, she scrabbled ahead through the boulders and started up the face of the cliff where the youthful Brilliade's clicking wove through the roar of the falls and the rapids below.

Though Sarah soon heard nothing more than the deafening rush of the water, other sounds were rapidly swelling and echoing into the night as well. Bats coasting down from the falls shrieked in terror while deep from within the cliff a melodious, oboe-like thrumming rose up with a fluty, joyous, high-pitched trill. And there were human voices, too, from the banks far below, from the river itself, and while all this was smothered under the watery turbulence filling her ears, if Sarah had turned before reaching out for the branch sweeping down from the cliff to the ledge, she'd have had a full view of the field where a gathering crowd was caught in the Brilliade's glow, and further down, bobbing around a bend in the river, a beacon of light, shining over the bow of a boat that sputtered along toward the treacherous rapids.

'What in God's name is that?' Mrs Liebling leaned from the bow of the tossing boat, but the only reply was the cough of the motor, straining against the battering currents, growing ever more dangerous now that they'd come to the river's head. She needn't have asked, however, for her companions were as bewildered as she, their mesmerized stares all fixed on the bubble of light that whirled about the falls. Then it spun away, splashing beneath them. Still, its light backlit the watery wall, turning the falls a brilliant blue except for a gaping black diamond shape.

'Keep bailing!' Sam's grandfather broke the spell as the river spilled over the pitching boat's sides. But their efforts were futile. This close to the falls, with the rapids roiling and foaming ahead, the currents went haywire, colliding with boulders, ripping apart then colliding again. The force of the river was split in so many directions it knocked the boat every which way. 'We've got to get to shore before we're scuttled!' old Mr Whittaker shouted, and turning the bow of the boat toward the bank, with the beam of the flashlight bouncing ahead, Mrs Liebling leaned forward again, tried to steady her hand and squinting, called back to the others:

'Are those people up there?' The beam of light didn't quite reach the edge of the river, but all along the bank and crossing the field by the house, which at last she could see, there appeared to be a moderate crowd gathering by the shoreline. 'Sarah!' she shouted. Although she was too far away to make out faces, the glow from the falls was sufficient to show that some were the height of children. 'Benjamin! Sarah!' she shouted again as the tiny boat struggled closer toward shore. 'Can you hear me?' And then it seemed one of them had, then another, and more, and they all began waving. 'They see us!' Mrs Liebling shouted excitedly. 'Oh, God, let the kids be there.' But as the boat dragged itself nearer the bank, it was nosing upriver as well, and soon they could hear the clamor of voices rising over the waving of arms.

'Go back!' they were shouting. The waving was not a welcome but a warning. But it came too late. A cross-current bounding away from the swollen embankment caught the boat by the bow, then spun it out toward the middle where several more currents clashed with the force of a riptide. At the eye of this violent collison, the river sucked back on itself, like a sink hole, dragging down to its spiraling center whatever debris had been caught in its pull.

For several endless seconds, the tiny boat rode the crest of the whirlpool, all its occupants dumbstruck and gaping over the side at the vortex below. Then the stern, weighted down by the outboard, dipped, and the four of them tumbled backward, spinning stern over bow, drawn inexorably down just as if it were one of Ben's black holes in space.

22
The Last Brilliade

'*Ben!*' Sarah hissed as she crept along the edge of the cavern, one arm overhead to fend off the glow-worms weightlessly swimming like vast schools of minnows through columns of rock. He was here, she was sure. She'd found his sweat-shirt left behind on the ledge. And there'd been traces of muddy prints starting into the mouth of the tunnel above. All the same, she'd almost lost nerve and nearly retreated back to the ledge when a flood of worms filled the tunnel, rushing up as if caught in some terrible current. But they only swept past her, as if they were being drawn to a far more powerful lure. And whatever it was that was luring them up to that hole in the falls was insatiable, for the flow of worms formed a river of light that never seemed to stop. The moment the cave would empty of one massive swarm, overhead, the mammoth Brilliade's belly would swell a bit and pulse with a deepening violet light. Then the gill-like ruffles beneath her bladder-like husk would start to flutter apart, releasing another great cloud of worms that drifted down with her musky breath. But in spite of their numbers, the worms in the cave seemed distracted, and those that swam Sarah's way seemed to do so more by chance than design, for they showed no interest in her. Perhaps they were confused by whatever it was that kept calling them up through the tunnel, whatever it was that beckoned them into that blackness which Sarah felt certain was Nightsea. The creature above, however, was another matter entirely. The moment she'd entered the cave it sent its great tendrils snaking out through the air, driving her back from the mouth of the tunnel, then oddly forgetting her once she'd moved. Perhaps, Sarah thought, it just meant to keep the route clear for the worms which kept flooding that way. But then she knew nothing about the timed explosives set into that part of the wall.

'Ben!' she hissed again on spotting a pair of jean-clad legs and boots jutting out from behind a sort of barricade formed by stalagmites. She had to wade through water to reach him, for winding through the columns of stone was a steamy underground stream that reflected the light of the luminous creatures above.

'Ben?' She splashed up from the stream, her heart in her mouth when she saw him, as still as her father, but curled in a fetal position, looking as though he were fast asleep.

'Ben!' she repeated urgently, dropping down to her knees and shaking his shoulder.

After struggling to stay awake through the night, awaiting his chance to escape – trapped as he'd been with one Brilliade guarding the tunnel while another inside had been stuck – exhaustion had finally won, dragging Ben down to a sleep so profound that it took Sarah several full minutes of shaking him and calling his name before he stirred. And when he did, he seemed different somehow, as distracted as the worms. Or maybe, she thought, it was only his waking confusion at finding himself in the cave. 'Are you all right?' she eagerly asked, helping him up to a sitting position. For a moment, he simply burrowed his fists in his eyes, his face and hands smeared with mud, as hers must be, she imagined, after her climb up the face of the cliff. His grubby fingers, however, had also smudged his ears with dirt, which covered the angry red welts from all of his scratching the evening before.

'I'm hungry,' Ben murmured groggily, and though it was more of a craving he felt, Sarah, finding his answer perfectly normal, hugged him with great relief.

'Oh, Ben . . .' the words then flooded out with all her pent-up fear. Still clinging to him, she told him of all that transpired since he disappeared. In the time it took her to finish her story, he seemed to come back to himself, in turn then telling her of all he knew, though his mind seemed to drift now and then. It was never for more than a second or two, and always off toward the tunnel, as though there was something beyond it, beckoning, just as it beckoned the worms. And while Sarah took it for simple preoccupation with their escape, Ben pointed to the small black box with the flashing red light hanging over the tunnel, and then his voice grew tight as a drum as he finally told her about the explosives and how the largest Brilliade drove him back every time he moved toward the tunnel. Then Sarah followed his gaze to the bladder-like creature hovering up by the ceiling, then down the length of its luminous arms, writhing like snakes through the blizzard of worms.

'If we run very fast – ' She scrambled back to her feet, dragging Ben by the arms up beside her.

'It's much too quick.' Ben watched the arms of the Brilliade sweep past the hole in the wall. 'I've tried it. I've tried to sneak to that last big stalagmite then run from there. But every time – '

'Then we have to try harder!' She cut him off, near panicked now that she'd found him only to hear that the cave could blow up any moment and that they were trapped inside. Ben gave a small, uncertain nod but his face grew even more doubtful. 'Now what?' Sarah snapped, near hysterical when he resisted her tugging.

'What if it blows up while we're in the tunnel?' he timidly

murmured. 'We can't even see what the time is on that thing, or if it's time at all. What if it's all hooked up to Marsden's cyclotron, what if it's set to go off when that thing – that chink in the falls – when it reaches a certain width?'

'What difference does it make?' Sarah tugged him again till he took a tentative step. 'One thing's for sure, the longer we stand around talking about it, the less chance we have.'

Then he finally yielded, stumbling down through the stream, slipping after her past the stalagmites until they came to the last, where the two of them paused to peer up at the creature above. Although she seemed oblivious to their presence, her violet gills fluttering lightly, releasing another shower of glowing worms drifting softly as snow through her arms, they both knew that the moment they started their dash for the exit, her arms would sweep out again.

'Ready?' Sarah, drawing a breath, met her brother's frightened gaze. Their hands clasped. 'OK.' Her voice came in a hush, but just as they started to sprint for the tunnel, they found themselves lost in a virtual blizzard of light as the worms rushed suddenly past them. It was just as if some dreadfully powerful mouth had inhaled from the chink in the falls, sucking every last one of them up as though the tunnel were one great straw. Still holding one another's hand, they blindly fumbled their way ahead. Then the rush of worms was past them, the tail of the storm swiftly vanishing into the hole while they found themselves off the mark by at least twenty yards, stumbling into a loop in the stream. 'Dammit!' Sarah scrambled up from the water as one of the arms swept down. It nearly reached Ben, but as soon as he started away from the tunnel, the great arm retreated.

'Now we're even further away than before!' he said as he

breathlessly joined her, drawing behind another row of stalagmites curving out from the wall.

'We'll just have to work our way back,' Sarah huffed, far more winded than he. And he saw then, as if for the very first time since she woke him, just how badly she looked. The day before, when she fainted, she looked as bad as she had her last hospital trip, but now . . . her sopping apparel was clinging so tightly it showed every jut of her bones, and her eyes seemed lost, sunken so deep in the sockets they seemed to peer out of a hole. It gave him the horrible feeling that Sarah was drowning inside of herself, like a pebble dropped in a murky well, sinking off to the dark and distant depths. And he knew it was her sickness she was drowning in, dragging her further away and inexorably closer to that thing she feared above all else. How she even managed to stand at that moment amazed him, her clothes were hanging so slack, almost as if they were empty and moved by little more than a stirring of air.

'Are you sure you can make it?' He reached for her arm, and it frightened him, feeling how frail she'd become.

'I'll make it.' Even her voice sounded more like an echo of itself, yet somehow, she still managed a small but confident smile. '*We'll* make it,' she corrected, and the glint in her eyes nearly convinced him. Again, she put her hand in his, squeezed weakly, then turned to look back at the tunnel. Then she made a small sound, like a hiss of air escaping from a punctured tire, and following her gaze, Ben squeezed more tightly on her hand.

Emerging from the tunnel were two creatures resembling great white bats, scrabbling on all fours, limbs crooked and webbed with fleshy wings. Although they had no ears, a mane of snow-white hair ran down their backs. Then he saw their manes bristle like cats sensing danger and both of them raised their eyeless heads.

'What are they?' Ben asked in a tremulous whisper.

'The Cotters.' Sarah drew him back, then both of them watched from their hiding place behind the row of stalagmites. The smaller of the two, the one called Rakkis, started up the wall, still scrabbling, gripping the rock with his suctioning fingers while pushing with padded, webbed toes. He seemed to be examining what Ben had thought was the detonator while down below, the other, crouched like a toad, lunged up on his powerful legs. Instantly, his fleshy wings unfolded, catching the air with a snap, and then he was flapping up to the vaulted ceiling, gracefully flying between the spires of rock that loomed from the floor like steeples, or like icicles, hung from above.

'What's he doing?' Sarah frantically whispered, her gaze still on Rakkis climbing the wall with its network of copper wires running out from the box with the flashing red numbers. But Ben did not hear, his attention lost on Cotter soaring high above, gliding around the great Brilliade, swooping after her young. It almost seemed as if he were driving them up, like a shepherd, and one by one, they rose, as buoyant as bubbles, gathering closer to the vast one above. Then the great Brilliade's arms began curling up as if to embrace her brood, and like Sarah that morning, Ben heard a warbly voice – or felt a voice-like vibration – as Cotter spoke in a language made up of visions, and feelings, to all of her offspring.

He saw a strange and watery world, like a movie projected into his head, and he had the oddest feeling that strange as it was, that it still looked somehow familiar – or not familiar so much as making sense in some peculiar way, as though he were seeing it all through the eyes of something that might call it home. But then, the images Cotter projected, along with the rest of the language he used, were being picked up by something both inside yet not a part of Ben. And this ocean of night he saw, like an ebony pearl, was called Nightsea, the Brilliades' home.

Great stretches of time were passing, eons of earth time, in Cotter's tale to the brood, for the lifespan of Brilliades and Sirenians was remarkably long. But none of the Brilliades, even the massive one, had ever been to their world, for even she was no more than a chrysalis when she was carried to this one.

Sirenians, it was explained in these pictures, were shepherds in their watery home, or more properly, they were guardians of the Brilliades, which were once bountiful. And though their world was far from any sun, the great Brilliades once brought it light, gliding through the Nightsea skies in vast luminous flocks. But Sirenian shepherds held them in the highest regard for more than this.

Just as solar energy nourishes the earth's vegetation, which in turn is integral to the food chain for earth's other life forms, Brilliade energy nourished the vegetation that fed other life forms on Nightsea. But on Nightsea, there was one difference. Unlike the sun, Brilliades couldn't survive without other beings like the Cotters to incubate their metamorphosing spores.

And this was the cycle of life in their world: the Brilliades nourished Sirenian crops; Sirenians received the Brilliades' seed; the seed, or larva, drew sustenance from the life-force of the Sirenian host; and then, on hatching, just before its husk was firmly set, the Brilliade thrust itself from its host with a backlash of its own lifegiving force, and thus, these two symbiont species of Nightsea were inextricably bound. And knowing the language of Brilliades was just one thing to come of all this.

Then Ben had the oddest sensation, a strange sort of warmth that made him think of his father, a bit like the affection his dad might convey by tussling his hair. It was almost as if a part of his father was somewhere above, and sensing Ben's presence, it sent out a sort of mental impression of something akin to tussling. But whatever it was, the feeling was faint and fleeting, and in the next moment he was caught up again in the spell of Cotter's tale.

The vision and sound pouring through him, however, now described a terrible blight. Like a cancer, this blight in the Brilliades' world, once infecting a thing, devoured it. But this blight was not from Nightsea. It came from a place called The Shadowlands, which Cotter described as the realm beyond worlds. He further explained that Nightsea and Earth were contained in a maze called The Wall Between Worlds. The picture Ben got was not unlike his teacher's demonstration in school, where a crumpled-up paper ball represented the universe wrapping around itself. But unlike this classroom model, Cotter's wall was a living membrane. And apparently Marsden's cyclotron wasn't the only way to get through it. But however this thing from The Shadowlands reached Nightsea, it preyed on Brilliades, and once it appeared, it stalked the vast flocks relentlessly till they were nearly extinct.

But fortunately, when Rakkis' and his father's flock was lost, Cotter was still incubating the last of their chrysalides. So, with their Brilliades gone, which put their farmlands in ruin, Cotter and his family set out to find a place untouched by the blight, hoping that when their last chrysalis hatched, they would be somewhere safe to start over. And in their roamings, they sensed such a place, like a radiant warmth in the currents of Nightsea. And they followed the current, believing it came from a place as yet untouched by the blight. And it led them to a crevice in a mountain in their world, and here, the image Ben received showed a gaping hole with a misty light. Then, as if he were there in the flesh and seeing it with his very own eyes, he watched the view turn away from the crevice and down the moutain slope where the glow cast over other Sirenians just like the Cotters. The tallest of these had the tiniest one of its group clinging to its neck while seven others, all smaller than

Rakkis, were gathered at its sides. Around them grew a lanky silver grass that wavered with watery currents while spreading below was a forest of something like coral that rolled away like waves – then vanished into a darkness like night, but deeper, and swimming with shadowy life. But this was after the brilliant flocks of Brilliades vanished from their skies. And then, Ben saw in a vivid rush of images how they came into *this* world.

Although there were many subterranean valleys that riddled the Nightsea terrain, the quality of the light through the crevice – its goldness – made Cotter uncertain. If it had come from a Brilliade flock in some hidden oasis within, there would be no predominant hue, but a swirling of colors, such as seen through a prism. For this reason, Cotter instructed his family to wait while he went through the crack with his oldest, wanting to be sure of where it led before the others followed.

But what they found was utterly unlike anything seen in their world before. They had come, in fact, to a place where the air was much thinner, for air in their world was like water, and water in this place fell in a wall at either side of the crevice, tumbling from a cliff overhead and winding below through a strange-looking landscape. And shining over all this was a blazing globe of golden light. Although, in time, they would learn that this dazzling light in the sky was called the sun, till that moment, the only stars they'd seen from their own world were distant pinpricks of light.

And this light, unlike the Brilliades', was blinding, and burned against their pale skin, and Cotter and Rakkis fled back through the wall of water to return to their family. But the crevice they went through now was not the one through which they entered this world. Instead, they found themselves in a much darker tunnel that led to this very cave. It was here that they first encountered the creature named Marsden, and the thing called a cyclotron, which had somehow opened the wall between their world and this one. But this, too, was not understood till much later, after learning the language of Ausable. At the time, they were only frightened and anxious to find their way back to their own world. But when they finally made their way back to the falls, the tear in the intra-dimensional wall had already repaired itself, sealing the chink and stranding them here.

From there, the story flew over the years, from the hatching of Cotter's chrysalis to gradually winning the friendship and trust of the people of Ausable. And then older Brilliades picked up where Cotter left off, projecting so many thoughts to the younger ones of what they'd learned, and what they'd taught, that Ben's head was spinning.

Through incubating Brilliade spore and the backrush that came with the hatching, human hosts in Ausable acquired some of the Brilliades' powers. It was because of this bonding that their hosts kept the outside world at bay, as much for themselves as their refugees from Nightsea, because the bondings had changed them. And together they came to understand what Marsden already knew, that Nightsea and Earth, and countless other worlds, were divided by fragile dimensions, that space and time extended, like the wall, in infinite directions. Then one voice silenced the others. Cotter told them about the explosives which he and Rakkis and Marsden had set long ago to go off when the chink in the falls reappeared and reached its maximum width.

Because of the need to stay hidden, both from the scorching sun and those who might not be as kind as the people of Ausable, they had passed many years in this cave. But now, the wall that imprisoned the largest of them was about to come crashing down, and together, they would soon be going home. But they were to be grateful, Cotter told them, for their time in this world. Without it, none of these Brilliades might ever have come into being, or if they had, they might have perished long ago from the Nightsea blight. Then Cotter told them he'd seen the mother of Rakkis through the weave between worlds – the image that came to Ben then he had seen before: an arm reaching out through the falls – and the mother of Rakkis told Cotter the chrysalis carried here long years before was in fact the last of the Brilliades of Nightsea. Now they would go back as many.

'Ben.' He heard his name called out from far away, like a distant echo, as if he'd been called a while ago and just now the sound was reaching him. He searched above, expecting to see Cotter looking back at him, or the thing he had sensed before, that had felt like his father fondly tussling his hair. But Cotter had been joined by Rakkis, and both of them were now gliding beneath the ruffled folds of the great one along with her young. And only as the massive Brilliade's sheltering arms curled up around them, as if to shield them from the coming explosion, did he feel Sarah's hand on his arm.

'Ben,' she whispered again. 'This is our chance. It can't possibly reach us now, not if we hurry before it brings its arms back down again.' She tugged him weakly, looking as if she could barely stand, let alone run, her glassy, sunken eyes urgently pleading. 'Come on! What's the matter with you?' For a moment, he looked at her out of a daze, scarcely feeling her feeble tug, but the images filtering down from above were fading as Sarah continued to plead, 'Please, we've got to go now!' He felt her breath on his ear as she whispered harshly, 'Ben, come on! We can't waste time!'

'It's too late. Didn't you understand? It's going to go off any second now.'

'You're just being chicken! Come on, we at least have to try!' She pulled him between the stalagmites.

'It's too *late*!' he repeated as if she were deaf. 'Didn't you understand?'

'Would you come?' she talked through him, her frightened gaze on the Brilliade's arms drawing tightly above, concealing her brood along with both of the Cotters. And he realized then that she hadn't received the projections Cotter sent, for some reason. But then, the chrysalis growing in him was too young yet for Ben to sense its presence, so he couldn't have understood that being joined to it helped him to pick up what Sarah could not. 'Please!' she begged, tears flooding her eyes, still trying to tug him along toward the tunnel. 'Please, Ben, I can't leave without you!'

'Sarah.' He grabbed both of her arms. 'It's too late! We'd be caught in the blast for sure! At least here, behind the stalagmites, we might have a chance!' But she pulled herself free from his hold.

'We don't even know when it's going to go off!' She backstepped toward the tunnel. 'Come on! We have to have a better chance running than if we stay! Please, before it sees and reaches down again! Oh please, Ben, hurry!' She waved him after, not knowing, of course, what he knew – that the only reason the Brilliade had repeatedly driven them back from the hole was because of the danger she'd started to sense as the rent in the weave grew wider.

'Sarah.' He started toward her, and misunderstanding the gesture, she finally turned, stumbling ahead, thinking he followed now, calling for him to hurry while Ben in turn began shouting for her to come back behind the row of stalagmites. Then both their shouts were suddenly lost in a deafening blast that shook the air, the shock wave slamming them both to the ground as rock shot through the cavern like gunfire. Loosened stone showered down from the ceiling, then stalactites, flying like spears, shattering into a rubble from which a great cloud of dust billowed up.

Winded, Ben rolled to his side, just glimpsing her gaunt frame, stumbling in circles now, one scrawny arm cast over her eyes, trying to find her way back through the dust. Then he heard the rumble above him, and just as his gaze leapt to the wall by the tunnel, jagged cracks darted out like lightning from every direction.

'Sarah!' he screamed through the deafening collapse of the face of the cliff, dropping in huge slabs that hit the floor with such force that the whole cavern trembled. More stalactites, loosened from the roof, came stabbing down and the air turned thick as smoke with crumbling, falling rock. Then, he heard the roar.

It was water, tons of it gushing down from the ceiling, beating back clouds of dust that rose from the rubble that littered the cavern floor. Blindly groping the ground around the stalagmites, trying to pull himself up, he felt the icy water from the ruptured falls lap at his knees. He grappled with the column of stone and dragged himself up to his feet, then wiping the filth from his eyes he squinted through a heavy glowing haze.

When the wall caved in, it took part of the ceiling, and out of the spray where the tunnel once stood, another wall, this one made of water, rose to the height of the cavern. With the flooding climbing higher by the second, he splashed across the floor of the cave, the light of the Brilliades gliding through the falls and to freedom guiding his way. Soon, the cavern floor would be no more than a terrace of water, spilling out to the river beyond like a crescent step in the falls.

Without hope, there's nothing, he heard a voice in his head as he crawled through the flooding rubble, trying to keep sight of the spot where Sarah had been. *You must never abandon hope*. It was what Gus had told his father that time in the car – the only time he'd ever seen his father cry. And crying now himself, he crawled directly toward the falls, oblivious to the icy water sloshing over his thighs, rising higher. *What is hope?* another voice, quite small, scarcely a whisper, asked. It seemed to come like Gus's, from inside, but not from memory. *What is hope?* it asked again, tiny, childlike, like tinkling glass, or a very young cricket's first tentative, creaking song.

Then the water had risen up to his waist, and the voice faded plaintively off as a terrible drumming filled his ears and something pummeled his head like nails. He had come to the edge of the falls, and the spray was blinding, and somewhere beneath the flooded rubble was his sister, and the thought of this crushed with a weight far greater than stone.

'Ben.' There came a new voice now, a delicate warbling right at his ear. Then water sloshed over his chin and into his mouth as he slipped from the rubble beneath him. Then something beneath the water slid firmly about his waist. It dragged him up, but he heard and felt nothing now, except for a numbing ache, and something else, inside him but not quite a part of him. A small echo of sadness.

23
The Starry Armada of Nightsea

While Sarah had pleaded with Ben to run for the tunnel, and Ben had begged her to wait, before the wall of the cave collapsed to end their tug of war, their mother, soaked to the bone and shivering wildly, sat on the bank of the river, staring insensibly up at the moon-like creature twirling through the falls.

'It's unnatural,' a low, suspicious voice said beside her, but her teeth chattered so badly, she could scarcely make out what the old man was saying. She hugged herself for warmth.

'I knew they weren't like us,' Mr Whittaker muttered away to himself. 'They changed. Ain't hardly human no more. No wonder they kept to themselves for so long.'

Still shaking so hard she thought she might fly apart, she clutched herself more tightly. How long she'd been in the river she didn't know. The last thing she recalled was rushing up to the water's surface, feeling as if her lungs would burst, then dragging at the air in aching gulps as she was carried ashore. She remembered the hands, small hands, but strong, that dragged her up from the murky depths, then the arm, a small arm, locking under her chin and the short legs that kicked out beside her. Somehow, whoever it was had drawn her back from that inexorable pull, then swam with her right through the turbulent currents with all the ease of a seal.

'Look at that. I tell you, it's unnatural,' old Mr Whittaker muttered, and turning her head, she saw Sam kneel by another woman who leaned over Gus. The woman, drenching wet, like Sam, had long black hair and looked vaguely familiar, as did a boy, also soaked to the bone, who was standing behind them. She might have remembered seeing them on her first day in Ausable if it weren't for a sudden rush of concern for Gus, sprawled on the grass, looking quite drowned. But even as she struggled up to her feet, she witnessed something even more astounding than whatever it was that was gliding in and out of the falls.

The woman kneeling by Gus had had the flats of her hands pressed to his back, but now they were lifting slowly away with a heavy steam rising directly beneath them. It appeared as if she were vaporizing and drawing the water out from his lungs using nothing other than her palms. Clare Liebling, staggering toward them, told herself she was imagining things. Everything that had passed since early that morning, from first meeting Gus to now, seemed such a jumble, she'd started to doubt that any of it was real.

'It's unnatural.' She heard Mr Whittaker behind her again, his tone low and suspicious, and then she saw Gus stirring and Sam looking up at the woman beside her.

'It's one of the Brilliade's gifts,' the woman said softly. 'It comes with the hatching.' But Sam looked about as bewildered by this as Ben and Sarah's mother felt. 'In us, it has its limits, though,' the woman continued. 'If he'd been any worse – ' But Sam was no longer listening, bowing her head to Gus's rising chest, and Clare, pressing on through the crowd, anxiously searched the faces raised to the falls.

'Sarah!' she shouted. 'Ben!' She was no longer even

aware of the thing they all watched, still whirling about through the falls, its brilliant light shining in all of their faces. But then, she'd been able to think of little else but for her children and husband, all of whom she prayed she would find in this crowd. '*Sarah!*' she shouted again, and then, across the field from the tiny house, a hoarse and shaky voice returned her call.

'Clare!' It was her husband. Stumbling up from the river and through the high grass, she shouted back, while behind her the young Brilliade ceased its cavorting about the falls. Slowly, it ascended, its tendrils trailing like glittering streamers while the radiant glow from its crystalline husk sent Clare's shadow slipping ahead of her.

Then the Brilliade's light fell across a tall, gaunt figure stumbling down from the house, and she ran across the final soggy stretch of ground and into his arms. For several long moments, they simply clung to each other, till Ray Liebling asked:

'Where are the kids?' And before she could speak, a terrible sound ripped over the river, and both of them reeled around to see water and rock shooting into the sky. Their hair whipped back with a sudden rush of wind and they held one another, both looking up with narrowed, stinging eyes as the falls appeared to leap back. The moonlike light pouring down from the creature hovering over the cliff changed color, turning vibrant blue, like dawn, and caught in its glow some distance below, rock and scrappy cliff-side shrubs cascaded from either side of the falls, and just before the blue-tinged wall of water, a huge black diamond hung. From where they stood, it looked as if the sky itself had shattered, and a monstrous fragment of night had fallen to earth, for the blackness within it seemed endless. Then the crowd from the shore was suddenly moving up through the grass and around them, for the rubble from the blast was swelling the river even higher.

'It looks like a coelenterate.' It was Sam Whittaker's voice they heard, and then they saw both her and Gus, her arm at his waist and his over her shoulder, straggling through the grass with backward glances at the young Brilliade, its deep blue light now throbbing as it glided toward the crowd.

'A what?' Sam's grandfather hobbled up as they stopped a few feet from the Lieblings.

'It's a phylum of invertebrates, like hydras and anemones.'

'Looks like a giant jellyfish to me,' the old man muttered, and then Sam laughed, a bit nervously, as people do when they're feeling uneasy.

'Grandpa, a jellyfish *is* a coelenterate,' she said in a low hushed voice, furtively glancing around at the crowd, clearly feeling that she and her group were outsiders. But everyone but the Lieblings and Gus and her grandfather silently watched the falls. Everyone but a woman and boy, both drenched, who stood a few yards away. The woman, who she'd watched revive Gus, was looking their way while she spoke to the boy. Sam, feeling more conspicuous than ever, turned back to her grandpa and added, 'It's all the same family, hydras, anemones, jellyfish – just like minnows and carp.'

'Minnows and carp ain't nothing alike,' he said, staring back at the woman and boy.

'They're both fish,' Sam distractedly told him. 'And don't stare back, they'll see you.'

'They'll see me whether I'm staring back or not. And I'll tell you another thing – ' But Sam, like everyone else, even Ben and Sarah's parents, turned her gaze away as the light from the head of the river grew suddenly brighter. More of the eerie creatures were appearing, splashing out through the falls. Gliding over the river in such a dazzling array of colors and light, the ever-swelling flock of Brilliades all but turned the night to day.

The one that had played in the falls, before the explosion, smaller than most of the others, had already drifted over the tops of the trees to the Marsden house and the field. Then it hovered there, its delicate tendrils quivering inches away from the crowd, almost as if it were searching for something, a bit like a kitten sniffing the air. And all the time, others, of all different sizes, coasted down from the falls, parting around the great diamond to sail down the river like some starry armada.

Clare found herself thinking of Ben by the woodpile that very first night, staring up at the fireflies, just as she now gazed up at this vision of light, for the two seemed alike. It had something to do with the sort of light, so luminous and pure that it seemed somehow to embody the very essence of life itself. And now, with the smallest one so close above, looking up through its crystalline gills, she felt she could actually feel that purity radiate over the crowd.

Even its simple anatomy seemed like a primal expression of life, she thought, like a miniature nebula whirling with stars enclosed in a fragile crystal ball. And the symmetry within it was as delicate as a snowflake – more so – with thousands of tiny specks of light flowing through an intricate web of intertwining vessels which resembled glassy, thread-like veins. And right at the core of this, like a pygmy sun, a sphere of warm light pulsed, and with every heart-like throb another starry surge flew through its veins. And while she felt her own heart longing once again for Sarah and Ben, she saw its tendrils sliding past her, down into the crowd.

Feeling her husband drawing her nearer, she stared with apprehension and awe as its arms curled over the youth whose face she finally recalled. But if he looked like death that very first day in Ausable Center, he now looked the picture of health, reaching up to the thing, his smile full of affection . . . yet sad. And then she sensed, not knowing how, that it was this boy who pulled her from the river – and he looked even younger than Ben, and that thought made her long for her children again.

An eerie clicking sound began to pour from the creature embracing the boy, then another sound, a deep and haunting oboe tone, like a rhythmic purr. Once more she felt her mind return to the very first night she stood in this field. With Ben's arms at her waist, trying his best to console her, they'd heard the same sound, like singing. But where was he now, she anxiously wondered, and Sarah, why weren't they here? And looking past the boy embraced by those delicate arms streaming with light, she scanned the other faces again, still hoping to see her children.

But now, other luminous bodies were gliding over the crowd, and like the first, their tendrils wavered in the air above as if they were searching as well. And then they were reaching into the crowd, and human arms and tendrils entwined. The night filled with their clicking and purring while she and her husband and Gus and the Whittakers huddled in a pocket apart from the rest.

'They're saying goodbye,' she heard Gus murmur, then her husband said:

'They've all shared something.' He sounded, like Gus, almost wistful, as if he felt somehow left out.

'Ray.' She turned to him and though his arm encircled her waist, he looked far away. 'We've got to find Sarah and Ben.' But whether he'd heard or not, before he could answer, a deep, vibrant hum from the falls echoed all through the night. As if this were a summons, the flock above began to draw away, sailing back over the river just as the falls vanished under a great, blinding light. Another of these creatures emerged, more brilliant than all of the rest, and rich in every color of the spectrum, like some great weightless prism of light. And the size of it – its proportions were mammoth, nearly as wide as the cliff itself, and the sound of more rock breaking loose from the cliff could be heard as it pulled itself through, growing larger. It seemed, in fact, to swell with the fresh night air as it rose, growing wider and wider, its streaming tendrils seeming to be without end as it drifted up through the sky.

The diamond of darkness beneath it was dwarfed by the thing, still inflating itself, still climbing, as if it had been confined a very long time and was stretching itself to its limits. And then its arms swept gracefully up, wavering with the evening breeze, unfurling across the night like undulating rivers of stars.

'I'm frightened.' Mrs Liebling shivered against her husband's shoulder. 'Ray, I'm so frightened for the children.'

And then it was as if the great brilliance above her had heard. Its ruffled belly opened like a flower, peeling away to reveal that solar core, pulsing, heart-like, and radiating a tingling warmth. It made Clare Liebling's hair stand out on end, but not from fear, for a thermo-electric field of some sort seemed to pour down from the thing, dancing in shivery streaks of blue light that bathed the crowd, bringing everyone's hair up as if the very air were charged with the Brilliade's energy. And the current of this energy field felt as if it were flowing through her. And it did, through them all. Just as Clare felt an annoying stiff knee which resulted from a jogging accident suddenly release its nagging tightness, old Mr Whittaker felt the aching, arthritic crook in his fingers fade, each of the gnarled appendages growing straighter before his widening eyes. And then there were things which none of them were aware of that were correcting themselves, like a cancer that would have been years away, dissolving in Dr Whittaker's chest. And in Gus's chest, the bud of what might have become a heart problem disintegrated while the start of emphysema in Mr Liebling's lungs was swept away. But few in the crowd were paying much attention to this healing force, for something else was happening in the heart of that brilliant creature above.

Already squinting, Ben and Sarah's mother had to close her eyes as the heart itself opened out with a light that blazed as bright as the sun. It wasn't till she felt the heat pouring down from it begin to fade and the crackling of energy dancing through the crowd grow weak that she opened her eyes. By then, the ruffled belly of the thing had closed again, and it seemed to be drawing into itself as it slowly streamed toward the river below. And as it neared, still seeming huge if steadily dwindling in size, she spotted a pair of kite shapes just beneath it, coasting toward the shore.

While the great one hovered just above the others, gathering them in her arms, the two Sirenian shepherds smoothly glided to the edge of the field. It was then that Mrs Liebling caught sight of her son scrambling down from one of their backs.

'Dad!' he shouted, darting across the field as the Cotters leapt back in the air, their great white wings flapping then filling like sails as they soared back over the river. Then Mrs Liebling was running toward him, followed by her husband and Gus, and then, at last, she saw the small figure behind him, moving slower, stiffly.

'Oh, baby.' She rushed ahead as her husband swooped Ben into his arms. 'I was worried sick when I couldn't find you.' Kneeling, she crushed the girl to her chest. 'Are you all right? What happened? Where were you?' she asked in a rush, still holding her tight.

'I was in the Brilliade,' her voice choked out. 'Mom, I can't breathe.' Then Mrs Liebling loosened her hold just enough to draw back and examine the girl.

'You're so pale.' Her worried gaze swam over Sarah's face, which, even without the light of the Brilliades, seemed to hold the faintest glow. 'And warm.' Her hands now smoothed the hair away from her daughter's glistening brow. And Sarah's hair, which had last been patchy and feathery, looked a bit thicker and darker. But Mrs Liebling scarcely took this in, conditioned from two years of worry to notice only signs of failing health, not unlikely improvements like this. 'And you looked as if you were limping.' She held the girl back a bit more, taking more of her in. And Sarah did seem different, but Clare could not see that her clothing was no longer hanging, that there was a bit more flesh on her bones, and that her eyes no longer looked so sunken in her pale moon face.

'I'm just a little stiff, that's all,' Sarah answered, and the light in her face seemed to concentrate behind her wide dark eyes, which shined in the Brilliades' light. But Mrs Liebling misunderstood, thinking it was her sickness again, while the stiffness was more like that stiffness that comes with awakening from a very deep sleep. And Sarah's sleep in the heart of the Brilliade had had the depth of an ocean, and what she had awakened from had been the mystery of death. 'Daddy!' The girl was pulling away from her then, rushing to meet her father as Gus and Ben walked toward the river's edge. And just for a moment, Mrs Liebling saw in her daughter's movement a growing litheness, and she sensed in that moment the subtle change in the girl: Sarah's life was not drawing to an end, but beginning all over again. And then, looking after her family all gazing out at the great flock of Brilliades, she started toward them, thanking God for their safety yet feeling strangely sad.

The sadness was the same she'd seen before in the smile of the Ausable boy, and which she felt all around her now, from the crowd in the field and the bright flock above. And then she understood the waves of feeling flowing between them, for they were saying goodbye for the final time.

The smaller Sirenian shepherd led the flock toward the gaping diamond of darkness. As soon as his wings slipped through, it was as if a flame had been suddenly snuffed. This same sudden darkening seemed to occur when the smallest Brilliades entered, as well, as though the blackness within were some terrible hunger that swallowed them whole. But then, as progressively larger Brilliades drifted through the hole, the faintest flickering of wings, like dozens of moths, appeared all around them. And then the dark itself seemed to waver and flicker, like the dawn in a liquid sky as the last great Brilliade, followed by Cotter, started gliding through.

Almost instantly, the watery sky of Nightsea caught the great Brilliade's glow, spreading over the world within in glittering rays like creeping frost. Ever-widening spears of light from the Brilliade spilled through the landscape around it, stretching over wintry dunes and valleys of silvery wavering grass. Over the hillocks, hundreds of Sirenian shepherds hovered like kites, and the blackness around them crept further and further away, over towering mountains and forests. And the forests, which spiraled up like great reefs of coral, seemed almost to lean toward the light, and their jagged bone-white branches began to unfold in a rainbow of colors, for life, long dormant in their limbs, was beginning to waken and bloom again.

Then the diamond's black edges began to waver. The scene through the hole became tremulous, blurring. And then it began to shrink, and the last thing seen was a glittering cloud of blue as the Brilliade showered her sleeping world with her spore, and as the worms sifted down, swimming through the forests of coral and skimming over the sandy hills, her deep oboe purr drifted back through the hole with a chorus of trilling, like crickets and bells, and then there was nothing, only the ghostly mist and roar of the Ausable falls.

'Sort of like getting a peek at the hereafter,' Gus said over Sam's shoulder, expecting to see Mr Whittaker still standing by her other side. But old Mr Whittaker, no longer hobbling but moving along quite sprightly now, was hurrying after the woman with long dark hair who had rescued Gus from the river.

'It's only one hereafter,' a small voice said to his right, where Ben had been. But looking down, Gus saw a strange boy between them with scraggly straw-colored hair. And the boy looked just as damp as Gus felt, as if he'd been swimming in all of his clothes. ''Cause after that, there's another hereafter, and more and more after that.'

'Where's he going?' Sam Whittaker watched her grandfather, rushing after the crowd, all moving through the high grass toward a cluster of beat-up pick-up trucks.

'After Gramma,' she heard the boy between Gus and Ben reply, and regarding him curiously, he off-handedly added, 'They was friends once, long ago.'

'But she's scarcely older than I am,' Sam pointed out, still looking past the boy. 'So I don't see how she could possibly know my grandfather if it was long ago. I mean, he hasn't even been up here since he was a kid himself, and that's nearly fifty – sixty years, I'd imagine, and I'm only twenty-eight.'

'Gramma's seventy-three and this August she's gonna be seventy-four,' the boy replied, but his attention seemed to be more on Ben, who'd grown somewhat withdrawn. 'They used to be kinda mushy together. That's what Gramma told me.'

'How old are you?' Gus then interrupted.

'Nine and a half,' he shyly answered, as if, like many young people, he secretly wished that he was already grown up.

'Well,' Gus murmured to Sam, 'at least *he* looks his age.'

'But my ma don't look much older than her.' The boy, sounding proud of this, pointed at Sarah who at the moment was being fussed over again by both of her parents. ''Cause she got the bright mark when she was little, like me, about fifty years ago, when my other Gramma and Grampa took her camping up here in a trailer. And *they* came all the way from Tennessee.' This he sounded proud of, too, as if to have come from just one state away was just as exotic in Ausable as someone from Borneo or the South Pole. But then, Gus realized the boy had probably never been off the mountain. 'But now, I got the bright mark, too. They was worried I wouldn't, 'cause she don't spawn too often. But soon as I heard she was I came right up and got myself a seed.' And of everything, he seemed proudest of this, so proud he seemed to lose interest in Ben, turning up his freckled face to beam amiably at Sam and Gus. 'Where's you from?' Gus and Sam exchanged glances.

'Who's "she"?' Sam asked, nonplussed by it all.

'The Brilliade.' The boy's gaze drifted off toward the falls for a moment, again looking wistful. But then it swung back again with the same broad smile. 'So, where y'all from?'

'Sam's from Reedsville, just down the mountain a bit,' Gus explained, 'and I'm from Cambridge.' Now it was the boy who looked nonplussed. 'That's a city in Massachusetts.' Still, the boy looked up at him with a frown, as though not knowing where this was and feeling badly about it, or ashamed, afraid they would think he was simple. Then the awkward moment of silence between them passed as the youth shyly told them:

'Can't never leave. Not that way, at least. So we got no cause to know all those places.' Gus supposed the boy was right, if indeed he would live out his life in these mountains. 'Guess some of you'll be stayin' on here, too, now,' he quietly, absently added, his gaze returning to Ben who still stared out at the river, as if in a daydream, and though the night had settled in all around them, his face held the faintest glow.

'For a little while,' Gus mumbled, thinking the boy had referred to their visit, his own gaze turning to Sam as they silently shared for a moment the wonder they felt. And then, at last, Ben added his two cents, which was not about staying or leaving.

'I'm hungry.' And well he should have been, not having eaten for nearly two days, on top of which, for another few days, he'd be feeling the hunger of two.

24
Visions and Voices

'It ain't natural,' old Mr Whittaker muttered, rocking by the woodburning stove while Clare and Gus and Sam all huddled around it, still cold from their dip in the river. 'Your great uncle ought to have known enough to leave well enough alone.' Gus's mouth dropped open to say something back, but Meg, who helped Sarah make supper, had taken the old man's remark even more personally, and spoke up first:

'Samuel, you're as big a fool as you was when you used to bring me those carp, like I didn't have a daddy and five brothers who fished the same river all day.' She crossed to the stove and using the ends of the shirt hanging over her jeans, she opened the oven door and pulled out what Sam saw with envy was Shoo Fly Pie, and looking even better than her own grandmother used to make. 'I don't believe you've changed one little bit since we was kids.' It seemed odd to everyone present – except for Meg's grandson, who sat at the table by Ben – that a woman who looked as young as Mrs Liebling should say such a thing to a man who looked, by contrast, old enough to be her grandfather. But then, it would take a while before all they had learned from the woman would finally sink in. 'You still think you know better than everyone else when you don't understand a thing.' She closed the oven door with a bit of a bang, just

207

for the emphasis. 'Don't you see, if it weren't for Matthew's cyclotron doing whatever it did, Nightsea would stay like it was, all dying away, till there was nothing but sand. If folks was always satisfied to just leave well enough alone, then how on earth could anything ever get any better?'

'Or on Nightsea,' Sarah, smiling, added, bringing two cups of milk to the table. Because it was made from powder and didn't taste particularly good, she'd added chocolate syrup, with extra sugar in the cup she gave Ben. He drained it almost instantly while Meg's grandson finickally sniffed around his. 'Want more sugar?' she asked.

'It's already too sweet.' He wiped a mustache of milk away from his upper lip.

'Then give it to Ben and I'll make you another.' As she turned, Ben gulped the second cup down. She hoped no one would take too much notice of how much and what Ben soon would consume. Meg and her grandson might understand, but her mother would only be frantic with worry. Just as she'd only start worrying – as soon as she finished feeling relieved – when she learned, as she would at Sarah's next check-up, that all of her daughter's sickness was gone. At least, Sarah thought, she had come by the 'bright mark' in far less an obvious way than Ben would, though having to slip as close to death as she did for the privilege was certainly harder. But now she was already what he had yet to become, once infused with the Brilliade's life-force. To bring her back went well beyond healing. The blood of the Brilliade flowed in her veins.

Returning to help Meg with the dinner, however, she still couldn't shake her concern – not for Ben, he'd be fine, but her mother would be in a frenzy if she suspected a thing. She might even try to have Benjamin's chrysalis killed, the way Uncle Gus's had been. Even she had been bent on destroying the one in her father before she understood. Pity, she thought, that the chrysalides were susceptible to high-frequency sounds and magnetic waves and other types of vibrations. And it was ironic, too. But then, the sounds of the chrysalides were of another world, so in a way it did have a symmetry – that their cry shattered glass while it just took a tape of rock music to shatter them. Fortunately, once a husk was set and a chrysalis finally hatched, the Brilliade emerging was impervious to all of that. Still, she wondered if the chrysalis growing in Ben would get that far. Maybe Meg and her grandson could help, she thought to herself as she glanced at the woman, now chopping bright red peppers to put in a pot full of crawfish being boiled into gumbo. If only she could speak with them alone. And not only about her brother. There was so much she wanted to know, like the powers she'd have as the force grew within her.

'They'll come, in time. Don't hurry things, girl.' It was Meg's voice, but her mouth wasn't moving. Sarah glanced apprehensively at the others, but no one else seemed to hear. 'Don't worry, this is yours and mine. It's special. Even my Danny can't hear.' But Danny, Sarah thought in confusion, had the bright mark, too. 'Not much longer than you.' As the thought was projected, Meg kept on chopping her peppers. Not once did she even give a sidelong glance as she continued on. 'Stop worrying, girl, and don't be so impatient. There's plenty of time.' Then she smiled, to herself. 'More time than you ever imagined, and that can be a big problem all in itself.' Now she did look at Sarah, one very brief moment, her eyes flicking over the girl with concern. And when she started chopping again, Sarah wondered if it had been about Ben. 'You both will have some hard roads up ahead of you, as time plods on. But that's what livin's all about. The easy way's just bidin' time. Like going along with it all, like havin' someone say you don't look well then feeling sick all day instead of just makin' your mind up to start feelin' good.' Sarah dropped the knife she'd been buttering bread with.

Meg had just described her life in a nutshell – letting everyone else decide what she was feeling and what she could and couldn't do. And then she couldn't even do what they told her she could, she got so helpless. Until she climbed the cliff and found her brother, even as weak as she was, and that she did on her own, before the blood of the Brilliade helped make her stronger. 'Those hard roads, though, now they're the ones that really make you grow.' And maybe even save your life, she thought, though she nearly well lost hers on that one. 'And they only look too hard to handle till you get a start. But once you make up your mind to a thing, the doing just about does itself. You'll see. The hardest thing of all's the choices, that's what it all boils down to. And I don't mean maybe one day this, and next day change your mind to that, but sticking with it right to the end, and if you done the best you can, the next choice comes along's a little easier. And while we're on boilin' down to things, you want to check my pot of gumbo?'

And Sarah did, and the stew was done to perfection, as Meg of course knew it would be. But all of Meg's talking, or thinking, still didn't ease Sarah's mind about Ben, and somehow, the most important thing to her then was that they'd both have the bright mark.

'Still, it ain't natural.' She tuned back into the argument between Gus and Sam's grandpa. 'Just look at her. They can't even age normal.' But Sarah sensed the old man was jealous.

'Grandpa,' Sam intervened, 'what's normal and natural won't always be just like you.' And Sam, Sarah sensed, was doing her best to understand all that she'd seen.

'And thank God for that or we'd sure be in one sorry state, if we was all like you.' It was Meg, in spoken words now, with a good-hearted laugh to follow.

'Grandpa, where do you think you get those tangelos from that you love so much?'

'You buy 'um for me,' he grumbled. 'How do I know? Florida, prob'ly. Who cares?'

'I don't mean *where* they're from. I mean how they got to be what they are in the first place.'

'God's design,' the old man declared self-righteously. 'Unlike *some* of us here.'

'It so happens,' Sam said lightly, 'that those tangelos you love so much are hybrids. What they are is a cross between a tangerine and a grapefruit.'

'We're not talkin' about some mixed-up fruits, we're talkin' about people who ain't – people, I mean. They're different than us. And if God had intended – '

'Speaking as an agnostic,' Gus interrupted, 'it would seem to me that if you believed that God created all things, then it would have to follow that all things created by, or between his creations were still his doing.'

Old Mr Whittaker's toady eyes had shrunk to all but slits and his mouth was pulled into a thin line over his dentures that matched the ruts in his brow. He looked, Sarah thought, as if he was either mulling it over or seized by a cramp. Then all the lines seemed to pull right into the center of his face and he said:

'I thought you was a gym teacher?'

'I am,' Gus replied with a grin. Of everyone there who did not have the bright mark, Sarah felt Gus was their strongest supporter. And then there was Ben, in the chrysalis phase, who was growing too distracted to have an opinion on much of anything that didn't pertain to which foods he would eat.

'I think the government might know a little bit more about this than a gym teacher.' Mr Whittaker fished a waterlogged pouch of tobacco and pipe from his jacket.

'Government? What's the government got to do with any

of this?' This was the first Sarah had heard her father speak in a while.

'When they find out, they'll have plenty to do about this, you can bet your boots on that!'

'Mr Whittaker, I don't think that's such a good idea,' her father said quietly, trying, she knew, to curb Mr Whittaker's shouting down to a civil tone. It was something he did both at home and with his students. Ray Liebling did not like to fight. If you couldn't discuss a thing quietly, he would say, then you shouldn't discuss it at all. Resolution required understanding, and understanding came from contemplation, and he hadn't met anyone yet, he would often point out, who could contemplate better while shouting. 'There'd be scientists and federal agents and all kinds of people poking around.'

'And military,' the old man smugly added, clearly approving of this.

'They'd pick this place apart and turn it upside down,' Gus put in forlornly, although the house had not been much to look at even before the windows blew out. Then his gaze turned to Ben, almost as if he knew, and he added more gravely, 'Then they'd herd everyone with the bright mark into a lab and throw away the key.'

'Better they shake things up around here than have *more* whatchamacallits slip through. All we need's to have another one of these wall things getting a hole.'

'But that's *exactly* what they'd be trying to do if they knew,' her father pronounced. 'Can't you see? As soon as they found out what happened, they'd want their own cyclotron.'

'They're already building one,' Sam pointed out, 'but they call it a super collider.'

'Matthew heard about that just before he lost the road,' Meg said in a tone that implied she did not think this other machine was in any way super. 'You can't just set one up and – boing – there's a hole to another world. It does it when it's good and ready, and Matthew's machine ran near three years before it happened the first time, and this last took another fifty. Could be it won't ever work with that other one, and anyway, Matthew said that's not even what they were making it for. It's for smashin' up atoms.' She said all this as if she were trading cooking tips, calmly stirring her stew. 'You can't just hop and skip from world to world.'

But Sarah then had the odd feeling that Meg was hiding something, and not from the others as much as from her, for she sensed her mind closing to her just as something poked through, not a thought projection exactly, but something that entered Meg Gallagher's mind unbeckoned. Something like a spontaneous image that popped up from her memory. And the image, though fleeting, had shown Sarah something that sent a chill running up her spine. It had shown Meg herself walking through a perfectly ordinary looking door and into a perfectly ordinary garden with fat ripe tomatoes on stalks, and just as she reached to pick one, her hand seemed to vanish into thin air, then, jerking it back, it was covered with something slimy and black that oozed to her wrist. If it hadn't been so formless, Sarah might have thought it was some sort of snail, but it fit her hand like a glove just as though it was trying to swallow it whole. Impulsively, she glanced at Meg, at the hand on the pot, then the one that she stirred with. Both, as best she could tell, and to her immense relief, looked quite normal.

'And anyhow,' Meg turned, avoiding her gaze, but smiling at all of the others, 'who'd be fool enough to believe such a story if you told them?' In the silence that followed, Mr Whittaker looked very small and wrinkled, except for his eyes, which bulged like a toad's, and a very disgruntled toad at that.

25
The Wall Between Worlds

'I'll drive you,' Gus offered after they'd finished the meal and Clare and Ray had cleaned up. And it had been a very long meal, with far more discussion than eating, except for Ben, who could not seem to get his mind on anything else, especially when Meg Gallagher pulled her Shoo Fly Pie from the oven. But it seemed to have ended with everyone in agreement, at least for the time being. Her parents, Gus and the Whittakers, though still trying to sort it all through, did not see any point in bringing other outsiders to Ausable. Even for Meg's 'healing', which had concerned Sam Whittaker most, but even as a physician she had to relent when Meg told her her 'gift' often failed, requiring special circumstances, like how much time must pass between each time she used it. But seeing Meg and her grandson Danny off made Sarah very anxious. She had no idea when her brother's chrysalis was due to hatch, but judging from the way he'd been through dinner and how distracted he seemed, she was counting the seconds till one of her parents noticed.

'How'd you think we got here?' Meg Callagher said to Gus's offer. 'Fly?' Everyone laughed a bit nervously at this, except for Sam's grandfather.

'Well, after you brought in that basket of crawfish and vegetables and all the trucks took off . . .' Gus shrugged. 'I just figured – '

'Not all,' Meg replied, now standing in the doorway, still looking a trifle damp as she pointed across the darkened field. 'That hump down there beside your van's my egg n' honey truck.'

'That's right. I remember.' Sarah's mother was standing with Gus by the door. 'When the children and I stopped in Ausable Center, you drove down in that truck.'

'Day I found Danny.' Meg Gallagher put her arm around her grandson, and with this reference to this other boy's being lost in the woods, like her father, for days, half out of his mind with the terrible craving that came from the chrysalis, Sarah again felt a budding of panic at being left alone to make sure Ben's survived. 'Incident'ly,' Meg added, not so much as glancing at Sarah's troubled face, 'I still have some honey and eggs in the back, if you'd like me to leave some behind.'

'Do you have your own hives?' Sarah's mother asked as she absently stroked Sarah's short, dark hair.

'And hens, and one very pompous little rooster.' Meg petted her grandson's scraggly head of straw-blonde hair, but something about the gesture did not seem as absent to Sarah as her mother's hand felt.

'*And* hogs and goats and a cow and a whole lot of other neat stuff,' Danny quickly piped up. Then looking at Sarah eagerly, 'You think you and Ben would like to come see it?'

'Now, that's a thought,' Meg began. 'In fact, if they'd like, they could come along now. Spend the night. Spend a couple o' nights if they want. I got plenty of room for them both. Why, they'd even get a real bed, too, if they don't mind sharin'. Be more comfortable, surely. More'n havin' seven of you all squeezin' together in here. And the way it's cooled down after all that rain, and with all of your windows blowed out, you'll be like a nest of snakes all tryin' to curl up around that biddy stove.' And Sarah could not help grinning from ear to ear, for it was all too perfect, the offer of honey and eggs, and Danny's impromptu invitation to visit, as if it had come to him all on his own out of the bright blue sky. Meg must have been planning it from the moment she saw that Ben had been 'seeded'.

'Oh, Mom, can we?' Sarah picked up her cue. 'It would be such fun. And it is going to be awful crowded. Oh, can we? Can we?' She could see it tugging at her mother's heartstrings. Sarah hadn't shown this much enthusiasm for anything over the past two years of starting each day as if it were her last.

'Give you and your man a little time alone to boot,' Meg murmured, winking.

'Oh, I don't know.' Sarah felt her mother's hand slide down and squeeze her shoulder, and knew on the spot that the primary hesitation was that she thought she was still ill. And then, of course, she would probably think it was also an imposition, and that they didn't *really* know much about Meg Gallagher after all, not to mention the business of Meg being 'different' – if only her mother really knew – and a hundred and one other reasons her mother could find to say no once she got the ball rolling.

'Well, I think it's a perfectly grand idea.' Her father saved the day. 'Especially the part about giving you and your man some time alone.' He'd come up behind them, putting an arm around Sarah and her mother.

'I don't know that five of us is going to feel much like alone,' her mother said wryly.

'It will when we close the door.' She heard her father whisper, and tilting her head, she saw him wink at her mother while nodding toward the bedroom door.

'Come on, Ben.' Sarah darted across to the table to drag

her brother away from the remnants on the pie tin which he scraped up with his nails.

'I have half of another one like that at home,' Meg taunted him from the door. 'And molasses cookies, too.' And doubtless everything else he'd need, Sarah thought. And before he could even register what was happening, Sarah was dragging him off, helping him stuff his backpack, then tackling her own and rushing him off to the door. 'Ray,' her mother still haggled it out with her father, 'I really don't know. I mean, we don't even understand – '

'We'll have the whole summer for that.' He winked at Sarah, and somehow, Sarah sensed he knew. If not everything, at least enough to know that they'd be safe. Then he caught Ben by the shoulders while her mother stooped to give her a hug, and she saw in his gaunt bearded face the same longing she'd seen when he watched the Brilliades go. 'You'll tell us all about it, now.' And he meant about more than Meg Gallagher's farm, and though Ben, since the meal, had been growing increasingly distant, she saw her brother nod. He knew, as well as Ben, about the change going on in his son, and if he'd had any choice, as Ben did now, he'd have carried his chrysalis right to the end. But the world of Nightsea needed all the Brilliades that the Cotters could bring, and watching him study her brother, she saw the boy in her father filling with wonder. Then her mother let go and turned to Ben and her father hugged her to his side. And then, it seemed her mother finally worked things out, and Sarah cringed.

'What's the matter with you?' she asked after kissing Ben's cheek. Then putting her hand to his brow, Clare Liebling looked up at Sarah and said, 'I don't think your brother's feeling too well.' But then she gave the boy another kiss and a bear of a hug and continued, 'No wince?' She was grinning. 'Not even a little groan?' And Sarah exhaled with relief, for her mother was only kidding about how he usually made such a fuss about kissing.

'Mom, Mrs Gallagher's waiting.' Sarah said promptly before she *did* catch on, then grabbing her brother's arm she tugged him hurriedly through the door.

'You behave now!' her mother called after them. 'And no fighting, you two!' Sarah pulled him along. Then she heard her mother, more quietly, say to her father, 'I still don't understand, but you know, I have a feeling about this place – as crazy as everything's been – that everything's going to start changing, and all for the better.' And Sarah, glancing at Ben, stumbling beside her through the darkened field, saw the palest moon-like glow of the bright mark and knew that her mother was right.

'Ben can sit back with Danny.' Meg stood by the tailgate of the beat-up truck, and after she'd given the boy a hand up and tossed in their backpacks, she led Sarah up front. 'Door's bent in on the passenger side. It's stuck. Swiped a tree diving down in the mud.' Meg opened the door on the driver's side. 'Watch you don't get stuck with the shift crawling in.' After Sarah climbed up and scooted across to her seat, she watched Meg fish for her keys. 'Don't worry so much. Your ma'll be fine.' She'd read Sarah's mind once again. 'And if she knew, with you at least, that getting you back like she did, that there just weren't any way without getting the bright mark, too, she wouldn't complain. And as for Ben, can't say I'm not glad there's a way now to carry on the line, but it's his choice of course, and he knows enough now to make up his own mind. Not like Gus and your daddy. They didn't know. And what they know now – well, people that know, if they don't stay on, we sort of help them forget.'

'What do you mean, help them forget?' Sarah asked uneasily.

'I mean,' Meg answered gently, still searching her pockets for the keys, 'that no one comes through here and leaves with our secret. Otherwise, like your daddy said, we'd have the whole world poking its nose around where it don't belong.'

'But you can't mean we have to *live* here!' Sarah was dumbstruck at the thought. 'I mean – you can't possibly mean – you don't mean to say we can't ever leave?'

'Ain't nothing wrong with living in Ausable.' Meg sounded a little offended. 'And those that have the bright mark,' she cryptically added, 'whether they want to or not find themselves slipping away for a spell now and then, but they always come back. But those that don't but know . . . well, we won't have a Brilliade spawning again for some time, and if your folks and their friends don't want to stay we can't really stop them. But one of the gifts – the 'sending', the one that lets us get in people's heads . . . now and then, we got no choice but to use it to change people's memories around. Sort of like plastering over the real ones with ones we make up, to help them forget. Now, where's those darn keys?' Meg poked through her pockets again, now pulling them inside out, while Sarah thought of the prospects of having her parents' memories changed around, unless they agreed to stay on, which she doubted they would, and got seeded themselves. She wondered if that's what Meg had meant about 'carrying on the line'.

'That Brilliade won't be spawning for years to come,' Meg, reading her mind, replied. 'And then, it'd be up to your people, of course, whether they got seeded or not. But by carrying on the line, I meant the children hereabouts. Not everyone in Ausable's hatched a chrysalis and worked the change, and the sad thing about it is most of our youngins are agin' faster than their folks. Like Danny was, until he hatched a chrysalis himself.' Then, as before, Sarah had the distinct impression that Meg held something back, that there was another reason to want a Brilliade here to keep the line going. And as before, it came to her in a fleeting glimpse of a thing in Meg's mind, another unbeckoned image out of Meg's memory that came with her words. It showed two walls, both thinner than thread while going on forever and ever, like walls of a honeycomb, filled with little pockets like a grid. And in one of the pockets, it seemed as if there were something gnawing away at the wall – a black and oozing slime like the thing Sarah saw on Meg's hand in an earlier glimpse. Sarah wondered if it might have something to do with the Nightsea blight. 'Now where in the world did they go to?' Meg had stooped over, searching the ground, and the unbeckoned image Sarah had glimpsed in her memory turned to an image of keys. 'Hope they're not at the bottom of the river.' Meg looked across the field and Sarah, on reflex – because it was something her own mother did all the time – glanced at the ignition and saw the key Meg was looking for dangling right there.

'It's here,' Sarah told her, and Meg, turning back, shook her head as she started to climb in the truck.

'It's a wonder I don't lose my head with the way I – ' And then she broke off as her foot came down, for before it could hit the floor, it vanished, followed by her leg to the knee. 'Whoops . . .' She hurriedly pulled herself back through the door and the leg and the foot reappeared, and her boot, to Sarah's swelling amazement, was covered with something that looked like snow – except that the substance was yellow and had a strange odor, like something was burning, and it melted like snow, and the odor grew stronger and sulphurous as it started to steam.

Meg, holding on to the door while she stood on one foot, shook the other furiously, as if the other had fallen asleep and the shaking was meant to bring back the sensation. The yellow-caked boot went blurry then solid again several times till it stayed that way, then she gave it a tentative tap on the ground as though testing to see if the feeling returned.

'That happens sometimes.' She glanced at Sarah sheepishly, giving the foot a good stomp, then dropping her gaze she stomped it again to shake off the last of the yellow snow. 'Wonder where that came from?' Meg then thought aloud, unperturbed, while Sarah still gaped. 'Sure does stink.' She even grinned a bit as though this astounding event was no more of a bother than stepping into something a dog had left behind.

'Gramma?' Danny then called from the back of the truck. 'Is somethin' wrong?'

'Slipped through into something,' Meg called back, meeting Sarah's astonished gaze. 'It's nothing to worry about. Passes off in a minute,' she said, looking sheepish again, but with Sarah still gawking speechlessly, Meg sighed and said, 'S'pose I should tell you the rest. You'll find out eventually anyway.' Then she climbed in her seat and closed the door. 'Now don't get your head in a twirl. It don't happen that often, and now you just saw how you stop it.'

'How *I* stop it?' Sarah finally heard her own voice, squeaking out like a frightened mouse. 'You mean, that's going to happen to *me*?'

'You been through much worse,' Meg gently reminded. 'And it's not all that bad, you know. You'll see. Times'll come when you'll want to go all the way through.'

'*All* the way through!' Sarah looked aghast. Then her eyes grew wider. 'Through what? To where?'

'Same thing the Cotters went through to here and back again, of course. You saw.' Meg started the engine. 'We better get moving before your folks think something's wrong.'

'But something like that can't just *happen*!' Sarah looked

off at the house, now half wishing she'd stayed. It was one thing to have the power to hear someone's thoughts, maybe even to heal, but quite another to have odds and ends of yourself disappear, and without any warning. 'You have to have a cyclotron. And even then, you said it's rare. And it's just in one place. Isn't it just in one place? It can't follow someone around!'

'No, it don't follow you,' Meg replied as she pulled the truck up the overgrown road. The tangle of branches crossing overhead scraped over the roof of the cab. And then, staring out through the windshield at the dim beams bouncing ahead through the night, Sarah saw what it was that Meg seemed so reluctant to explain. It was *in* her. 'It's part of you now,' Meg said, very gently. 'It passed on down, with all the rest. You see, the first time, when Cotter carried the chrysalis through, it changed it. It happens when a thing goes through. And all of us with part of the Brilliade in us got that in us, too.'

'Got what?' Sarah asked, still struggling to comprehend this unwelcome development.

'Don't know what it is, exactly. Sort of like catching a cold, I s'pose. And whatever it is that makes it happen, it starts like an itch in a hand or a foot. Or an elbow. Sometimes, you can be leanin' against a tree or a wall or the side of a car, and all of a sudden you find that you're on the way to slipping through.'

'Slipping through what to where?' Sarah asked again anxiously.

'Don't never know where it's to. Each time it's different,' Meg quietly told her. 'If it could take you where and when you wanted, the Cotters would have got home long ago. But I can tell you one thing, wherever you go, you get there through the wall between.' Then she opened her mind to the girl. With a sinking feeling, Sarah saw the night grow darker all around till everything, Meg and the windshield and even the woods beyond it disappeared. In place of this, a great double wall stretched endlessly all around her, the same vast honeycomb which Sarah glimpsed by accident before. Only this time, it wasn't a glimpse, but like she was actually caught in the middle. And though the wall was as fragile as parchment, it shivered a bit just as if it breathed, and she knew somehow that the wall was alive and each shuddering heave it gave was a sigh. And with each sigh, the tiniest sparks flew in through every facet, streaking past one another like shooting stars and out through the other side. And through Meg's vision she sensed that each spark represented the ends and beginnings of life, departing from or about to arrive in those worlds beyond the honeycomb wall. And through those tiny portals, Sarah had fleeting glimpses of some of those worlds, but the wall's two sides kept slipping in different directions, and the sparks flying through made her dizzy.

'If you give yourself in to the itch,' she heard Meg's voice, 'you go all the way over, and then you're stuck till it goes away, but you always come back where you started from.' Then, as if Meg read her mind as before, Sarah heard her gently scolding, 'If it weren't for this thing Cotter's chrysalis caught and passed on, you wouldn't be here now. Don't you see, before it passed over the first time, all it could do was help things grow. It's only this thing that it caught in the wall between that gave it the power to heal. And the power,' Meg solemnly added, 'to put the spark back in you. Otherwise, that spark would have gone through the wall for good, like Matthew's did.'

'Where did it go – Matthew's spark?' Sarah uneasily asked.

'No one but Matthew could tell you for sure. But my guess is it got born all over again into something else in another world. Not that there's anything wrong with that,'

Meg was quick to add. 'After all, Matthew was already way too old, even with the aging slowed, and no matter how long you stay in a place, the day comes when it's time to move along. Like Matthew said, one place is as good as another once you're a part of it, 'cause how good it is only depends on what you make of it while you're there.' Sarah wondered if he'd have still thought that if his spark got in something like the slime. But then, she supposed if slime could think about such things as well, maybe it wouldn't be all that excited at turning into a person. All the same, she couldn't imagine wanting to be anything else, especially if it meant that one day she would have to leave her family.

'But that's just it,' Meg told her, sounding surprised Sarah hadn't seen it herself. 'We're *all* family, Sirenians, Brilliades, Ausable folk and even your family and you. That wall's the thing that binds us all together. Did you think it just kept us apart?' Sarah didn't know what to think. There was just too much to take in all at once. 'Then don't try so hard,' Meg said as the honeycomb wall began to fade. 'Things like where you'll be headin' for next don't make much sense to fret about now. You won't know where you're going till you're there, and anyway, now you're here.' And Sarah then wondered just how long she was going to be stuck in Ausable, not at all sure how she felt about actually living here, if it came to that. 'What it comes to depends on your folks and Gus and the Whittakers.' Meg had heard her thoughts. 'And then how the folks in Ausable feel when they sit on all this for a spell. So you might just as well put it out of your mind till we have some idea how it's going to turn out.'

'But that's just what I'm worried about,' Sarah told her. 'That you'll put it *all* out of my mind. I don't *want* to be made to forget everything that happened here if we move back home.'

'And you won't.' Meg looked at her in a way that

reminded her of her mother. 'Even if we wanted to change you and your brother's memories around, when the gifts the Brilliade passed on got strong enough, they'd all come back. But that's a ways off. You've got plenty of time – the whole summer, in fact – to work it all out. So stop all this worrying over tomorrow. You'll just go missing the rest of today.'

And Meg was right, there was time for it all, and for the first time in a very long while, Sarah no longer dreaded the endings tomorrow might bring, for in endings were always beginnings.

The beginning of Book II in The Ausable Odysseys

Books in the Methuen Teen Collection

UNDER DIFFERENT STARS : Carolyn Bear
ROUGH MIX : Denis Bond
AMONG FRIENDS : Caroline B. Cooney
DON'T BLAME THE MUSIC : Caroline B. Cooney
THE NIGHT WALKERS : Otto Coontz
IN LOVE : Jennifer Curry (editor)
NIGHT MAZE : Annie Dalton
OUT OF THE ORDINARY : Annie Dalton
GOOD AS GOLD : Brian Finch
THE SINGING BOWLS : Jamila Gavin
GROOSHAM GRANGE : Anthony Horowitz
SPIRIT RIVER : Monica Hughes
TOO MUCH GOLD : David Johnstone
FUNNY, HOW THE MAGIC STARTS : Sam McBratney
DREAM PALACE : Anthony Masters
TAKING ROOT : Anthony Masters (editor)
A HAUNTING REFRAIN : Alison Prince
MUSICAL CHAIRS : Jean Richardson
YOU'VE GOT TO BELIEVE ME : Judith St George
PLAGUE 99 : Jean Ure
HIDDEN TURNINGS : Diana Wynne Jones (editor)